PRAISE FOR *THE GUILTY COUPLE*

'I loved *The Guilty Couple* so much I was up until 2 am finishing it. Twisty and compelling, tense and fast-paced and thoroughly unputdownable.'
Angela Marsons

'A brilliantly written, fast-paced and very clever thriller – I couldn't put it down!'
Susi Holliday

'When you sit down with this book, you won't be getting back up until it's finished. Fast-paced, fun, packed with twists, this is a gem of a read.'
Jo Spain

'Pacy, surprising and with some brilliant twists – C.L. Taylor's best yet. Brilliant.'
Catherine Cooper

'Compelling. Compulsive. Crafted. Cleverly calculated.'
Jane Corry

'A clever, suspenseful story about secrets, blurred boundaries and a whole lot of betrayal. C.L. Taylor is a master at writing twisty thrillers, and this one is no exception.'
Samantha Downing

'Twisty and gripping – another brilliant book from C.L. Taylor.'
Jane Fallon

'Cancel your appointments, kick off your shoes and get comfortable. There's a new C.L. Taylor book in town – and it's a corker.'
Cass Green

'Absolutely ripped through this belter of a story. A pacy plot full of her trademark twists, and characters that don't leave your head until long after you finish the final pages. C.L. Taylor has smashed it out the park with this one.'
Lisa Hall

'A one-sitting read. Breathless pacing from the opening chapter to its twisty turny conclusion. Taylor is a writer at the top of her game and never disappoints.'
John Marrs

PRAISE FOR C.L. TAYLOR

'Claustrophobic and compelling.'
Karin Slaughter

'I was glued from start to finish!'
Shari Lapena

'Fans are in for a treat.'
Clare Mackintosh

'Clever, surprising and nuanced – C.L. Taylor is at the top of her game.'
Gillian McAllister

'Clever and unsettling, with a brilliant cast of characters.'
Rachel Abbott

'Utterly sinister and compelling.'
Mel Sherratt

'A compelling, addictive and wonderfully written tale. Can't recommend it enough.'
Louise Douglas

'A masterclass in character. Clear to see why she's a million-copy seller.'
Sarah Pinborough

'Twisted, unbearably tense, and a shock ending.'
C.J. Tudor

'Cally is the absolute queen of the page turner.'
Elizabeth Haynes

'A gripping, intrigue-packed thriller.'
B.A. Paris

'The intricate plotting, vivid characterisation and the exciting intrigue combined to make a most entertaining read.'
Liz Nugent

'Another twisty, chilling and unpredictable thriller . . . I couldn't put it down. Excellent from start to finish.'
Claire Douglas

'She's done it again. A complex, compelling page-turner set at a wellness retreat, with lots of twists and turns.'
Mark Edwards

'An addictive page-turner that kept me reading through the night.'
Lucy Clarke

See what bloggers are saying about
C.L. TAYLOR . . .

'I devoured *Strangers*. Twisty and clever, utterly compelling
characters and a superb edge-of-the-seat finale.'
Liz Barnsley, *Liz Loves Books*

'My eyes were simply glued to the page, I couldn't
tear them away!'
The Bookworm's Fantasy

'An intriguing and stirring tale, overflowing with family drama.'
Lovereading.co.uk

'Astoundingly written, *The Missing* pulls you in from the very
first page and doesn't let you go until the final full stop.'
Bibliophile Book Club

'Imaginative, compelling and shocking – *The Fear*
is a highly engrossing read.'
The Book Review Café

'*The Fear* is a dark tale of revenge and just when you think you
know where the story's going, the author takes you by surprise!'
Portobello Book Blog

'[*The Missing*] inspired such a mixture of emotions in me and
made me realise how truly talented you have to be to even
attempt a psychological suspense of this calibre.'
My Chestnut Reading Tree

'Tense and gripping with a dark, ominous feeling that seeps
through the very clever writing . . . all praise to C.L. Taylor.'
Anne Cater, *Random Things Through My Letterbox*

'C.L. Taylor has done it again, with another
compelling masterpiece.'
Rachel's Random Reads

'In a crowded landscape of so-called domestic noir thrillers,
most of which rely on clever twists and big reveals, [*The
Missing*] stands out for its subtle and thoughtful analysis of the
fallout from a loss in the family.'
Crime Fiction Lover

C.L. Taylor is a *Sunday Times* bestselling author. Her psychological thrillers have sold over a million copies in the UK alone, been translated into over twenty languages, and optioned for television. Her 2019 novel, *Sleep*, was a Richard and Judy pick. C.L. Taylor lives in Bristol with her partner and son.

C.L. TAYLOR

The Guilty Couple

avon.

Published by AVON
A division of HarperCollins*Publishers* Ltd
1 London Bridge Street
London SE1 9GF

www.harpercollins.co.uk

HarperCollins*Publishers*
1st Floor, Watermarque Building, Ringsend Road
Dublin 4, Ireland

A Hardback Original 2022
1
First published in Great Britain by HarperCollins*Publishers* 2022

A catalogue copy of this book is available from the British Library.

ISBN: 978-0-00-837926-1 (HB)
ISBN: 978-0-00-849573-2 (HB)
ISBN: 978-0-00-839406-6 (TPB)

This novel is entirely a work of fiction.
The names, characters and incidents portrayed in it are
the work of the author's imagination. Any resemblance to
actual persons, living or dead, events or localities is entirely coincidental.

Typeset in Sabon LT Std 11.75/14.5pt by Palimpsest Book Production Limited,
Falkirk, Stirlingshire

Printed and bound in UK using 100% Renewable Electricity by CPI Group (UK) Ltd,
Croydon CR0 4YY

MIX
Paper from
responsible sources
FSC™ C007454

This book is produced from independently certified FSC™ paper
to ensure responsible forest management.

For more information visit: www.harpercollins.co.uk/green

To Joe Wood

Chapter 1

OLIVIA

2014

Only one member of the jury glances in my direction as they file back into the room: she's early-forties with long dark hair and a soft, round face. She looks like a Sarah or a Helen and her heavy gaze has rested on me for the last five days. We're around the same age and I hope that's made her sympathetic towards me; *there but for the grace of god go I* and all that. Or maybe she believes that I'm the monster the prosecutor has painted me out to be: a liar and a cheat, a woman riddled with hatred and obsessed with money and death.

The truth is, I have no idea how Sarah-Helen views me, or what she's been thinking over the course of my trial. If our roles had been reversed and I were on the jury rather than in the dock, I'd have been watching the defendant for signs of guilt: fidgeting, nervousness, swallowing and shifty eyes. I have avoided doing any of those things. I hold myself still,

1

shoulders back, feet wide, hands interlaced, fighting the urge to lick my dry lips.

The only time my composure slipped was when my husband took the stand yesterday to give evidence for the prosecution. I hadn't seen him in weeks and he looked tired and sallow-skinned. His hair needed a cut and the skin around his jaw looked ruddy and dry from a hasty shave. Dominic and I had not been in a good place before I was arrested but I trusted that he'd rebut the prosecuting barrister's suggestion that I was a woman so keen to keep my house, my lifestyle, my daughter and my lover that I'd arranged to have my husband killed. Dominic did *not* defend me. Instead he talked, at length, about how toxic our marriage had become (true) and how much he'd wanted to mend things (not true) and how horrified and shocked he'd been to discover that I'd increased his life insurance policy and attempted to contact a hitman on the Dark Web (not as shocked as I was).

I gnawed at the raggedy cuticle on my thumb and beamed my thoughts at the witness box: *Dominic, tell them the truth. Tell him!* In my mind my thoughts were as powerful as a haulage truck's headlights floodlighting a dark countryside road, but my husband didn't look at me once. His eyes flicked from the barrister to the jury, to the judge, to the gallery, but they never rested on me. It was as though there was a force field masking me from view or maybe I wasn't there at all; I was an invisible woman, or dead.

When Dominic finally left the stand, my cuticles were bleeding.

Now, as the jury take their seats, it isn't my husband's face I seek out; my fate is no longer in his hands. Sarah-Helen meets my gaze for a split second before she looks away sharply but what I see hits me in the guts like an anvil. My fate is written across her face.

THE GUILTY COUPLE

Before the session my barrister Peter Stimson had told me he was still very optimistic that I'd be found not guilty, that he'd given the jury enough cause for reasonable doubt. I want to believe him but the look I saw on Sarah-Helen's face is making it hard.

Hope is the only thing that's got me through these last few weeks. Hope that the jury will see beyond the story the prosecutor has concocted, hope that they'll realise I've been set up. I'm a thirty-nine-year-old woman, a mother, an art gallery owner, a wife and a friend. I can tell a Jan van Goyen from a Rembrandt and make a lovely batch of brownies for the school PTA sale but I can't get past week five of Couch to 5k without running out of puff.

A frisson of excitement fills the courtroom. The judge has beckoned the court usher to come forward. Her low heels clack on the wooden floorboards as she crosses the room; the sound reverberates in my chest, matching the pounding of my heart. The judge speaks in a low voice as the usher approaches the podium. My barrister and solicitor both sit up taller in their seats.

The usher turns to address the court and a wave of fear crashes over me. It doesn't feel real, this, me in a courtroom, waiting for a verdict. If they find me guilty, I'll get between seven and ten years. Grace is only seven. She'll be a teenager before I am free.

The usher turns to the jury. 'Would the foreman please stand.'

Sarah-Helen rises from her seat and smooths the crumpled skirt of her cotton floral dress. She's nervous. That makes me feel worse.

'Madam Foreman,' the usher's voice rings out through the wood-panelled courtroom. 'On this indictment have the jury reached a verdict upon which you are all agreed?'

Sarah-Helen clears her throat lightly. All eyes are on her and the stress of the spotlight pinkens her cheeks. 'Yes, we have.'

'On count one,' the usher says, 'do you find the defendant guilty or not guilty?'

Time slows as Sarah-Helen's lips part. *Please*, I silently pray, *please, please*. I didn't conspire to have Dominic murdered. I don't know who did but it wasn't me.

'Guilty.' Sarah-Helen's voice rings out clear and loud then I hear nothing at all. The judge's lips move and the usher stalks back across the floor. There's motion from the gallery, shifting and whispering. Faces, faces, faces, all looking at me. The dock, once so solid beneath my feet, becomes marsh-mallow soft. A hand to my elbow keeps me upright, leads me out.

I seek out my husband as I am ushered towards the door that leads to the cells. He's sitting next to Lee, my business partner, and they're deep in conversation. *Stand up.* I turn on the headlights again, beaming my thoughts into his. *Tell them you set me up. Tell them that I'm innocent. Tell them what you did.* My husband shifts in his seat and glances across the courtroom, as though he senses the weight of my gaze. His eyes meet mine and he smirks.

Chapter 2

DOMINIC

2014

Dominic Sutherland braces himself as he approaches the side exit of the Old Bailey and hears the roar of the press pack outside as his solicitor opens the door. Over the last five days of the court case, he hasn't been able to enter or leave without being surrounded by journalists and photographers, all shouting his name, firing camera flashes in his face and blocking his way. So far he's managed to avoid giving them a single comment, despite the shouts of 'Can you ever forgive Olivia?' and 'Will you stand by your wife if she's found guilty?' that trailed after him wherever he went. But he's going to have to say something now.

The press have been chasing the story for weeks, intrigued by the tale of the suave chartered surveyor in his late thirties, his adorable ringleted daughter, his blonde wife, her lover and the crime that nearly cost Dominic his life. They've been picking over the details of the case: Liv's affair, the life

5

insurance policy she increased, the unknown hitman she tried to hire on the Dark Web and her confession to Danielle Anderson, personal trainer at Fit4Life gym and a serving detective in the Metropolitan Police.

Why? That was the question the press returned to. Why would a woman who had it all choose to have her husband murdered? Why not just leave him instead?

'Everything okay, Dominic?' Melanie Price, the CPS's solicitor, puts a hand on his shoulder. 'If you need a couple of minutes to—'

'I'm fine.' He smiles tightly and steps through the door.

Flash bulbs fire in his direction, making him blink, and a chorus of voices shout his name.

'Dominic! How do you feel?'

'Are you pleased with the verdict?'

'Dominic! Rosie Jones from the *Mirror*, can I—'

'Ladies and gents!' Melanie raises a hand and the noise abates. 'Mr Sutherland has prepared a statement. There are to be no questions afterwards, thank you.'

Dominic snatches a breath as he reaches inside his suit jacket for the statement he scribbled out at the kitchen table that morning as Grace banged around upstairs, getting herself ready for school. He's already dreading the conversation he'll have to have with her when he collects her from her friend's house later.

He clears his throat and reads. 'I would like to thank the Metropolitan Police Force, the CPS and the judge and jury for ensuring that justice has been done today. The sentence awarded to Olivia means that, for the first time in a long time, I will be able to sleep soundly tonight. Whilst our marriage was not perfect, I cannot fully express the horror I felt when I discovered that my wife and her lover were conspiring to have me killed.' He pauses to take a breath. 'It was down to the swift action of the police that their plan was foiled and I am able to address you all today. I would like to request privacy at this time as my daughter and I come to terms with what has happened and attempt to pick up the threads of our life. Thank you very much.'

There's a lull of no more than a split second then the questions from the press start up again. Dominic ignores them.

'Thank you.' He shakes hands with Melanie and his family liaison officer and then squeezes his way through bodies, microphones and television cameras to reach the black BMW waiting for him further down the road. He slides into the back seat, closes his eyes and blows out his cheeks in a noisy sigh.

'You all right there, mate?'

The driver is watching him in the rear-view mirror. His shoulders are wider than his seat and his neck is thick and lined beneath close-cropped hair. Dominic can almost imagine the man reaching into the glove box, pulling out a gun and twisting round to point it directly between his eyes. He chuckles at the irony of the thought.

'I'm good, thanks. Oakfield Road, please. Crouch End.'

As the car pulls away he reaches into his inside pocket. His fingers touch the sleek, narrow shape of his mobile phone then slide away, to an altogether chunkier, cheaper phone. He takes it out and taps at the rubber buttons to access the unread text.

It's just a single word: Well?

He taps out a reply: She's not a problem any more. She got ten years.

Chapter 3

OLIVIA

Now – 2019

A fight has broken out in the middle of C Block. It's been rumbling for a while and the wing's been buzzing all day. You know when a fight's coming because the air thrums with tension, like it does before a storm. For a lot of the women it's something to look forward to, a break from the mundanity of the daily routine. Given all the screeching and shouting from the circle of onlookers, the two women scrapping in the middle aren't the only ones releasing their anger and frustration during the fight.

I'm not entirely sure why they're scrapping. Something about Sabrina disrespecting Gardo's girlfriend Chanelle. They're really going for it – grappling with each other and throwing punches, arms whirling, all elbows, nails and fists. Sabrina's the shorter of the two women but what she loses in height she makes up for with her bulldog-like physique. Gardo's landed some hard punches but Sabrina's giving as good as she gets, despite her bloody nose and torn lip.

Out of the corner of my eye I spot Vicki Kelk darting into a cell that isn't hers. I step out of my own cell to take a closer look. Kelk is a crackhead who'd rob her own granny to get money for drugs. She's cruel too. She coerces girls into smoking spice then films them twitching and shuffling and staring like a zombie before uploading the videos onto YouTube via her smuggled mobile phone.

The cell beside the one Kelk's raiding belongs to Janet and Theresa. Janet's a lifer in her sixties. She's not much of a talker but she can give you a look that makes you feel like someone's walking over your grave. Theresa's new and if she's not in her cell she's skulking around looking terrified.

In a lot of ways she reminds me of me.

It was the noise that got to me when I arrived, all the screaming and shouting and wailing and banging. I tried to hide in my room but my cellmate told me that if I didn't go out onto the wing and mix with the others I'd be viewed as weak and attract the wrong kind of attention.

There's no sign of Janet but Theresa is standing alone at the back of the circle surrounding the fighters. Her mousey hair is tucked behind her ears, her arms are crossed over her heavy chest. She's watching what's going on from beneath her eyebrows. As Kelk darts into Theresa and Janet's cell Theresa turns her head sharply to look at me, then heads after her. I slide closer so I can see what's going on. I wouldn't get involved normally but I'm getting out tomorrow so if Kelk decides to wage war on me the fight won't last very long.

'What are you doing?' Theresa's voice rings out as I approach the doorway. Kelk is over by the kettle with two packets of ramen noodles in her hands.

Kelk's gaze slides towards me then returns to Theresa. 'I'll pay you back.'

'Put them back please.'

Kelk lifts her sweatshirt and sticks the noodles into the waistband of her joggers then pulls the sweatshirt over the top. She smiles, her top lip curled back to reveal her teeth. 'Take them back.'

Theresa does nothing. She's paralysed by fear when what she needs to do is stand up to Kelk. If it ends up in a fight it ends up in a fight. It's the only way she'll earn her respect. But Kelk is dangerous. I wouldn't put it past her to have a toilet brush rammed into her joggers, the brush removed and the plastic moulded into a spear-like point.

'Give me one.' I step into the cell, pulling the door partly closed behind me.

'Eh?' Kelk shoots me a curious look.

'She's got more ramen on the shelf. Chuck me one. And that bag of teabags while you're at it.'

A smirk spreads across Kelk's face. 'I thought you were getting out tomorrow.'

'I am. I want to give Smithy a leaving present.' I glance at Theresa who's still hovering near us, the base of her throat flushed red, her hands fluttering at her sides.

Kelk throws a packet of noodles and the clear bag of teabags at me.

I tuck them under my waistband then push past Theresa. 'What else have you got?' I rummage around under her bunk. 'Got any sweets? Stamps? I know Smithy would really—'

The words are knocked out of my mouth as my head hits the cell wall. Theresa just gave me a shove.

'Give my stuff back,' she shouts as I twist around and duck out of the bunk. She lands her first punch as I straighten up. Smack! Right on my cheekbone. Adrenaline floods through

10

me as I fight to regain my balance but she's on me straight away, small fists thumping at my stomach, my head and my chest. I weave my fingers into her hair and pull her head back then lift my knee to her stomach to create a space between our bodies. I land a couple of punches but they glance off her. Theresa shows no such restraint and each time her fist makes contact my body sings in pain. As we continue to grapple I hear voices from the doorway: Kelk, and a couple of other women discussing our fight.

After what feels like the longest two or three minutes of my life I shout, 'All right, all right. I'll give you your stuff back' and Theresa shoves me roughly away.

She watches as I throw my spoils onto her bunk, then turns to confront Kelk. 'And you,' she says.

Kelk's eyes narrow, but she rummages around in her joggers and tosses two packets of ramen noodles onto the bunk.

'Out!' Theresa takes a step towards her. 'Show's over. You can all fuck off now.'

As Kelk and her cronies retreat I wrap a hand around my body and groan softly. Theresa really put some welly behind those punches and my ribs and cheekbone are throbbing like hell.

Theresa closes the door. 'Sorry Liv. I got a bit carried away.'

'You're not kidding.' I touch a hand to my nose to check for blood. 'You weren't supposed to shove me into the wall. You were supposed to wait until I grabbed the stamps and then swing for me.'

'Sorry.' Her face twists with regret. 'I was so nervous I forgot the plan.'

'It's fine.' I give her shoulder a squeeze. 'It made it look more realistic. Are you all right? I didn't hit you too hard?'

She shakes her head but she's quivering like my daughter's

11

hamster did, just before it died. The adrenaline's wearing off and she needs to get her shit together before she goes back out onto the wing. She'll have gained enough respect now to stop Kelk nipping into her cell but new inmates arrive all the time. Theresa's going to have to keep standing up for herself if she's going to get through the next few years unscathed. I learned that the hard way.

'I was so nervous that Kelk was going to jump me,' she says.

'No. The beating you gave me put her—'

A siren interrupts me. Up in the CCTV room someone's spotted Sabrina and Gardo's fight. In between the beats of the alarm I hear the thunder of trainers on concrete as the women outside scamper back to their cells.

'I'd better go.' I make a move for the door.

'Thank you, Olivia,' Theresa says. 'I owe you.'

'Yeah, you do.' I squeeze her hand in goodbye. 'Stay safe, okay?'

'Well?' Smithy reaches a lazy arm over her bunk and ruffles the top of my hair. 'Have you decided what you'll have yet? McDonald's, KFC or Nando's?'

Food is something Kelly Smith has talked about at great length over the last three years we've been padmates. I spent my first two years in prison sharing with an older woman called Barbara who'd been convicted of GBH. She looked like she worked in a charity shop or a library but she had a mean right hook. Ninety-five percent of the time she was pleasant enough but if someone crossed her and she lost her temper she'd smash up our cell. On the one, and only, occasion I tried to stop her she broke my nose.

After she was moved on Smithy moved in. She appeared in the doorway of my cell and looked me up and down, her thin, mousey hair pulled back into a loose ponytail with a straggly halo of escaped strands framing her hard, angular face. I'd heard from one of the other girls on the wing that she was a thief so I was on my guard.

'I'm pretty easy to get on with,' I told her as she slid inside, a clear plastic bag containing her belongings in her hand. 'But if you nick my stuff we're going to have a problem.'

She looked at me from beneath sparse untidy eyebrows, her pupils pinpricks in sharp green eyes, and I readied myself for a row. There aren't that many fights in a female prison but a new cellmate is always an unknown quantity. For all I knew she could be a psychopath as well as a thief.

'All right your Majesty,' she said, her thin lips breaking into an amused grin, her throaty East London voice filling the small room.

Queenie. Posh Bird. Chelsea. I'd been called it all by the other girls. I'd never thought of myself as posh. I was from Brighton, the daughter of a nurse, but I went to Exeter to study Art History and polished up my accent to try and fit in. It stuck, even after I moved to London when I finished my degree. Not that many of the other inmates knew that about me. To them I was 'the posh blonde who tried to have her husband killed'. By the time Smithy turned up I'd long since given up correcting them, on the poshness or my guilt.

The only thing that's been keeping me going for the last five years is the thought of seeing my daughter again. Grace is seven in the only photo I have with me: she's sitting on a bench in Hyde Park in the sunshine, a 99 ice-cream in her hand and such a look of joy on her face it's as though all her dreams have come true. She was such a mummy's girl back then. She'd go to Dominic for a bit of rough and tumble (she loved being flipped upside down and spun around and around) but it was me she came to for cuddles.

Aged seven she was already a keen artist and a straight talker. She knew what she liked and what she didn't and she wouldn't hold back if I bought a painting she thought was ugly. Every Sunday we had 'art and craft afternoon' when we'd sit around the kitchen table and paint pictures, sculpt air-drying clay or make necklaces and bracelets with beads. We'd read together every night before bed. I'd read part of a chapter and she'd read the rest. Afterwards she'd shout down the stairs, 'Make sure you put it in my reading record, Mum.'

On my first night in prison I stuck Grace's photo on the wall of my bunk with toothpaste. That way her face was the last thing I saw before lights out and the first thing I saw in the morning. She's twelve now and I don't even know what she looks like. The last time her grandparents brought her to see me she was ten. I've called George and Esther, I've written to them – my friend Ayesha even visited them to beg them to please bring Grace in to see me – but they always said the same thing: Grace doesn't want to visit me anymore and they can't force her to come. I don't know why she's changed her mind about seeing me. The last time I saw her she was sullen and withdrawn but I put that down to a hard week at school or a bad night's sleep. Afterwards there was a tiny, terrified part of me that was worried Dominic had succeeded in turning her against me. If I'd known that would be the last time I'd see her for two years, I'd have hugged her like I'd never let her go.

'Present for ya,' Smithy says now, reaching under her pillow. She pulls out a thin, battered paperback; the pages are browned and wrinkled with age and several of the corners are turned down where she's bookmarked a page that she likes.

'No.' I shake my head. 'I can't take that.'

14

'Course you can.' She waggles it in my face. 'I want you to have it.'

The book in her hand is *The Right Way to Do Wrong* by Harry Houdini. It's partly about the magic he did and the secrets of sideshow circus acts but it's also about the methods of deception involved in burglary, pickpocketing and various swindles. Smithy found it in the bottom of a rucksack she nicked and it's been her talisman ever since.

'It'll bring you good luck,' she says, hitting me on the arm with it until I snatch it out of her hand.

'Will it give me the last five years of my life back too?'

She laughs loudly, exposing the large gap between her front teeth. 'It's not a fuckin' time machine, Liv. I told you, mate, you'll drive yourself mental with what ifs and if onlys. You gotta look to the future, not the past. That's long gone.'

'Sutherland!' Two weighty thumps on the door to our cell make me jump. A key scrapes against the lock and the door opens.

'Come on then.' Davies, one of the guards, crooks her finger and jerks her head to one side. 'Say your goodbyes. It's time to go and—' She narrows her eyes. 'What happened to your face?'

'I walked into my bunk, miss.'

'Did you, now?' She rolls her eyes. 'Good job you're getting out then.'

I take Grace's photo from the small pile of my belongings and drop the rest onto Smithy's bunk.

'It's not much, but you won't need any commissary for the next week. Thank you, Smithy. I mean it. I couldn't have got through the last few years without you.'

'Ah, piss off.' She laughs good-naturedly and pushes me away. 'I'll see you in a week.'

'I meant what I said, Kelly. I'll help you out. I'll give you

15

the money I promised you so you can do that carpentry course.'

'Yeah, yeah. That's what they all say.' She waves a dismissive hand through the air. 'We'll do it,' she adds as I head for the open door. 'Promise you.'

Davies raises an eyebrow. 'Do what exactly?'

'Olivia was fitted up, miss, and we're going to prove it when I get out.'

'Framed, were you, Sutherland?' The prison officer smirks as she moves to one side to let me out. 'Course you were. Come on, let's go.'

Chapter 4

OLIVIA

Ayesha gets up from the sofa that will be my bed for the night and crosses her tiny North London living room. She picks up the glass water spray on the mantlepiece and squirts the fern on the window sill. I shift in my armchair, tucking my feet under my bum. The jogging bottoms and sweatshirt she gave me yesterday so I could get changed after my shower are too small in the arms and legs, but at least I no longer smell like my cell.

'Aysh?' I ask again. 'Please.'

She sighs and puts down the water spray. 'It's a terrible idea.' She returns to the sofa and pulls a cushion onto her lap. 'If someone sees you and reports you you'll—'

'I know, my probation officer already made that perfectly clear.'

'You'll get sent back to prison. You won't see Grace for years.'

'No one will see me.'

'Liv, you've got a supervised visit with her on Tuesday. You only need to wait another three days.'

'I need to see her *now*, Aysh.' I grind my knuckles against my sternum but it does nothing to lessen the burning sensation in my chest. 'It's been two years . . .'

It's been killing me, not knowing how she is. I *need* to see her. I need to know she's okay.

Ayesha rubs a hand over the back of her neck. Her resolve is crumbling.

'So will you?' I ask. 'Take me to her school? In time for pick-up? I won't talk to her, I promise. I'll just sit in the car and watch. You can put on the child locks if you want.'

'I haven't got child locks.'

'Please Ayesha, you're my best friend.'

Indecision clouds her eyes. She's torn between wanting to help me and wanting to protect me from myself.

'What if Grace sees you? Or calls the police?'

'She won't.'

'How can you be sure?'

'Because she's my daughter.' Desperate tears fill my eyes and I swipe them away. 'And she loves me. I know she does, even if she hates me too. Please. Please just let me look at her. I won't ask anything of you, ever again.'

Ayesha laughs softly. 'Why do I get the feeling that's a promise you're not going to be able to keep?'

It's a no-parking zone outside Longacre Academy so Ayesha pulls up in a side street nearby. It's the only street with a bus stop and if Grace still lives in our old house she'll have to walk directly past the car to catch the bus home.

'You okay?' Ayesha turns off the engine.

'Yes, no. No, mostly no.' I feel jittery and unanchored and my feet are pounding out a frantic beat on the rubber mats in the footwell. I've dreamed of this moment for so long it feels like a scene from a film.

18

'They're coming out.' Ayesha squints into the distance. 'I just spotted a couple of navy blazers.'

I've never seen this uniform before. The last time I did the school run Grace was wearing a deep red jumper with the emblem of the school stitched over her heart. She barely reached my shoulder back then. I've got no idea how tall she is now.

Teenagers I don't recognise cross the road and saunter towards us, their eyes on each other, or their phones. As they pass us not a single one of them glances our way.

Ayesha reaches for my hand and squeezes it. 'You're shaking. Take a deep breath. Try to calm down.'

I'm not sure I know how to do either of those things anymore. I just want to see my girl.

More kids now, in a huge group, cross the road and then peel off to the left and the right. I can't see all of their faces. One of them could be Grace. She might be walking to her new house or catching a lift with a friend. She might not be getting the bus at all.

'Remember what you promised me,' Ayesha says as my fingers reach for the door handle. 'You said you'd stay in the car.'

I press both hands between my knees but my right leg won't stop jiggling. The heels of my trainers are pounding the footwell so violently I'm probably wearing a hole in the mat.

'There she is!' Now my hands are over my mouth. 'Ayesha that's her, with the blonde hair, with those two dark-haired girls.'

Ayesha leans forward in her seat, looking for her. Along with Nancy she's Grace's godmother but, because Dominic was an arsehole about letting her see Grace while I was in prison, she hasn't seen Grace for over five years. Ayesha and

I were both interns at Sotheby's, the year before I met Dom, and we got on brilliantly right from the off. Ayesha left after six months to do a Master's in business but, unlike most work friendships that wane and drift when you no longer spend eight hours a day together, ours went from strength to strength. We went out to bars and clubs, and to yoga and spin class to try and counteract the late-night bags of chips and the bottles of wine. We went speed dating together and left, laughing our heads off at how cringy it was, halfway through. After I started dating Dominic she was one of the first people I introduced him to. Her opinion mattered so much to me that I was nervous the whole way through dinner. Afterwards, when she told me she really liked him, I couldn't have been more relieved.

The two dark-haired girls peel off after they've crossed the road and Grace pauses for a second, watching them go. She's too far away for me to see the expression in her eyes but the set of her face makes her appear worried. Is she lonely, just living with Dom? Does her heart sink when it's time to go home? Maybe she's envious of her friends' families? There's so much about my daughter's life I can only guess at, so much I don't know.

For one terrible second I think she's about to go after her friends, then she pulls her phone out of her jacket pocket, crams her earphones into her ears and walks down the street to where we're parked.

I will time to slow down as she draws closer. I need to look at her, to take in every last detail, to keep me going until I see her again. Her hair's longer than it was when she was a child, but she's still got the same wild, corkscrew curls. Her skin looks pale, gone is the ruddy healthiness of a child who'd play outside at every given opportunity, and the soft round-ness of her cheeks and jawline has almost faded away. She has high cheekbones like Dom, a smaller nose than either of us, full pink lips and my dark shadows beneath her eyes. She's a beautiful twelve-year-old girl but she's still my child, my confident, chatty seven-year-old, my giggly, silly three-year-old, the baby I held in my arms.

'Liv?' Ayesha's voice is a background hum as I reach for the door catch. 'Liv, don't! Liv, oh for fuck's sake no!'

Grace glances up from her phone, startled and unsure. There's confusion in her eyes as she looks me up and down then wariness and a dawning recognition as her gaze rests on my face. My heart leaps. This is the moment I've spent five years dreaming about, when she throws herself into my arms and everything that's happened is gone in an instant. Smithy was wrong. You can rewind time.

Smiling, I take a step closer, but the light dims in Grace's eyes and I draw to a halt. Her lips have tightened and her expression has hardened. We stare at each other, so close physically, the closest I've been to her in years, but never further apart.

'Gracie,' her name leaves my lips on a frightened whisper. This isn't how it was supposed to happen. I didn't expect her to look so angry. 'Gracie, I've missed you so much.'

She twists around to look behind her, to check her friends aren't watching or to look for help? But the street is empty, all the other kids have dispersed.

Her gaze returns, warily, to me. 'What happened to your eye?'

I touch a hand to the tender skin above my cheekbone. Before I left Ayesha's I plastered concealer onto the purple/green bruising but I may as well have put Tippex on a mural for all the difference it made.

'I knocked into something.'

21

My daughter's eyes narrow suspiciously. 'You look like you were in a fight.'

'I got out of prison yesterday.' The words come out in a rush. 'I know I'm not supposed to see you like this, that I should wait for a visit with Granny and Grandad, but I couldn't do that. I've missed you so much. I thought about you every single day I was away. The only thing that got me through it was the prospect of seeing you again.'

Grace recoils, shoulders hunched, head down as though every word I am saying is so repugnant, so cringeworthy, she just wants to disappear.

'I know it's a shock,' I continue, 'seeing me again, like this, but—'

'You tried to kill Dad!' The words explode out of her and her eyes, the palest of blue, just like Dominic's, glint with anger.

'I didn't. I promise you. Someone made it look as though I did but I really, really didn't.'

'The jury thought you did. People don't get sent to prison for something they didn't do.'

It's a phrase she's used before, when she was seven, in the first call I made to her from prison. It sounded to me as though she was parroting someone else's words, her grandparents' perhaps, or Dom's. Back then she accepted my explanation that sometimes mistakes are made and Mummy was trying very hard to get the judge to look at her case again. Seconds later we were talking about a dream she'd had the night before and the games she'd played at school with her friends.

'Gracie.' I take a step towards her and a spark of fear crosses her face. She thinks I'm going to hurt her. The thought sends a spike of pain through my heart. 'It's okay,' I step back again, hands raised. 'I'm not . . . I'm . . . I just . . . I just

22

wanted to hug you. I'm sorry, I know this is a shock and I'm not dealing with it the right way.'

Tears spark in my eyes and I glance back at the car, not wanting her to see them. Ayesha is sitting forward in her seat with her elbows on the steering wheel, worry written all over her face.

When I turn back to look at my daughter she's got her phone in her hands once again, her eyes fixed to the screen.

'Please,' I say, 'don't tell Daddy or Granny that you've seen me.'

'You don't get to tell me what to do.' Her voice breaks mid-sentence and I see a glimpse of the daughter I left behind as she fights to stay in control of her emotions.

'You're right. I don't, but I do love you, Grace. I need you to know that. I know you're angry with me and I understand why. But if you tell anyone about this then I'll be sent back to prison.'

'Good.' The word is a grunt from her throat but there's no force behind it.

'Ayesha gave me one of her old phones,' I add, 'and she bought me a Giffgaff SIM so I've got a new number. I wrote it down for you.'

I dig into the pocket of my sweatshirt and pull out a folded piece of paper. Grace glances up as I hold it out towards her, then looks back down at her phone.

'I'll just put it here, shall I?' There's a bin to my left with a broken umbrella resting against the base. I tuck the paper between the bent fronds. I can tell Grace is paying attention, despite the phone in her hands. Her body is tense, primed to run or react.

'I'm going to go back to Ayesha's flat now. I've written her address down too, just in case. It would be nice to text each other, sweetheart. I have missed you so much.'

My heart pounds as I walk back to Ayesha's car. *Please*, I will my daughter, *don't let me go*. But Grace doesn't look up and she doesn't run and hug me. She continues to stare down at her phone as Ayesha wordlessly starts up the engine and pulls into the road. I twist round in my seat staring desperately at the angry, hunched shape of my daughter as she grows smaller and smaller, and then disappears.

Chapter 5

DOMINIC

It is seven thirty in the morning and Dom is in bed with his arms above his head and his gaze fixed on the ceiling. He should be basking in a postcoital glow, but instead he is irritated. DS Danielle Anderson shouldn't be lying naked beside him, the duvet bunched over her hips. She should be in her own house, not his.

His plan had been to take her to a nice little eatery in Clapham for lunch then break the news that the on-off relationship they'd been having for the last five years was over. He knew she wouldn't make a scene in a public place, she had too much self-respect, and, true to form, Dani hadn't made a scene. She'd accepted the news with a shrug of her shoulders and a 'c'est la vie' little laugh then she'd ordered another bottle of wine and changed the subject. Three hours later Dom had an arm around her shoulders as they tumbled into a taxi. Thirty minutes after that, they were in bed.

Now what's he supposed to do? He doesn't want her to assume that he's changed his mind about them splitting up so they're probably going to have to have another conversation. He never meant to start up a relationship with Dani. She was his trainer, a side job she fitted in with her police work, and theirs was a strictly professional relationship. Well, it was until Dani asked him if he could lend her some money so she could send her sister to a private drug rehab clinic. At the time his stock market investments were doing well so he gave her five grand and said she didn't have to repay it. She was adamant that she'd pay it back in instalments, but she only gave him two hundred pounds and Dom didn't chase her for the rest. He'd been doing pretty well financially at the time and had liked the fact his money could help someone out. It had also struck him that it wouldn't be a bad idea to have a cop in his pocket, just in case he ever needed her help.

It turned out that he did.

Their relationship – not that he'd ever use that term, what they share is a far more casual affair than that – began with a drunken shag after Dani met him for a drink following Liv's trial. The sex is good – passionate and varied without the weight of love to complicate it. He's never enquired whether Dani is sleeping with anyone else and she's never asked him.

He pushes the duvet off and sits up, swinging his legs over the edge of the bed. Ghosting Dani would infuriate her. He's going to have to bite the bullet and explain that what just happened was a spontaneous goodbye shag. She appreciates plain speaking, it's one of the things he's always liked about her.

'Dani—'

'Dom—'

Their voices overlap and Dom hesitates. Maybe they're thinking along the same lines. If she wants to get there first then she's welcome to.

He nods. 'You go.'

Dani sits up, cradling the duvet to her chest, and Dominic feels a pang – not of regret per se, but of longing for something he'll never have again. With her pale brown eyes, slim but curvy body and shoulder-length chestnut hair swept into a side fringe, she has a look of forties film star Gene Tierney in the film *Laura*, but more bed-rumpled and real than primped and polished. Not that Dani would have the first idea who Gene Tierney is.

Once, when Olivia was in prison and Grace was away at school camp, he and Dani spent a whole evening together. He put on the film *The Ghost and Mrs Muir* and, partway through, Dani disappeared off to the kitchen to get another bottle of wine. When she didn't return after fifteen minutes he went looking for her and discovered her sitting on a stool at the counter, halfway down a bottle of red, scrolling through Instagram on her phone. It was the last time he tried to introduce her to one of his favourite films. It wasn't that her reaction made him feel *old* – he was only thirty-nine, and he was pretty sure there must be some twenty-six-year-old women who loved old black and white films – but it made him realise he'd overstepped the mark. Sharing your passions wasn't something people who were casually screwing did, that was boyfriend/girlfriend type shit.

The next day he told her he thought they should take a step back, give each other a bit of space. Dani looked surprised but didn't argue. Dominic's resolve lasted all of two months until he had too much to drink at a work do. He texted her, asking if she wanted to come over for a nightcap. She didn't reply until the next day: I was on shift but I might be free Sunday night. Any good?

No recrimination, no anger, no angst, nothing – she turned up, shared a bottle of wine with him then led him upstairs to the bedroom. The next morning she left before he or Grace got up and she didn't bother to text to say thanks or 'That was fun' or 'When can we do that again?' She was so laid-back it was refreshing. He'd never met a woman quite like her.

'Right so, first off have you got any paracetamol?' Dani presses a hand to the side of her head. 'I've got a shitload of case work to get through today and I haven't got time for a hangover.'

Dom nods and waits for her to continue.

'Also, don't freak out about *this*.' She waves a hand back and forth over the stretch of bedsheet between them. 'What happened happened. It was fun, as always, but, um . . .' for the first time since she began speaking she looks uncomfortable, 'I was going to mention this yesterday but you got in first and dumped me.' She laughs. 'It didn't seem appropriate to mention it after that. I feel like we're friends, in our own way, so I'm asking you now, before I go.'

'Asking me what?' Dom steels himself. It's either going to be money, or she's found something out. He *really* hopes it's money.

'It's Casey,' she says. 'She's relapsed again, in a big way.' She runs a hand through her hair, teasing her fingers through the tangled ends. 'She needs to go back to Carmichael House for treatment. I've done everything I can to save up but I've got nowhere near enough – a couple of thousand tops – and she needs to stay there for six months this time. Whatever causes her to take drugs, is still there, inside her. It hasn't gone away.'

Dom drops his gaze. He couldn't give her that kind of money even if he wanted to. He just hasn't got it anymore, not since his investments crashed and burned five years earlier. Ironically it was shortly after he gave her five grand because he was feeling flush. He lost everything, nearly every penny of his and Olivia's savings. He's been living off his earnings as a chartered surveyor ever since, not that there's much of his pay packet left after he's bought food, clothes and flute lessons for Grace, paid the bills, given his parents the rent for the house, and forked out for his rental car. Not that Dani knows any of that. To her, and to almost everyone else he knows, he's a big shot in the City with a large house in Crouch End and an Audi Spyder in the driveway.

He kneads his temples and closes his eyes. She's not the only one with a hangover.

'I'm sorry Dani, I can't.'

'Are you sure?' There's surprise in her voice. 'I know thirty grand is a lot but we can draw up another arrangement. I'll pay you back every penny, I promise.'

Dominic stands up and pulls on his dressing gown, keeping his back to her so she can't see the expression on his face. 'Have you tried the bank?'

'They don't lend money for this sort of thing.'

'Say it's for a car.'

'I can't get a loan.' She says each word separately, the emphasis on *get*. 'My credit history is shit. I've got a five grand overdraft and I pay the minimum amount of interest on my credit card.'

'I thought you said you had a couple of grand saved up?'

'It's not enough. I still—' she breaks off with a sigh. 'Is this because Olivia's out?'

Dom stiffens. 'How do you know about that?'

'I rang someone I know in the prison service.'

Alarm bells clang in Dom's brain. In the five years he and Dani have been sleeping together she hasn't brought up his ex-wife once.

'Why?' he asks tightly.

'Because I heard you on the phone to your daughter's

school, the last time we hooked up. You said you were worried about Olivia turning up at Grace's school.'

He remembers the phone call. It was to Grace's head of year. He's been in frequent contact with the woman since his daughter started secondary school – mostly about the bullying.

'What's that got to do with you?'

His tone is barbed and Dani raises her eyebrows. 'Because I had a hand in Olivia's conviction and if she's getting out I want to know about it.'

'By earwigging private conversations?'

He's not entirely sure why he's so angry with her but he's under a lot of pressure, his head's ringing and he wants her gone. It was a mistake to let her stay the night.

'Look Dom.' Dani swings her legs out of bed and yanks on her jeans. 'You don't want me to interfere, I get it, and I'm gone. After today you won't see me again. But you're not the only one with responsibilities here. If I don't get my sister private care she'll overdose and die and you're the only person who can help me.' She pulls her T-shirt over her head and stuffs her bra and knickers into her jeans pocket.

'I told you,' he says. 'I can't.'

She stares at him from across the bed, bristling with frustration. 'Can't or won't?'

He stares back, anger bubbling in his chest like lava. Everyone wants something from him and he's sick of it. He wants to run as far away as he can from his claustrophobic, penny-pinching life and never look back.

'Won't,' he says steadily.

Dani's eyes flare with rage. 'Fuck you, Dom. If Casey dies it's on you.' She storms out of the room, slamming the door shut behind her. A split second later the door opens again. 'And if that happens I'll make sure you spend the rest of your life in prison.'

Dom's pulse quickens. 'If I go down, Dani, so do you. You're in it up to your neck and I can prove it.'

'Prove what?' Her eyes narrow.

'You didn't think I'd hand over all that money without recording our little chat for posterity, did you?'

Her lips part but, instead of responding, she turns sharply, swears, and disappears out onto the landing. Dom crosses the bedroom, pulling his dressing gown tightly around his body, and heads for the open door. What did she see that spooked her? He stands in the doorway and looks left, towards the stairs, but Dani's already disappeared downstairs. He looks to his right, towards his daughter's bedroom, and rises up on his toes, a gasp of surprise catching in his throat.

'Gracie?' His daughter is in her school uniform, her hair smoothed back into a ponytail, her eyes cold. 'What the hell? I thought you were at Louisa's house?'

'I was. But I forgot this,' she jerks the flute case in her hand. 'Louisa's waiting for me downstairs.'

'Did, um . . . did you see . . .' The words tumble out of his mouth as his brain frantically scrabbles to keep up. 'That was Dani, my personal trainer.'

'Why was she in your bedroom?'

'I had a shower after we worked out and she popped in to tell me something.'

Grace's judgemental expression doesn't shift. 'Your hair isn't wet.'

'Before.' He runs a shaky hand through his hair. 'She needed to tell me something before my shower.'

His daughter gives him a lingering look then strolls past him, flute case swinging from her hand. She pauses at the top of the stairs and crouches down, her hand stretching for something that Dom can't see. When Grace stands up again she casually hangs whatever she found around the knob of

31

a banister and makes her way down the stairs. Dom waits in the doorway, heart pounding, as his daughter calls to her friend. Seconds later he hears footsteps on the polished tiles in the entrance hall. When the front door slams and the house falls silent he steps across the landing and plucks the discarded item from the banister knob.

It's Dani's sheer black gossamer bra.

Chapter 6

DANI

'Fuck!' Dani breathes the word into her hands, her fingers steepled over her nose, then twists at the waist and smashes her fist into the peeling gym punchbag. 'Fuck, fuck, fuck.'

Ever since she left Dom's house, a little after 7.30 a.m., she's been feeling like she wants to beat the shit out of someone or something – her computer when it took forever to return a search result; DS Reece Argent for staring at her during the team briefing; the woman behind the deli counter when she got her lunch order wrong – and now she's taking it out on the punchbag in the gym.

For every punch she mentally aims at Dom's face, she adds two to her own. What was she thinking, assuming he didn't have anything on her? She drew up a repayment plan when Casey entered rehab and paid Dominic back two hundred pounds of the five grand he'd given her. It was a stupid thing to do in retrospect but, at that point, Dani hadn't done anything dodgy. Unlike Olivia, Dominic knew she was a cop and there were no strings attached to the money.

As far as Dani knew, Dominic Sutherland was a legitimate businessman. She'd entered his name into a database at work and nothing had come up, not even a minor affray. When he'd confided in her that he thought something dodgy was going on with his wife she still thought he was a decent bloke. She knew Liv was having an affair, but it wasn't her place to tell Dominic. They were both her clients and she wasn't going to get involved in their private lives. But then Dom told her about the life insurance document he'd found – Liv had increased the payout she'd get in the event of his death – and how he'd grown suspicious after overhearing phone calls his wife had made to her lover.

Most worrying was Dominic's admission that he was being followed by a man dressed in black, and that he feared for his life. He begged Dani to intervene, suggesting she take Liv out to the pub. If Olivia was drunk she might become loose-lipped and he needed a concrete confession to take to the police. As a thank you he'd give Dani another five grand so Casey could stay in rehab for two months rather than just one.

Dani refused. She was on shaky ground as it was, accepting the first five grand as a gift when he knew she was a cop. Actively accepting more money in return for providing evidence that could lead to a conviction was a massive no no. It was corrupt practice and she could end up in prison herself. But then Casey ended up in hospital after an overdose. The doctors told Dani that Casey would almost certainly die if she overdosed again. She had to get clean. That night Dani asked Olivia to go for a drink. Twenty-four hours after that, Dom handed over five grand and Dani booked her sister into Carmichael House, the most secure private rehabilitation unit she could find. As Casey screeched and wailed as she was led inside Dani could only pray that two months would be enough to save her sister's life.

Jab, jab, upper cut. She smashes her fist into the belly of the bag.

She's been ignoring her phone all day because she knows her mum Brenda is at home with Casey, waiting for an update. When Dani said she'd sort the money for treatment Brenda nodded tightly, her lips pressed into a thin, tight line. She didn't ask where she'd find thirty grand, she just wanted Casey to be well.

Dominic Sutherland was Dani's last option. She hadn't wanted to ask him for money again, not when sometimes she woke in the night feeling like she'd sold her soul to the devil to save her sister's life.

She liked Dominic and she enjoyed sleeping with him. No-strings sex suited her – whenever she got into a relationship normally the bloke would moan about her hours and question her relationships with her male colleagues – and seeing Dom every few months meant she could check the lie of the land.

The first time she met Dom she was more focused on his fitness goals than checking him out. She registered that he was attractive – tall, dark with piercing blue eyes and an athletic physique – but he was a client, thirteen years older than her, and married. He was also a bit of a Jekyll and Hyde. One day he'd be charming and funny, the next snappy and irritable. She began to understand why he was so irascible when he began quizzing her about his wife's movements – had she been going to all her sessions, had she ever mentioned another man's name?

Jab, hook, jab, hook. Dani gives the punchbag everything she's got with her arms then attacks it with her legs, smashing out a roundhouse kick then jump-kicking the bag until her quads are burning and she's gasping for breath. She sits down on a weights bench, her head between her knees, and takes

35

long, slow breaths until her heart stops hammering. She's screwed up. Threatening Dom was a mistake. Now she's got to find thirty grand, save her sister's life, *and* watch her back.

Chapter 7

OLIVIA

I knock on Nancy's red front door then check my phone. There's still no message from Grace. Yesterday, as Ayesha drove away from the school, there was a part of me that hoped Grace would pluck my phone number from the fronds of the umbrella, driven by curiosity or love. That dream has faded with each hour that's passed since. Life has shaped my daughter into someone I no longer know. I don't know what she's experienced, how much she hurts, or how many lies she's been fed. We've got a supervised visit tomorrow but how can I rebuild Grace's trust in me with her grandparents hovering around?

'Olivia?' The door swings open. 'Olivia, oh my god!'

I almost don't recognise Nancy as she lunges towards me for a hug. She's dyed her brown hair bright red and it's almost down to her waist, her skin is healthy and glowing and she looks so elegant I want to cry. I return her hug, trying not to feel self-conscious in the cheap, shapeless viscose dress I picked up from Primark this morning. My roots need doing and my fingernails are bitten down to the quick but more than just my appearance has changed since we last saw each other. I'm rougher on the inside too.

Nancy pulls away to look at my face. 'I can't believe you're out. Are you a mirage?' She laughs her throaty laugh. 'Oh it's so, so good to see you, Liv. I've missed you so much.'

Looking into her sparkling, laughing eyes again I feel as though I have stepped back in time, as if I've popped round for a bite to eat or a quick coffee before I collect Grace from school. Instead I'm here to say hello after five years in prison and to pick through the belongings Nancy's been keeping in her garage since Dominic threw them out. Momentarily I'm the woman I used to be, living the life I used to have, and it makes my heart ache.

'Come in, come in.' She grabs my hand. 'I've got champagne in the fridge.'

I follow her into the living room, a room I know almost as well as my own (or what used to be my old living room). Dom and I used to come round at least once a month, hanging out with Ian and Nance, drinking wine, chatting, laughing and, way before Grace was born, passing around a joint. The sofas have changed since I was last here – Nancy's finally convinced Ian to get rid of those horrible old leather things – but everything else is pretty much the same. There's an impressive wooden fireplace with the original tiled surround, the paintings Nancy bought from my gallery hanging on the crisp white walls, an elegant glass coffee table and a sixty-inch TV with secret hidden speakers that Ian installed in the walls to give cinema-effect surround sound.

I was wary of Nancy when we first met fifteen years ago. Not only was she the loudest person in the restaurant with a cackle that made the other diners openly stare, she was the first woman Ian had introduced us to since Helena, his previous girlfriend, had died eighteen months earlier, and Nancy had some pretty big shoes to fill. Dom and I both adored Helena, a diminutive blonde from Manchester whose lust for life made her presence fill every room she entered. They'd been together for only two years when she was involved in a car accident on the M6 as she travelled home to see her parents. She died at the scene. Ian was heartbroken, as were we.

Ian Ritchie is Dominic's best friend from uni and he's one of those people you warm to within minutes of meeting them. Jovial, unpretentious and scruffy, he's not the sort of person I would have expected to be friends with Dominic but their relationship works. They're like a double act when they're together – quoting from films and feeding each other lines with Ian playing the fool to Dominic's straight man. I was hugely nervous the first time I met Ian because I knew how much Dominic valued his friend's opinion, more so than his own parents', but Ian put me at ease immediately, pushing a shot of tequila into my hand after a hearty hello.

I felt protective of Ian's heart after he lost Helena and Nancy's ebullience made me worry she might not be serious about him, but I couldn't have been more wrong. She was warm, kind and funny and when she looked at Ian I could see in her eyes how much she loved him. By the end of the meal I adored her and I hoped she felt the same about me.

'Here you go!' She hands me a glass of champagne and takes a seat on the sofa beside me. 'I want to know everything. How do you feel? How was prison? Have you seen Grace yet? Have you heard from Jack?'

'I'm fine, prison was pretty awful and . . . what else did you ask?' Unlike Ayesha, whose calm manner and soft voice have an almost soporific effect on me, Nancy's loud voice and machine-gun conversational approach can either make me feel energised or steamrollered.

'And Grace?'

'I'm seeing her tomorrow, a supervised visit to the zoo with Dom's parents.'

She raises her eyebrows. 'That'll be nice.'

We both laugh. She's met George and Esther. She knows what they're like.

'So, how are you anyway?' I ask. 'How's Ian?'

'He's good. Still busy with work. On top form, as always.'

'And you two? Are you still happy?'

'Depends what we're talking about.' She laughs and takes a sip of her champagne but her gaze swivels awkwardly away. I don't have to ask what the source of conflict is in their marriage: it's me. Ian didn't go to my trial, and he didn't make contact with me afterwards. It breaks my heart to think that the man I adored, who made me cry with laughter and hugged me like I was his favourite person in the world, has taken Dominic's side. But why would he do otherwise? Dominic's his best friend. And Nancy's one of mine. I can only imagine the arguments they've had. Weaker marriages would have collapsed completely under the strain.

'Anyway,' Nancy waves a manicured hand through the air, 'tell me about Jack. Have you heard from him at all?'

Nancy, Ayesha and Dani were the only people I told about my affair with Jack. Nancy was there when Jack and I first met, at the Louise Hayward exhibition in my gallery. She saw how he looked at me, how he smiled, how he spoke. I think she liked that Jack put a smile on my face. Whenever I saw her afterwards she'd tease me, asking if I'd had another visit from the handsome art connoisseur. When I told her I hadn't seen him since, she read the lie on my face. When I confessed that I was falling in love she didn't judge me once.

'No,' I say. 'I haven't heard from Jack.'

The last time I saw him, we had lunch at the Shard. I'd

made up my mind to tell Dominic everything when I returned from a Paris art fair three days later. Grace would be away at Brownie Camp and Dominic and I would have the house to ourselves for a few hours. The guilt I'd felt since my first kiss with Jack had grown so large, so heavy, it was as though a new organ had grown in my belly, and I wanted it gone.

Dominic had become unbearable in the months before I began my affair with Jack. Our marriage been limping along for years – neither happy nor unbearable but in a lacklustre limbo in-between – but when he lost our savings it imploded. It wasn't just money for holidays or a rainy day that he'd thrown at the stock market. It was money we'd both saved so we could buy our own home and cut the apron strings with his mother and father. We had enough for a deposit on a modest house with just enough left for Grace's future and for me to put into my gallery. Dominic wanted our own place as much as I did but he hated that we had to be careful with money in order to save. He wanted to be like the partners at his company: flying away on exotic holidays, putting their kids in private school, driving the best cars, wearing expensive watches and ordering Cristal champagne without a second thought. I guess that's why he did what he did. When he confessed we were in a restaurant in town. It was my birthday but, instead of giving me a present after we'd finished our meal, he handed me that bomb. I'm fairly certain he timed his confession so I wouldn't make a scene. I didn't. I was too shocked to speak. I said nothing as he paid for the meal and I stared mutely out of the window during the taxi ride home.

The moment the front door closed behind us, denial kicked in. The money couldn't all be gone, could it? There had to be a way to get it back. Some kind of ombudsman or compensation scheme? Dominic shook his head, telling me over and over again that it was gone. When denial slid into anger I ranted and raged until Dominic threw me across the room in frustration. As my tears dampened the carpet he announced that he was going to pick Grace up from Brownie Camp and that I should sort myself out before our daughter returned. The next day I moved out, telling Grace I had to go to an art fair. I went to Ayesha's for forty-eight hours and Dominic bombarded me with texts. He was sorry. He'd made the biggest mistake of his life. He wanted me to come home. Grace missed me. So did he.

I moved back in – more for my daughter than myself or Dominic – and, for a couple of weeks, Dominic became the man I'd fallen in love with so many years before. He was thoughtful and gentle, clever and funny, and then, just as I began to soften, he wasn't. He began sniping at me and he criticised every decision I made – whether it was to do with the business, the Tesco order, or Grace. His temper, which had always been short, became explosive. A simple request to hand me a mug from the cupboard would either be ignored or result in a cup being thrown across the room. When I told him I'd decided to sleep in the spare room for a bit, he put his fist through the wall. What began as irritation morphed into something much worse. He resented me. I was the reason his life hadn't panned out the way he'd planned. I was the reason he felt like a failure. Being with me made him feel trapped. I felt it as powerfully as a heatwave. And then I met Jack.

Over lunch, Jack said he'd come with me when I told Dominic about us. He was worried that, this time, it wouldn't just be the wall that Dominic punched. I was touched by his protectiveness but there was no way I could agree. To tell my husband I was leaving him was one thing; to parade the man I was in love with in front of him was another. Jack and I hugged at the entrance to London Bridge station and told each other we loved each other. I promised to text him from Paris and let him know I'd arrived safely, and again, after I'd seen Dom.

'He didn't write to you in prison?' Nancy searches my face. 'Not a single letter to explain why he ghosted you?'

'No.'

'What an absolute bastard.'

Tears prick at my eyes but a sudden rush of anger dries them. I promised myself a long time ago that I'd never cry over Jack Law again.

He responded to the text I sent him from Paris but he didn't reply to the ones I sent when I returned, from the spare room at home, my eyes red and puffy and my throat raw after the most awful conversation of my life. He didn't pick up when I rang the next day and he didn't answer the intercom when I stood outside his flat in the rain with my finger on the buzzer. The last text I received from him was three days after I ended my marriage to my husband: I'm sorry, Liv. I love you but I can't do this anymore.

I replied, begging him to meet up, but my WhatsApp messages went unread. I rang, only for each call to go to voicemail. I wrote him letters and virtually camped outside his flat, ringing his bell over and over again. But he never caved, and he never replied. I'd destroyed my marriage, my daughter's stability and my life for Jack, and in return he ran away.

I didn't think I could feel any lower, any more wretched or any more broken.

And then three weeks later I was arrested for a crime I didn't commit.

We sort through the cardboard boxes and bin bags stacked up in one corner of the garage, the silence occasionally punctuated by Nancy saying, 'This dress is nice. Do you want to take it with you?' or 'Do you need books? I'm sure Ayesha has loads.' I say no to most of her suggestions. What I'm searching for are photographs of Grace but it looks like Dominic has kept them all.

'Are you going to confront her?' Nancy asks, out of nowhere, as I sort through a bag full of underwear, toiletries and jewellery, all thrown in together.

'Who?'

'Dani.'

A shudder ripples through me. 'God no. If she could screw me over once she could do it again. If I'm going to confront anyone it's Jack.'

The thought of seeing him again floods my mind with memories: his eyes searching mine before he leaned down and our lips touched for the very first time; the weight of his arm across the back of my neck as we walked along the Southbank; the studied concentration on his face as we looked through second-hand books under Waterloo Bridge; the deep rumble of his laughter in a Chinatown restaurant as I stared in horror at the plate full of chicken feet that had been placed in front of me; and the warmth of his body as it curled around mine. I'd been trudging through life for months, weighed down by worry after Dominic had squandered our life savings, shackled to a man who seemed to view me as an irritation in his life. Being with Jack was like I'd thrown off those chains, like I was suddenly free. I felt alive, I felt young, I felt like anything was possible as long as Jack was by my side. Then he disappeared when I needed him most.

'But aren't you curious?' Nancy says, whisking me back into the dimly lit garage. 'To hear Dani's side of things?'

I spent days, months, in prison analysing my relationship with Dani and the events that led to me being arrested. I hadn't expected to build a friendship with my personal trainer – how could you like someone who caused you pain on a weekly basis? Then there was the fact we had nothing in common. I was a flabby mum of one in my thirties who spent her days balancing childcare and trying to get her gallery off the ground. Dani was mid-twenties with a rock-hard body and drive and determination that I could only dream of. But we did become friends, in the gym at least. Looking back I can see how one-sided that relationship was. She knew loads about me and I knew next to nothing about her. I didn't even know she worked for the Metropolitan Police. When she invited me out for a drink one night, I was so flattered I immediately said yes. She was a fast drinker and nipped off to the bar before I could offer to get a round in. We mixed our drinks – gin and tonics, cocktails and then shot after shot after shot. I couldn't remember a thing the next morning, not even how I got home.

I don't need to hear Dani's side of things. I can't remember what I said that drunken evening when she claimed I said I wished my husband were dead but I know she lied and I'm pretty sure Dominic paid her to do so. Initially I assumed that he was so angry at me for leaving him for Jack that he framed us both. He couldn't bear the thought of Grace living with another man. I told Ayesha my theory the first time she visited me in jail. She regarded me dubiously. Wasn't framing someone a pretty extreme way of enacting revenge? Dominic was risking a prison sentence himself if he'd got caught. Why not fight me in the courts and make out I was an unfit mother? The more I thought about it the more convinced I became that she had a point. It *was* an extreme thing to do. There had to be a reason he wanted me out of the way.

'Olivia,' Nancy says now. 'Don't you think that—'

A cough from across the garage cuts her off. Ian is standing in the doorway to the kitchen, his six-foot-four frame almost filling the space. He's grown a beard since the last time I saw him. It's wiry and gingery like his mop of wild hair. He's wearing a navy suit with his tie loosened and the top button of his shirt undone. His murky green eyes flick from me to his wife.

'What's she doing here?'

'Hi, Ian,' I say before Nancy can speak. 'Sorry to surprise you like you this but I needed to get a few things.'

'Liv—' Nancy starts, but Ian talks over her.

'I'd like you to leave, please.'

I take a step towards him, horrified by the tight set of his face. He looks nothing like the Ian I knew and loved. Who is this coldly polite man who can barely bring himself to look at me?

'Can we talk about this? Please? I really don't want to lose your friendship. I know what you think I've done but—'

'Just go. Please.'

Nancy drops the bin bag she's holding and joins my side. 'Ian, don't be like this. At least hear her out.'

'I don't need to hear anything she's got to say.'

Five minutes ago I felt comfortably warm from the champagne and sorting through the bags, but the temperature has dropped since Ian appeared.

Tears prick at my eyes as I pick up the small pile of things I've selected from the box of underwear and jewellery, then I turn to Nancy. 'I'll call you later, okay?'

'Of course.' We hug tightly then I walk towards the doorway. Ian steps out of my way.

'I don't know who you are anymore,' he says softly as I leave the kitchen and enter the hallway. 'I wish you'd never met Jack.'

Chapter 8

DOMINIC

Dominic sits in his car in the underground car park beneath the shining tower block in South London where he works as a chartered surveyor, his burner phone in his hand. He really, really wants a drink. He's spent the whole day stewing about Grace and her fucking flute, and what she might have overheard. Then there's the threat Dani made. He's been distracted in meetings all day and he even swerved an appointment to survey a multi-million-pound town house in Chelsea for an important client, making his PA ring up with a pathetic health-related excuse. If he doesn't anaesthetise some of the stress he's feeling, he's going to explode.

D wanted more money. He bashes out a message, using the buttons of the phone as miniature punchbags for his thumbs. I said no.

His phone pings with a response.

And?

He types back.

She threatened to shop me.

His phone pings again.

She won't. She's got too much to lose.

Dominic runs a hand over the back of his neck. It's tacky with sweat and the collar of his shirt feels too tight. He loosens his tie then turns his attention back to his phone.

She's knows L is out.

So?

He turns the key in the ignition and puts the air conditioning on full blast. It's not a hot day but it seems airless in his car and he feels claustrophobic, sitting in the low light of the car park with thousands of tonnes of glass and metal above his head.

It feels dangerous.

DO NOT LOSE YOUR SHIT NOW, the reply arrives, all in caps.

But Dominic is losing his shit. He's on the verge of bankruptcy, his daughter hates him, his ex-wife is out of prison and he's pissed off someone who could bring the fragile pile of cards that is his life tumbling down.

Another text flashes up on the screen.

There is a way out of this.

His stomach churns. He knows exactly what the sender is referring to. It's something he's been saying no to for years but he's running out of options.

Ok, he types back. Tell me what to do.

Chapter 9

I feel as though I'm being tailed by two geriatric private eyes. Esther and George Sutherland are pretending to be interested in the Gorilla Kingdom but, whenever the distance between us increases by a metre or two, Esther gives George a sharp little nudge and they trail after us again.

Grace hasn't said a word to me other than the quietest of 'Hi's when we met at the entrance. She looked like a comma, head down, spine curved, her body language screaming, 'I want to be anywhere but here.' But it was me she chose to walk beside, after her grandparents paid for her ticket, not them. I'm taking it as a positive sign. I'll take anything as a sign right now.

My social worker told me that London Zoo, the setting for my first supervised meeting with Grace, was 'a neutral location where the distractions may help ease some of the awkwardness and pressure that you and Grace might feel'. I suspect the zoo was Esther's suggestion. If I thought my ex-daughter-in-law had tried to have my son killed I wouldn't be in any hurry to let her into my house either.

My mind buzzes as we walk, in silence, past the Gorilla Kingdom and towards Penguin Beach. I should say something – it's down to me to knock down the invisible barrier between us – but I'm worried that if I get it wrong I'll add even more bricks to the wall. Every question I think of sounds trite. Grace won't want to tell me about school or her hobbies. She won't want me to know about her friends or any boys she might like. We've got five years to fill and I don't know where to start. So much has happened in the last twenty-four hours that I can't hold onto a thought for more than a couple of seconds before another one crowds it out.

Yesterday, I returned from being booted out of Nancy's house to Ayesha's empty flat. She'd told me she was going away on a work trip but I'd forgotten and the silent flat, and the sounds of life – footsteps, shouts, laughter and random bangs and bumps – in the rest of the block, unnerved me. For the first time since I'd left prison I felt misplaced and unsafe. My thoughts turned to Smithy, lying on the top bunk of our cell with someone else in the bed below her. My bed. Smithy would be laughing, chatting and taking the piss. A wave of loneliness washed over me. I had no one to talk to and very little credit on my phone so I kept myself busy, watering Ayesha's plants and cleaning the flat.

I slept fitfully and when my alarm went off a little after seven I peeled myself off the sofa, tired and sore. My appointment with the job agency was at 9.30 a.m. It was a 'monitored appointment' – part of my probation terms – and if I missed it I'd be screwed. Besides, I was skint.

I'd used up a huge chunk of my savings paying my defence team. The rest went to my solicitor after Dominic filed for divorce. The house belongs to his parents and I received next to nothing in the settlement. There was no money in the art gallery I co-owned with my friend Lee either. He'd dissolved it when he couldn't keep up with the debts.

'I've got an interview for a job,' I tell Grace.

Her blue eyes flicker in my direction. 'Doing what?'

'Cleaner.' The member of staff at the job agency for ex-cons had laughed when I'd requested a position in the arts. 'I need to save up some money so that—'

Two shadows sweep over my feet. Esther and George have crept closer. They can hear every word I say.

'So I can rent a flat of my own,' I continue. 'Somewhere big enough for you to stay too.'

There's a spark of anger in my daughter's eyes. 'Don't bother. If I can't stay with Dad I'd rather sleep on the streets than live with you.'

The heat hits me full in the face as I follow Grace through the plastic flaps at the entrance to the Butterfly Paradise enclosure and a large black and white butterfly swoops past, making me duck.

'Grace!' I touch her on the shoulder. 'What did you mean, if you can't stay with Dad?'

She spins around as though stung. Her cheeks are pink from the heat but her eyes are narrowed and cold. 'Don't pretend you care.'

She stalks through the enclosure and tucks herself into the small space between a butterfly feeding station and a window that allows visitors to look at developing cocoons. In her black leggings and close-fitting pink T-shirt she looks much slighter than she did in her school uniform, but she's nearly as tall as me. The last time I saw her her cheek would press against my stomach when we hugged. Not that there's any chance of a hug now, she can't even bring herself to look at me. Her body is angled towards the butterfly feeding post, forcing me to talk to her back.

'Grace, of course I care. That's why I went to your school to see you, it's why I'm here now.'

She mumbles something I can't hear.

'What was that, love?'

'If you hadn't gone to prison, you'd have run off with Jack and left me behind.'

My breath catches in my throat. There's no way she can have known about my affair. She never met Jack, I was really careful about that. How many lies have Dom and his parents fed her over the last five years? How much damage have they done?

'That's not true.' A woman with two kids, one in a buggy, one holding her hand, passes between us and I lower my voice. 'I did fall in love with Jack but I'd never have chosen him over you. If I'd left Dad I would have taken you with me.'

'Liar. I can't trust any of you.'

'Grace, that's not true.'

'How would you know?' She turns sharply, her eyes shining with emotion. 'You don't know anything about my life. You don't know anything about me.'

The urge to reach out and touch her, to comfort her, is so strong I have to push my hands deep into my pockets.

'You're right. I don't know anything about your life now but I do know you, sweetheart. For seven years I loved you and I looked after you and—'

'And then you left me. Just like Dad's going to.'

'What?'

'There you are!' Esther's voice rings out from somewhere behind us. 'George, would you hurry up? I don't care what you've spotted. We're supposed to be keeping an eye on Grace.'

52

'What do you mean, Dad's going to leave you?' I ask my daughter but she's slipped past me and is heading for the exit.

'Grace.' I hurry after her. 'Where's Dad going?'

'Leave me alone,' she snaps as she pushes her way out through the plastic flaps and a blast of cool air hits my face.

'I will if you tell me where your dad's going. Because if—'

'Prison!' she bellows in my face. 'He was arguing with his stupid personal trainer and Dad said that if he goes down, so does she. And then she left and I found her bra on the stairs. So she's not his trainer at all, is she?' She pauses a beat, her eyes shining with angry tears. 'Stop staring at me like that. I don't want you in my life. I don't want anyone. I just want to be by myself.'

Chapter 10

DANI

Dani is at her desk, reviewing the disclosure schedules for one of her colleague's forthcoming trials. She's trying to block out the sound of her workmates chatting, tapping at their keyboards and speaking on the phone, but it's not just the office noise that's making her struggle to concentrate. She's thinking about Casey. When she went to Brenda's house last night she'd been shocked at just how much her sister had deteriorated in a couple of weeks. Casey was stumbling around the kitchen, red-eyed, pale-faced and thin. She was trying to make a cup of tea and her hand shook as she took a mug from the counter. Dani was so scared of Casey getting burned, she had to pour the water from the kettle for her.

Her sister had been so happy when she left the private clinic nearly five years earlier. She was still very slight but the hollows had disappeared from beneath her cheekbones and her eyes were bright, not dimmed. She was healthier, physically, but the biggest change was in her personality. She no

54

longer looked at Dani or their mother with empty, blank eyes, dismissing their suggestions to go somewhere or do something together with the smallest shake of her head. For the three years, from eighteen to twenty-one, that drug addiction had held Casey in its grip Dani had felt like she'd lost her sister. All the hobbies they'd shared – horse-riding, karate and swimming – no longer interested Casey and the things they used to laugh about no longer raised a smile. When Dani had gripped her sister's hands and begged her to get help Casey looked straight through her and said, 'I don't know why you care. We were never very close.' Dani fled to the bathroom and screamed into a towel. It was the addiction speaking, not her sister.

And now she's losing her again.

'She's always sleeping,' Brenda told Dani. 'She barely eats and if she does go out it's to buy drugs. She's killing herself and I don't know what to do.'

Dani could kill Joshua, Casey's ex-boyfriend. If he hadn't cheated on her none of this would have happened. They wouldn't have split up, Casey wouldn't have moved back in with their mum and she wouldn't have started using again to try and numb the pain.

Dani sighs heavily and puts down the pile of papers in her hands. She's read the same document three times and hasn't taken a word of it in.

'You all right, Dan?' asks Jess, the detective constable sitting at the computer opposite her.

'Yeah.' She pushes her chair away from her desk. 'Shit night's sleep, that's all. Do you want a coffee?'

'As if you need to ask.'

Dani weighs up her options as she makes her way to the little corner of the office that serves as a kitchen. None of her mates could lend her three grand, never mind thirty, and she can't ask the guys in the department to do a whip-round, not for a sister on drugs. She could go to a loan shark but then she'd spend the rest of her life paying off ten times the amount. She thinks, fleetingly, about all the seized cash that's bagged up in the evidence store, then immediately dismisses the thought. Even if she could do it – and it would be near impossible – the possibility of being caught by a colleague makes her feel sick.

She unscrews a jar of cheap instant coffee and spoons it into two mugs. It's looking increasingly like Dominic Sutherland is her only option. It was a pretty firm no but she could try him again. They were both hungover last time and things escalated. If she doesn't lose her shit again maybe she can talk him round. She puts two spoonfuls of sugar into Jess's mug then opens the fridge for the milk.

'Danielle?' She stiffens at the sound of a familiar voice. Detective Sergeant Reece Argent has sidled up behind her, stinking of aftershave with a smarmy look on his unshaven face. He asked her out a couple of months ago and she said no. He seemed to take it well but she keeps catching him staring at her in briefings or across the office. Wherever she is, he is too, like a literal bad smell. She ignores the fact he called her by her full name. He does it to get a reaction and she's not going to give him one.

'What do you want, Reece?'

'Fielding wants to see you.'

Her heart rate quickens. She can't be the only copper who assumes they're in for a bollocking when their boss calls them in for a chat. Unless . . . her stomach clenches. Unless Dom's come good on his threat. She straightens up, the milk carton still in her hand.

'Why?'

Reece's eyes flick from her face to her chest. 'He's probably discovered what you've been up to.'

She tenses. 'What's that supposed to mean?'

'It's a joke.' He smiles, his thin lips pulled tightly over coffee-stained teeth.

Chapter 11

OLIVIA

It's pouring with rain as I exit Wood Green tube station and hurry down the street, hood up, head down. Nearly twenty-four hours have passed since I saw Grace but her words are still ringing in my ears: her dad said that *if he goes down, so does she*. I couldn't get any more out of her and, after we left the butterfly enclosure, Esther and George stuck to us like glue.

What Grace said has confirmed my suspicion that Dominic and Dani were behind the plan to frame me. I thought it was a purely financial agreement but it looks like they've been sleeping together all along. It explains the long dark hair I found on our bed shortly after their PT sessions began. I plucked it from my cotton pillowcase, held it up to him and jokingly asked if he was having an affair. Dominic rolled his eyes. It was a hair, not an earring or a pair of knickers, he said. Either one of us could have brought it home with us, stuck to our clothes or our skin, after a long day at work. He'd taken my jokey accusation far more seriously than I'd expected him to. It was obviously guilt.

A man knocks into me and swears as I'm hit by a thought and stop walking. Dominic sleeping with Dani also explains what I found.

Two months before I was arrested I popped into Dom's home office to get my passport. We kept all the family passports together, shoved between two books on one of the shelves. I was due to fly to Paris for the Salon du Dessin art fair. Lee had argued that he should be the one to go because he knew one of the artists and thought he could charm him into letting us show his work. I countered saying I hadn't been to a fair for ages and he'd been to one recently in Madrid. He eventually agreed that I should go but there was a frosty atmosphere in the gallery for the rest of the day.

Dom's office was as neat and tidy as usual but there was a new addition to his uncluttered desk: a book about nutrition and exercise, lying next to his mouse. I picked it up, curious. My husband had never been a big reader, films were more his thing. Dani's name was scrawled on the inside cover. She must have lent it to him, it wasn't the sort of thing he'd buy for himself. There was a piece of paper, peeking from between the pages, so I pulled it out. It was an A4 sheet from a notepad, folded in two. At the top someone had scrawled '£5,000' and beneath it were three columns – dates, money, balance, all written by hand. The first entry was dated that day; £200 had been paid leaving a balance of £4,800. I initially thought it was something to do with his lock-up. We didn't have a double garage and, when Dom had bought a motorbike a few years earlier, he'd insisted on forking out a small fortune for a private lock-up to keep it safe.

'What are you doing?' His barked question from the doorway made me jump.

I held up the piece of paper. 'What's this?'

He crossed the office and snatched it out of my hand.

'Nothing important,' he said after he'd looked at it. 'I've set up a bank account for Grace.'

'But we already pay into an ISA, I opened it on her first birthday.'

'Yeah well,' he tucked it into the inside pocket of his jacket, 'this is different.'

'Different how?' There was something about the tense set of his shoulders and the way his gaze kept shifting from me to the book, still lying on the corner of his desk, that wasn't sitting right.

'My parents are paying into it.' He looked at me, steadily now, daring me to question him further. 'When Uncle Bernie died and they cleared his house they found twenty grand in cash under his bed. They're paying it into all the grandkids' accounts, bit by bit to avoid death duty.'

Interesting, and unlikely. Esther and George were comfortably wealthy – they could have made double the rent we were paying them on our town house on the edge of Crouch Lane if they'd gone through an agent. So wealthy that they'd set up trust funds for Grace and the other grandchildren when they were born. So to start sneaking a windfall into the grandkids' accounts seemed out of character. George used to work in the City and had been a magistrate for years. Esther was the deputy chairwoman of her local WI.

'I'll make sure I thank them,' I said, 'the next time I see them.'

Dominic's steady gaze faltered and I saw a flash of fear. 'I wouldn't. You're not supposed to know.'

That was more likely. Esther had always been coldly polite to me. I could have put it down to the fact she was a cold, reserved woman but she was smiley and demonstrative with the people she loved. She adored her daughter's hedge fund manager husband. I'd always felt she thought I wasn't good enough for her son.

'She doesn't think I'd steal it, does she?' I stared at him, appalled. 'I know the gallery is struggling but I wouldn't steal from my own daughter for god's sake!'

The conversation descended into an argument with Dominic accusing me of ostracising his parents and we didn't talk for the rest of the day.

Dad said that if he goes down, so does she.

If Grace heard that correctly then maybe Dominic's still got that repayment schedule. He'd need something tangible to prove that he paid Dani to lie. His word against hers wouldn't wash.

I step into a shop doorway. It's raining more heavily now and my cheap Primark jacket is sticking to my skin. I push back my sleeve to check the time but there's no watch on my wrist. I definitely put it on this morning. Did the strap snap and I didn't notice? It wasn't expensive but I don't want to waste money replacing it. I dig around in my bag for my phone instead. But it's not there. It's gone, and so has my purse.

I've checked my bag three times and my purse and phone are definitely missing. Was I pickpocketed on the tube? Or was it that man who knocked against me and swore? Did he slip my watch off my wrist then ease his hand into my bag when I was too lost in thought to notice? When we were cellmates Smithy told me all her little tricks and scams – how thieves often work in pairs and one will distract you by knocking into you or asking you a question or giving you a hug when you're drunk while the other one robs you blind. It happens to tourists in London all the time.

A thought hits me and I step out from the shop doorway and scan the faces of the commuters, scurrying to get out of the rain.

'Smithy!'

No one stops or answers my call.

'Smithy, I know it was you.'

A scrawny figure steps out from the underground station and weaves her way between the scrum of bodies. A beanie covers her ratty hair and she's wearing a big black puffer jacket, skinny jeans and oversized trainers that I've never seen before, but I'd know that grin anywhere.

'Smithy, you absolute shit!'

She launches herself out of the crowd, turns to shout 'Piss off!' at a disgruntled commuter, then throws herself into my arms.

'Didn't I teach you nothing?' She raps her knuckles against the crown of my head. 'Mate, you were in your own fucking world. I could have nicked your coat and your shoes and you wouldn't have noticed.'

'You did it just now?' I feel a strange mixture of horror and respect. 'When that man knocked into me?'

'Yeah.' She digs into her puffer jacket and pulls out my watch, purse and phone and hands them to me. 'I was gonna jump on you and surprise you but I thought this would be more fun. I thought I'd trail you all the way to Ayesha's and ring on the doorbell and say I had a delivery.'

All the air leaves my lungs in a rush. I've been so caught up in my strange, new life that I completely forgot Smithy was getting out today. We arranged weeks ago for her to come over to Ayesha's at six o'clock on the day of her release. We're going to Nando's and the celebration meal's on me.

*

'Oh my god.' Smithy tears into her piece of chicken, pulling chunks of white meat from the bone with her teeth. 'This, right here, is heaven.'

She hasn't stopped eating since we sat down and she's already made her way through five chicken wings, peri-salted fries, a portion of garlic bread and now she's starting on her main of half a chicken, corn on the cob and macho peas. I've barely touched my boneless chicken thigh meal because I've been talking since we sat down, telling her everything that's happened since I left our cell.

'How was Theresa?' I take a sip of Coke to wet my dry mouth. 'Did Kelk leave her alone?'

'Uh-huh.' Smithy nods as she chews on her food.

'What about you? Have you got somewhere to stay?'

'It's all good. I'm looking after a mate's studio flat,' she reaches for her Coke and takes a swig, 'while she's up North looking after her mum. It's in Elephant and Castle, above an antique shop. That's what the old bint who owns it calls it anyway. Looks more like a junk shop to me. Loads of old crap.'

'Is it all right? The flat?'

She shrugs. 'I've stayed in worse.'

'I haven't forgotten about you,' I tell her. 'About the money for your course. It's just . . . it's going to take a while. There wasn't as much in my bank account as I thought and I need to get back on my feet, get a job and then rent a flat that I can share with Grace when I get custody—'

Smithy waves a dismissive hand through the air. 'Don't worry about it, mate. Like I said, I'm good.'

My shoulders sag in relief. I've been stressing about this conversation since I checked my balance. I don't want to be the sort of person who makes promises they can't keep.

'Have you seen your probation officer yet?' I ask, changing the subject.

'Course.' She takes another bite of chicken then shovels

some peas into her mouth. She chews for an age then pushes her plate away. 'I'm done. I can't get another mouthful in. So you were right then? About your old man and the cop? They were in it together?'

'Looks that way.'

'What are you gonna do?'

'There's nothing I can do.'

She wipes her mouth with a napkin then drops it onto her plate. 'I thought you said there was something that proves she's bent?'

'Might prove she's bent. I don't know for sure.'

'You'd better take another look at it then.'

'How?'

She raises an eyebrow. 'How'd you think?'

'Smithy . . . I can't go back into my old house. Even if I still had a key, which I don't, I'm not allowed anywhere near it. Dom took a restraining order out on me. I could end up back inside.'

'You won't if no one catches you.'

'Forget it.' I dip a couple of chips into peri-peri sauce and chew on them. 'I'm not a criminal.'

'How's that working out for you?'

'What's that supposed to mean?'

'You're innocent, right? You spent five years in prison, lost your business, got shafted by your divorce, you're sleeping on a mate's sofa and you can't spend time alone with your daughter. And you still want to play by the rules? Be legit? Why don't you just bend over so they can shaft you again?'

'Fuck off, Smithy.'

'I think you'll find I'm not the one getting fucked.' She sits back in her chair and folds her arms over her chest. 'Honestly, take a look at yourself. You told everyone who'd listen that you were going to prove your innocence the moment you got out, you stood up to your dickhead padmate and you took a punch to help Theresa out. And now you're a pussy who's going to roll over and let your ex win?'

I lean forward, elbows on the table. 'I'm not a . . . I'm not letting him win.'

'No? Then what has he lost? Look,' she unfolds her arms and counts on her fingers. 'Your ex shafted you. The police shafted you. The legal system shafted you. No one's gonna gallop up the King's Road on a white horse and save you. You need to save your fucking self.'

'But I . . . I haven't got the first clue how to break into a house.'

She grins. 'Well then, it's a good job you know me.'

Chapter 12

DOMINIC

Dom strolls from one room of the sizeable Chiswick house to the other, his notepad in one hand and his Dictaphone in the other. His messenger bag is slung across his body; in it are his electronic moisture meter, a torch, a laser tape measure, compass, digital camera and various other bits and bobs he needs in order to complete a valuation survey. His phone, in the inside pocket of his suit jacket, has been vibrating inter-mittently ever since he left the office but he's ignored it. He told his PA, Maira, that he was going home early with a migraine and gave her strict instructions not to contact him until the evening, even if it was urgent. That hasn't stopped some of his clients from ringing him directly and he knows he's going to have a shit ton of work to catch up with once he's finished this job.

It's the third house he's visited since he left work and it's the most stunning one yet. It's a recently completed chapel conversion with period features, three bedrooms, four bath-rooms and two reception rooms. His jaw actually dropped as he walked into the spherical living room with its white arched columns and stained-glass windows. It was like being in an ancient Greek domicile rather than a converted church. Not that the conversion hasn't modernised the place – it's full of glass and light with a chandelier made up of interlinked glowing circular hoops. It's more like a work of art764 than a light. For all its beauty, though, it's not the sort of house he'd want to live in, even if he could afford it, but he could imagine a film or rock star living here, or a family member of a UAE sheikh.

He lifts his Dictaphone to his mouth and is just about to make a comparison between this house and other homes in the area when his other jacket pocket bleeps. Sighing, he reaches in and pulls out his burner phone.

Well? the text message reads.

He taps out a response. I'd agree with the £5.5 million valuation.

His phone bleeps again. And what are you going to value it at?

He grits his teeth – he can feel the last vestiges of his professionalism draining away – and types back. £7.5.

There's no going back now. When he files his inflated valuation he'll have crossed the line between professionalism and criminality. His signature on that document will make him an accessory to mortgage fraud.

Chapter 13

OLIVIA

It's been two days since I took Smithy to Nando's and now we're sitting in a bus shelter about two hundred metres from my old home. Dressed in dark colours with our hoods up we look like a couple of teenaged boys on their way to the skate park. It would be funny if I wasn't so terrified. It's nearly twelve thirty and Smithy's spent the last ten minutes trying to talk me out of going back to Ayesha's. The plan we made that had me buzzing with excitement as I filled my belly with peri-peri chicken now feels fraught with danger. I shouldn't be this close to my house, it violates the terms of my licence, and if anyone reports me to the police I could find myself back in prison.

'Liv,' Smithy gives me a nudge. 'Your ex is at work, your daughter's at school, we can nick the memory stick from the security cameras, and you know the code to the alarm.' She pauses. 'You sure the CCTV system doesn't upload to the Cloud?'

Another ripple of fear passes through me. So much could

go wrong. 'The old one didn't. Hopefully Dom hasn't replaced it.'

'Hope.' She grimaces. 'Never a good idea. Just keep your head down as we go up the drive. If there is a new system we can't let our faces be picked up by the cameras.'

'I can't do this.' I move to stand up. 'It's too risky.'

She grabs my hand and pulls me back down onto the bench. 'Look, I'm not trying to freak you out, Liv. I'm just making sure we've got everything covered. It'll be fine. I've done this loads of times.'

'And you've been caught.'

'Only when I was sloppy.'

'But is it worth it? What if Dominic's destroyed the repayment schedule? What if we find it and it doesn't prove he paid off Dani?'

'Then we keep looking until we find something that does. Come on, Liv, don't lose your bottle now. I spent three years listening to you whitter on about how you were gonna prove your innocence when you got out. Now's your chance. Nothing's gonna go wrong.'

'But . . .' A new worry hits me. '. . . what if Dom's changed the alarm codes.'

'One step at a—' Smithy breaks off. She's just spotted what I've noticed too: Rosa, my old cleaner, walking out of the gates of my old house. She's got a bucket of cleaning supplies in one hand and a vacuum cleaner in the other. Her handbag is strapped across her chest with the body of the bag resting above one slim buttock. I feel a strange rush of nostalgia as I watch her walk down the street in search of her red Mini. I took on Rosa when I was pregnant with Grace. I had Symphysis pubis dysfunction and it was hard to walk, never mind clean. We'd have a coffee and chat in the kitchen before she started cleaning, and by the time my maternity leave ended and I went back to work I felt like I knew Rosa's family as well as my own.

'You were right,' Smithy hisses. 'She still cleans on the same day.'

Rosa is the reason we're sitting in the bus shelter rather than breaking into the house. Over our Nando's dessert of gooey caramel cheesecake I spotted a flaw in our plan. If Rosa still cleaned from 9 a.m. until lunchtime on a Friday we'd either have to break in on a different day, or at a different time. When I said the word 'cleaner' Smithy's eyes lit up. If we had Rosa's keys we wouldn't have to smash a window, we could just let ourselves in. We'd take off our shoes just inside the front door, search through Dom's study and be long gone by the time Grace came back from school. Rosa would assume she'd lost her keys, Dom would get some more cut and no one would be any the wiser.

There was just one problem.

In order to avoid Rosa recognising me, Smithy would have to provide the distraction while I lifted the keys. I'd never stolen from anyone before, unless you counted an ice-cream eraser I'd 'accidentally' borrowed from a friend in primary school and taken home in my bag. Sitting in our cell listening to Smithy describe how she swiped wallets, purses and phones was one thing but rifling through some-one's handbag myself was another. And I didn't even know if that's where Rosa kept our spare house key. It might be in her pocket for all I knew.

Last night I barely slept for worrying. What if Rosa caught me in the act? What if she screamed and alerted a neighbour? What if someone called the police?

I got up at 5 a.m. this morning to go over what Smithy had taught me in a side alley beside Nando's. I fashioned a 'person' out of a pair of Ayesha's jeans stuffed with pillows and propped them up against the kitchen counter, then I hung my bag around the hips, with a pan full of water securing the bag's strap to the counter top. The first time I tried to get into the bag the 'mannequin' fell over. The second time the bag fell off. Finally, after twenty or thirty attempts, I managed to twist open the clasp, scoop my hand around the bag and withdraw a key.

'You ready?' Smithy nudges me with her shoulder.

An image flashes up in my mind, of Grace's terrified face when the police turned up to arrest me, then I see Dominic's mouth, twisting into a smirk when my sentence was announced.

'I'm ready,' I say.

We peel off, Smithy crossing the road to cut Rosa off before she reaches her car while I head down the street in the opposite direction to approach her from the rear. I keep my hood up, face averted so Rosa can't see my features if she glances across the street. When I've passed her I hurry across the road and jog after her, keeping my footsteps light. The plan doesn't involve hurting Rosa in any way but I feel wretched anyway. However I try and excuse it it's a mugging; we're going to steal something that someone doesn't want stolen.

When Smithy put the plan to me I suggested that I ask Rosa for the keys instead of taking them from her. The words had barely left my mouth before I realised what a foolhardy idea that was. Like almost everyone else I know, Rosa thinks I tried to have Dom murdered. There's no way she'd hand over the keys. She'd ring him the moment I was out of sight and he'd ring the police. I considered texting Grace to ask her to let me in after she got back from school but our relationship is too fragile to suggest something like that. She might have issues with her father but she doesn't trust me either.

I'm no more than a couple of metres away from Rosa now and over her shoulder I can see Smithy is a similar distance in front of her. Surely Rosa must be able to sense me behind her? She's weighed down with the hoover and her bucket of cleaning products but she's moving at a pace, eager, I imagine, to put everything down once she reaches her car.

My heart's beating so quickly now I can feel it in the base of my neck. As soon as I've got the keys I'm to turn and walk quickly in the opposite direction. Smithy will follow and we'll let ourselves into the house without Rosa ever suspecting a thing.

We're nearly at Rosa's Mini and I'm starting to panic. What's Smithy waiting for? Why hasn't she knocked into her yet?

I jump as a car horn sounds. A black BMW is driving slowly alongside us and the driver of the white Fiat Uno behind it is getting impatient. As both cars pass us and turn left at the end of the street, Smithy shoulder-barges Rosa, who lets out a cry of surprise and drops her bucket. It tips onto its side and cleaning materials spill out onto the street.

'Oh my god, sorry, are you okay?' Smithy grips Rosa's arm, her tone friendly yet concerned.

That's my cue to go for the shoulder bag, strung across Rosa's body and resting against her right buttock. It's a bucket-style canvas bag with a zip across the top. I'm so close I can smell Rosa's perfume and see the streaks of grey on the crown of her head. She must be able to sense how close I am. My hand shakes as I reach for the zip. I can't do this. It doesn't feel right.

'I'm fine.' Rosa gives herself a small shake to dislodge the hand on her arm but Smithy's going nowhere. She's talking nineteen to the dozen, something about her terrible day and why she wasn't looking where she was going.

72

'Please,' Rosa says. 'I need to get my things. I have another job to go to.'

She takes a step backwards, pulling away from Smithy, and I leap backwards to avoid a collision.

'Of course of course.' I can hear the tension in Smithy's voice. She's frustrated that I haven't got the keys. I'm taking too long.

Rosa jerks her shoulders one way, then the other, trying to shake Smithy off. 'I told you. I am fine.'

I look over her shoulder at Smithy and shake my head sharply. I can't do it. This was a mistake. I can't steal from people. That's not the kind of person I am.

In an instant Smithy lets go of Rosa's wrists, apologises profusely and ducks down to pick up the bucket and a bathroom cleaner. As Rosa bends to pick up a collapsible duster I take a step backwards, preparing to leave. Her handbag swings to the side of her body and then I see it – a piece of material, poking out of the rear pocket of her jeans. It's one of the lanyard straps we used for staff during an exhibition, bright yellow with blue stripes. Dominic must have put a spare key on it for her.

Smithy heads towards me, pauses, turns back and then hoiks the lanyard out of Rosa's pocket in one swift move.

Chapter 14

DANI

Dani indicates left, turning the BMW into Elyne Road. The chat with Detective Inspector Matthew Fielding turned out to be nothing more worrying than her annual appraisal. She was praised for leading a small team in successfully investigating burglaries that targeted the elderly, and asked to develop the management of the team's overtime budget. The meeting had ended with a handshake and a 'Good work' from Fielding. Dani headed back to her desk, told Jess that she had a witness statement to collect and, a few minutes later, strolled casually out of New Scotland Yard.

Mood lifted by her boss's feedback, her plan was to drive past Dom's house to see if his car was parked up outside. She'd ring the doorbell if he was in. Texting or ringing wasn't an option. He'd ignored every attempt she'd made at communication since their argument a week earlier. She'd calmed down since then, maybe he had too.

She'd decided to show him the photo of Casey looking gaunt and thin that Brenda had WhatsApped to her a few days earlier. Telling Dominic that Casey needed urgent help was one thing but seeing how ill she really was was another. Casey was only six years older than Grace when she fell in with the wrong crowd and started using drugs, and if Dani appealed to Dominic as a father, rather than a lover, surely he'd soften and offer to help. The house he lived in had to be worth nearly two mill and he drove an Audi R8 Spyder for god's sake. Thirty grand was nothing to someone like him. If he was worried about Olivia stirring up trouble, or trying to get more cash out of him after the divorce, Dani would reassure him. When she saw him last week he was panicking, plain and simple, and she knew how to deal with people like that, and which strings to pull.

Only Dom's black Audi isn't parked up in the driveway of his five-bedroom house as she drives past. Wherever he headed after he told his personal assistant that he was ill, it certainly wasn't home. Irritated, Dani continues driving down the street, then spots something that makes her pause. Walking along the pavement, dressed in a hoodie, skinny jeans and white trainers, is Kelly Smith, a career thief and waste of space that Dani's arrested and interviewed multiple times. Even with Smith's hood pulled up she'd recognise the hard planes of her face anywhere.

She slows the car. Smith's heading for an older, dark-haired woman struggling under the weight of cleaning supplies. Surely Kelly isn't planning on stealing the Henry Hoover? She'd be lucky to get twenty quid from Cash Converters for it. Dani glances into her rear-view mirror, in search of an accomplice. Sure enough, there's another woman in a dark hoodie, trailing the cleaner, head down. The accomplice senses she's being watched and turns to look at the car, giving Dani a good view of her face. Olivia fucking Sutherland. Dani's breath catches in her throat. It couldn't be, could it? Liv's barely been out of prison for a week and she's on licence. What the hell is she doing strolling down her ex-husband's street, dressed like a teenaged boy? Dani glances back at Smith who's dressed almost identically. Do they know each other? Has she just stumbled on them in the midst of a job? She touches the brake, mind racing. Should she get out and have a word or should she—

The driver of the Fiat Uno behind her sounds his horn and she has no choice but to continue driving. If she jumps out both women will scarper and she wants to know what they're up to. There are only so many reasons why Olivia Sutherland would return to her old street, and none of them are good.

Chapter 15

OLIVIA

I'm shaking so much I can't get the key into the lock then, when I finally do, the key doesn't turn, no matter how much I wiggle it.

'Are you sure you're using the right key?' Smithy asks, making me jump. She was supposed to be at the end of the path, keeping a lookout. 'You're taking forever.'

'Yes, look.' I show her the two other keys on the lanyard. 'That one with the black piece of tape on it is for the back door. Dom always did that so he could tell the difference between the front door key and the back. And this one,' I touch the smaller of the three keys. 'It's not a Yale. He must have put a padlock on the shed.'

'Let me try.' Smithy nudges me out of the way and grips the key in the lock. It turns effortlessly and she raises her eyebrows as if to say, 'See!'

I reach for the door handle but she knocks my hand away. 'You definitely remember the code for the alarm? Because it's going to start the second we open this door.'

'Yeah. Unless he's changed it.' I glance back towards the street to check no one's watching. To a passing stranger we probably look like two friends hanging out, but it's not strangers I'm worried about. We didn't know many people on this street when I lived here but we were friendly with the neighbours on either side of the road. I'm almost certain they'll have taken Dom's side. Then there's the black BMW that cruised past us earlier. I couldn't see who was inside.

'What's the code?' Smithy asks. 'And where's the keypad?'

'It's Grace's birthday. And the keypad is in the cloakroom, first door on the left.'

'Cloakroom.' She snorts in amusement. 'You got groomsmen too?'

'Yes, but they live in the outhouse with the horses. The maids are in the attic with the ghosts.'

Smithy's grin widens as she reaches into the pocket of her hoodie and pulls out a pair of latex gloves. 'Good, you've still got your sense of humour. Means you're calming down. Now, put your gloves on and let's get this shit done.'

The alarm is louder than I remember: a frantic beeping that makes my ears pulse. I don't look around as I slip into the house. All my attention is on stopping the beeping and making sure the police don't turn up. I head for the cloakroom and kick my way through piles of Grace's shoes to reach the keypad. Smithy follows me. She's unusually quiet but her breathing is shallow and quick. I can't believe she used to do this regularly. I'm crapping myself and this used to be my house.

I flip down the panel that covers the rubber keypad and jab at the numbers then hit the enter button. The display panel flashes red. Two more attempts.

'Do it slower,' Smithy urges. 'Take your time.'

I take a steadying breath then tap in Grace's date of birth again. I hit enter.

Incorrect.

'Shit.'

The constant beep, beep, beep of the alarm fills my head and I freeze. If I enter the wrong code a third time the security company that installed the alarm will be alerted. Even if we manage to escape before they get here Dom will be told there was a break-in and, at some point in the next week, Rosa will tell him that she lost her keys. He'll put two and two together and realise it was me.

'Tell me what Grace's date of birth is,' Smithy shouts over the sound of the alarm.

'Fourth of February 2007.'

She looks from me to the keypad. 'That's not what you entered. You did the second of the fourth.'

'Are you sure?'

'Yes.'

'A hundred percent sure? What if Dom's changed the code?'

'I'm sure.' An urgent tone enters her voice. I'm not the only one who's nervous now. 'I watched you enter it twice. Do it again but do it right. Even slower this time. Zero. Four. Zero. Two. Zero. Seven.'

'Zero.' I tap the keyboard. 'Four.' I tap it again. 'Zero. Two. Zero.' I exhale heavily before I press the last digit. Please let Smithy be right. Please, please. 'Seven.'

The alarm cuts off as suddenly as it started and I double over, pressing my hands to my thighs as I suck air deep into my lungs.

'Save the dramatics for later,' Smithy says as she heads out of the cloakroom. 'We've got evidence to find.'

*

To my relief the CCTV system is the old one with two cameras trained on the drive and none in the house. I push open the door to Dominic's study with the memory stick clutched tightly in my hand and discover that the room is as minimalist and uncluttered as it was the last time I was here. I'd assumed, after the divorce, that Dominic would rip every trace of me from this house but, from the glimpses of the living room and the kitchen I saw as I hurried after Smithy down the hall, nothing's changed. The soft-pile grey carpets are the same, the furniture's the same and the artwork I bought remains on the walls. It's like stepping back in time. There are traces of me everywhere. I'm not just an intruder, I'm also a ghost.

'Right.' Smithy pulls at one of the desk drawers. 'What are we looking for? A piece of paper with some numbers and dates on it, right?'

'Yes.' I head for the bookshelves and scan the books. It's unlikely Dom would have returned it to the same book but he's always had a terrible memory. If he put it back he'd know where to find it again.

Although . . .

A new thought hits me as I move from bookshelf to bookshelf, looking for a neon spine amongst the faded green and navy vintage hardbacks that Dom bought for decoration but has never read. If Grace was right about what she heard and he has threatened Dani he'll have hidden her repayment schedule well. It might not even be in the study anymore. It could be on him for all I know. I join Smithy at the desk as she yanks open the bottom drawer and carefully flicks through each of the A4 pads she pulls out.

'Nothing.' She carefully replaces them and closes the drawer. 'You?'

'The book's not here.'

'Crap. Where do you want to look next?'

'Bedroom? You take the living room?'

She nods and we peel off in different directions, padding silently on socked feet.

I speed up the stairs and my heart twists as I pass Grace's bedroom. It's the only room in the house that has changed. Gone is the mountain of soft toys on her bed, the unicorn bedside light and the posters of woodland animals. There are anime and manga posters everywhere now: Japanese school-girls in short skirts with huge expressive eyes. Only two teddies remain on the bed: a large white rabbit we gave her for Christmas when she was three and a glow-in-the-dark musical seahorse I bought when she was two months old in a desperate attempt to get her to sleep. It didn't work but she took it everywhere with her – to nursery, to the park, for a bounce on our garden trampoline. I lived in fear of her losing it and, for the longest time, two other seahorses lived in a cupboard under the stairs. I scan the room, looking for other traces of me, but there's not so much as a photograph. I move away, heart stinging. That is why I'm doing this, not just to clear my name and get revenge on Dom and Dani, but to repair the damage that's been done to my relationship with Grace.

I burst into the room I used to share with my husband and head for the chest of drawers. I'm rummaging through the sock drawer when I hear a shout from downstairs.

'Smithy!' I hurry down the stairs so quickly I lose my footing and have to grip the banister to stop myself from falling. As I right myself Smithy appears in the hall.

Her face is taut with fear. 'We need to get out. Now! There's a cop in the driveway and she's staring right into the house.'

Chapter 16

DANI

Dani is pressed up against the side of Dominic's house, not moving a muscle, listening for the sound of footsteps or voices. She doesn't know if they'll come from the front of the house or the back but she hopes to god that, if they do come out of the back door, they don't choose this side of the house to make their escape.

There was no sign of Olivia Sutherland or Kelly Smith as she drove slowly back down Oakfield Road. She circled around a few nearby streets, scanning the alleyways and gardens for two female figures dressed in black, but they'd vanished.

There were three possibilities: either they'd made their escape, they were hiding, or they were breaking and entering. She was pretty sure neither of them had spotted her, which made escape or hiding unlikely. That left one option – they were up to no good. Knowing what she did about Olivia it was unlikely Smithy had turned her to a life of crime so, if they had illegally entered a house, it had to be Dom's.

Dani parked up a little way down the street and strolled back to the house. The gates to the short driveway were open. They'd been closed on her first drive past. Glancing around to check she wasn't being watched, she approached the front door and tested the handle. Locked. If Liv and Smithy were inside they'd found an alternative way in. All the windows to the front of the house were closed and secure and when she checked the sides of the house and the back, slipping down the narrow fenced walkway that separated the building from its neighbours, there was no sign of forced entry. Dom was AWOL and it was early afternoon which meant Grace was still at school; the house should be empty.

As she returned to the front she started to doubt herself. Was it really Smith and Sutherland she'd seen? Given the conditions of her licence, it would be a bit fucking stupid of Olivia to return to the family home. She'd have to be desperate or . . . a thought hit her . . . or there was something inside the house that she was desperate to get hold of. There was no way Olivia could know about the recording that Dominic claimed to have. Or could she? Dani felt a flicker of fear. If Dominic's ex-wife was out to prove that she'd been framed then it wasn't just him she had to watch out for, it was Olivia too.

She'd been about to walk back down the driveway when, out of the corner of her eye, she saw a flicker of movement in one of the ground-floor windows, a dark shape darting from one side of the room to the other.

Someone was in the living room.

She shifted out of sight, down the walkway at the side of the house, then crept towards the back. Instinctively she reached for her radio to call for back-up, then paused. Arresting Olivia would remove one threat but it wouldn't remove both. Dom would still have the recording and the handwritten loan agreement. Sending Olivia back to prison wouldn't magically provide Dani with the thirty grand she needed to save her sister's life.

Was there some way she could use what she knew to her advantage? Did Olivia have money? She didn't think so. Beth, Dani's mate who was a guard at the prison, had told her that Olivia's release address was a flat rented by someone called Ayesha Okoye. The name didn't ring a bell and it didn't come up on the PNC. If Olivia was loaded surely she'd have got her own flat?

That just left Dom. He'd told Dani he wouldn't lend her cash, not couldn't, which meant he'd got the finances. He just needed a nudge in the right direction.

Now, her pulse quickens as she hears the sound of a door closing and a lock being turned. They're coming out the front, at least she hopes it's 'they'. She only caught sight of one hooded figure that she *thinks* was Smith. She needs Olivia to have been in the house too.

She inches closer to the front of the house so she can get a good look at whoever just came out and a slow grin spreads across her face as she spots two hooded figures crouching behind the garden wall. They're having a silent argument, gesturing at each other about something Olivia is holding in her hand. Could there be a key on the end of that lanyard ribbon? Olivia keeps trying to drop it but Smithy shakes her head, no. Slowly Dani slides her phone out of her pocket, zooms in on the figures and takes a photo. Her smile widens. That should be worth thirty grand.

Chapter 17

OLIVIA

I can't breathe. I'm doubled over and I'm sucking in cold, damp London air but none of it seems to be getting into my lungs. I don't know how long Smithy and I just ran – ten minutes, fifteen? – but it's longer than I ever managed on Couch to 5k. Smithy was miles ahead of me the whole way, glancing back as she reached the end of each street to check I was still with her. I've never run so fast in my life. Amazing what the threat of prison can do for your athletic ability.

When Smithy shouted that there was a cop in the front garden I flew down the stairs, heart thundering, but I couldn't see anyone when I peered from behind a curtain. It was a woman, Smithy hissed, a plainclothes detective that had nicked her a couple of times over the years. She couldn't remember her name. I didn't need her to. I knew exactly who it was.

'Smithy, I think I'm feeling better now.' As I straighten up I get a whiff of whatever's rotting in the dumpster we're crouching behind and double over again.

'Urgh.' Smithy jumps away as I throw up. She retreats to

a safe distance and leans against a wall, arms crossed over her chest. She's not even breathing heavily.

I wipe a tissue I found in my pocket over my mouth and straighten up. 'Where'd you learn to run like that?'

'Dunno. Always been good at running. You should have seen me on sports day at primary school. I cleaned up. You all right?' She steps closer then recoils, wrinkling her nose.

'I'm fine.' I gesture for her to follow me out of the alley.

'Oi, you twat, you dropped this.' Smithy crouches down and picks up the lanyard that must have fallen out of my pocket when I was looking for a tissue. We argued about whether to ditch it or take it with us before we made a run for it. I thought we should drop it in the driveway to make it look like it had fallen out of Rosa's pocket as she left the house. Smithy said we should keep it in case we needed it again. I was so scared I was hyperventilating. We hadn't found anything and there was no way I was going to break in anywhere, ever again. But there was no time to argue so I pocketed the key and we ran.

'Sorry.' I take the lanyard from her and shove it deep into my pocket.

'So what happens now then?'

'I go back to Ayesha's and you go back to your flat.'

'That's not what I mean.' She shakes her head. 'What's the plan about getting the evidence?'

'Nothing.'

She looks at me incredulously.

'There's nothing we can do. We didn't find anything so . . .' The adrenaline's starting to wear off and I feel tired and empty. I just want to get back to Ayesha's and have a glass of wine.

Smithy must be able to tell how exhausted I am because she shrugs and says, 'All right then. Give us a text later.' She lightly punches me on the arm. 'Have a shower and clean your teeth when you get back, yeah? You bloody stink.'

I'm about to make a comment that she doesn't exactly smell like roses either when my phone buzzes in my back pocket. I slide it out and unlock the screen, expecting to see a message from Ayesha, Grace or the recruitment company. But the email notification that's flashed up isn't from any of them. It's from the man who broke my heart and betrayed me. It's an email from Jack.

Chapter 18

DOMINIC

The lift doors open and the damp, diesel smell of the underground car park floods Dominic's nose. He rubs his hands over his face and steps out of the lift. It's been a long day and he's had a shitload of work to catch up on after taking yesterday afternoon 'off sick'. If one more person says his name ('Dom, could you . . .' 'Dom, I don't suppose . . .' 'Dom, one second of your time . . .') he's going to lose his shit. He's sick of people, of their voices, their faces, their bodies and their smells. He'd like to up sticks, move to a jungle and make his living taking photographs of rare plants and animals. Not that he knows the first thing about photography but how hard could it be?

He pauses in the entrance to the car park and scans the cars for Dani's black BMW. This was never supposed to happen. When she stormed out of the house the other day he thought that was it, he'd never see her again. They were at stalemate; they both had too much to lose to ever make good on their threats. It was part of the reason he hadn't given her the thirty grand – he didn't need to. He didn't have to buy her silence when he had enough on her to put her in jail. So when she'd texted him last night to say she needed to talk he'd ignored her. Of course she wanted to talk. She wanted thirty grand. But her second text made him sit up.

Something happened today that you need to know about.

His curiosity was piqued but he didn't trust her. She knew which buttons to press to get him to respond. Another text arrived a couple of seconds later:

Someone's digging around and you're going to need my help.

A muscle twitched in his cheek.

Meet me in the car park at your work at 6pm tomorrow.

Still he didn't reply. Was it some kind of trap? Was Dani making good on her promise to make sure he spends the rest of his life in prison? Or was it a pitiful attempt to extort money from him? There was no way he was going to meet her.

Fifteen minutes ago he changed his mind when a new text appeared:

I'm downstairs. If you don't want to lose Grace you know what to do.

Rage spiked through him. How dare she use his daughter as leverage? Was that a threat? He'd forward the text to her boss and sit back and watch her whole life explode.

Fuck you, he texted back. Don't ever mention my daughter's name again.

As his thumb moved towards the 'Send' button a thought hit him that made him pause. He read through the series of texts that Dani had sent, his brow creasing as he picked over the information. Maybe she wasn't threatening him after all. If she'd seen or heard something worrying it had to have something to do with Liv. Why else would she insinuate that he might lose Grace?

Now, he squints into the distance as a car's headlights flash repeatedly, cutting through the gloom. Dani's waiting for him.

Dominic opens the passenger side door of Dani's BMW saloon and climbs in. There are empty Costa cups in the footwell and the air in the car is a repugnant blend of coffee and synthetic air freshener.

'Well?' he turns to face her. 'What's this about?'

Her eyes sweep over him. 'Show me your phone.'

'What?'

'Show me your phone and close all the apps. I need to know you're not recording this.'

'Oh for god's sake.' Dom twists in his seat and pulls on the switch to open the door. 'I haven't got time for this shit.'

'Fine. Then we'll both go to prison and Grace will go and live with her mum.'

Dom turns back to look at her.

'Close the door, Dom.'

'What's this about?'

'Close the door, show me your phone and I'll tell you.'

Teeth clenched, Dom does as she says. 'There, see,' he closes the apps on his phone as she watches, 'not recording.'

'Okay, turn it off.'

Bit late to shut the gate on the horse when it's already bolted, he thinks irritably as he turns his phone off. He's already got more than enough evidence to put her away.

'Pockets,' she says and he sighs as she pats him down.

'What's this?' She plucks the burner phone from inside his jacket but he snatches it away from her before she can look at the screen. 'Anything I should know about?'

'No.' He tucks it back inside. It's the phone he uses to text her but he's not going to tell her that. She's getting on his tits.

'Are you sure about that? Because if you get arrested—'

'It's nothing dodgy. Okay? Who I sleep with is my business.'

Dani's lips tighten. 'That's classy, Dom.'

Inwardly he grins. His words landed just as he hoped they would. So much for Dani's claim that she could have sex without emotions getting involved.

'Just tell me what this is about.'

'Fine.' She shows him the screen of her own phone. It's a photo of two hooded characters, teenagers probably, crouching by a wall.

Dominic sighs irritably. 'Are you going to tell me what this is or am I supposed to guess?'

'It's your ex-wife,' Dani touches the screen, zooming in on one of the hooded figures, 'and her cellmate, Kelly Smith. That's the wall at the front of your house and that . . .' she touches the screen again '. . . I'm guessing, is the key.'

'Let me see that.' Dom reaches for the phone but Dani snatches it back.

'No, no, no. You can look but don't touch.' She shows the photo to him again and this time he keeps his hands in his lap.

She's right, it is Liv. Even in a shapeless black hoodie that hides her hair he can clearly make out the profile of her face.

'What the hell was she doing?'

Dani tucks her phone inside her jacket. 'Olivia and Smith were in your house at approximately two o'clock yesterday afternoon.'

Dom stares at her, his eyes wide, a cold chill coursing through his body. 'In? Doing what?'

'Your guess is as good as mine.'

He mentally searches the house. He's got a couple of nice watches, his great-grandfather's war medals and a fair amount of tech but he doesn't keep cash at home. Was Olivia looking for something of hers? He packed up most of her shit when she was sentenced: clothes, jewellery, make-up, that sort of thing. Nancy collected the boxes to keep in her garage. Ian wasn't keen. He said Dom should burn the lot. Unless . . . he stares out into the gloom of the car park. Unless it wasn't something of Liv's that she was looking for.

'What did they steal?' he asks. 'Did you arrest them?'

'I don't know.' Dani's looking at him like he's a piece of crap. 'And no, I didn't.'

He sits up taller in his seat, puffed up with indignation. 'Why the fuck didn't you—' he breaks off as a thought hits him. 'What were you doing at my house anyway?'

'Looking for you. According to your PA you'd gone home early because you felt unwell.' She raises her eyebrows. 'Go anywhere nice?'

Dom ignores the question. It's none of her business where he was but he's going to have a word with Maira when he gets back to the office. She needs to be more careful about what she says.

'So,' he says, 'why didn't you arrest them?'

'Good question.' Dani gives him a long look.

'Send me the photo. I'll get them arrested. Liv's not supposed to go within a mile of my house.'

A small smile creeps onto Dani's lips. 'I'm not going to send you the photo, Dom.'

'Why the hell not?'

'I have my reasons.'

He sits back in his seat. He's bored of the game-playing now. 'What is it you want?' Even as the question leaves his mouth he knows what the answer will be.

'I want to help you, obviously. I take it Liv doesn't have her own key to the front door.'

'Of course she doesn't. I changed the locks years ago.'

'You might want to do that again because I saw them in the street, surrounding your cleaner. Were her keys on a brightly coloured lanyard?'

'Oh shit.' Dom runs a hand over the back of his neck. It's slick with sweat. Those were his spare keys. When he had the locks changed he'd got only three keys cut. One for him, one for Grace and a spare set. He gave the spare set to Rosa meaning to get more cut but he never got round to it.

'Is Rosa all right?' he adds, suddenly aware that Dani's looking at him strangely.

'I doubt she even realised what was happening.'

'Well, that's something. Who was Olivia with?'

'Kelly Smith, career thief. She can sniff out money a mile off and if she thinks you and Liv have got some you're not going to get rid of her any time soon.'

'This just gets worse.' Dom doesn't even bother to hide the weary tone in his voice. Liv's up to something, he knows it. His mum told him that Olivia managed to have a private conversation with Grace in the butterfly enclosure at the zoo. His ex-wife isn't going to settle for supervised visits for long. She'll want Grace to live with her again; that's why she was poking round the house, looking for something she can use against him. She won't have found anything but if she was determined enough to break in god knows what else she'll be prepared to do. He's been struggling to sleep since Olivia was released from jail and when he does he wakes up gasping and thrashing, still gripped by nightmares about the police turning up at his door. The only way he's ever going to sleep well again is to get out of the UK and he's been given an out – a way for him and Grace to have the future they deserve, free from fear. He just needs to get through the next few weeks and Olivia will be out of their lives for good.

'I'll keep an eye on Olivia and her little friend but . . .'

Dani pauses as though she doesn't know what to say next but Dom doesn't buy it. She knows exactly what she wants. '. . . But my time doesn't come cheaply. I'd have to give up all my PT clients for a start. And then there's the risk involved, nipping out to keep an eye on them when I should be doing case work.'

'Let me guess,' Dom says. 'You want thirty grand?'

Dani tilts her head to one side and flashes her eyebrows at him as though to say, 'clever boy'.

'I haven't got it.'

Her expression hardens. 'Then I suggest you find it. And quickly. Now get out of my car.'

Chapter 19

OLIVIA

I've done a lot of crappy jobs in my life – working in retail at Christmas, serving pervy middle-aged men drinks in a golf club and interning at Sotheby's – but cleaning office blocks isn't one of them. It's half past ten at night, I'm knackered and I've still got another half an hour to go, but the rest of the team are efficient, if not hugely chatty, and our supervisor doesn't seem to be the hovering type which is good. I was a bundle of nerves during my interview two days ago. After my inability to find any evidence that proves my innocence it was more important than ever to get some money coming in. I shouldn't have worried. I'd googled the types of questions that might come up and managed to answer the majority, fudging anything I wasn't sure about. A couple of hours later I received a phone call telling me I'd got the job and that I should pop into the office at some point to fill out some forms and collect a polo shirt and ID. I had a minor heart attack when I was handed my rota and The Radcliffe Building – the soaring skyscraper where Dom works – was on the list but

95

there was a blank space where my shifts should have been. Out of the seven buildings C&C Cleaning Services contract for, I'd only clean two.

Now here I am, hoovering under desks, wiping down surfaces and emptying bins. It's good to be out of Ayesha's flat and doing something useful instead of lying on the sofa, refreshing my phone.

The email Jack sent was short: I'm sorry for everything I put you through. J x

My reply was equally succinct – Where are you? – but I did consider sending: *You are a cowardly, selfish bastard and I'll never forgive you for abandoning me when I needed you most. Never contact me again.*

How dare he get in touch with me now after five years of silence and so many lies?

If he hadn't vanished the way he had I might never have gone to prison. We'd have had two defence barristers to prove our innocence and two alibis, not one. The arrest warrant was in both our names but, instead of choosing to fight beside me, Jack packed up his passport, wallet, toothbrush, laptop and a few clothes – and he fled. It was all over the papers, the lover who'd gone on the run. There were sightings of him in various parts of the country and, according to my solicitor, the internet was awash with theories that he'd smuggled himself on a ferry to France by hiding in the back of a van.

For the longest time I convinced myself that Jack was dead. His last text had said, I'm sorry, Liv. I love you but I can't do this anymore. At the time I'd assumed he was ending our affair but what if it wasn't that? What if what he couldn't do anymore was live? There were moments, when we were together, when he'd go quiet, seemingly lost in thought, and his mood would sour. I'd tiptoe around him when he was like that and give him space. Then, all of a sudden, something within him would switch and he'd be the playful, laughing, joyful Jack I loved so much. Were the signs he was in a dark place always there but I'd chosen to ignore them? I wasn't sure what was worse, believing that Jack had betrayed me or choosing to believe that he'd taken his own life.

My phone vibrates in my back pocket, making me jolt. It continues to vibrate as I reach for it; someone's ringing me.

I abandon my hoover and hurry out of the room. 'Hello, who is this?'

The sound of sobbing fills my ear and there's no mistaking who it is.

It's cold and dark in the stairwell but I don't bother to turn on the light.

'Grace? Take a deep breath, sweetheart. I can't understand what you're saying.'

There's a pause, a sob, then a shaky attempt at a breath. I am simultaneously concerned that she's upset and joyful that it was me she turned to for help. She must have taken my phone number from the umbrella after all. She's had it all along.

'M . . . Mum,' she manages my name, then a sob steals the next word away.

'What is it, sweetheart? You can tell me.'

'I . . . I . . . I had to see my head of year today.'

'Okay. What about?'

Her crying intensifies for a few seconds then she calms herself down again.

'I'm . . . I'm being bullied. It's been going on for ages but they're too clever. They're making it look like it's me.'

'That what's you?'

'That I'm the bully.'

'Who's they, Gracie?'

'Ava, Daisy and Brooke. They've set up fake accounts on social media in my name and they showed Mrs Hargreaves all the horrible messages I was supposed to have sent. And she . . . she believed them. So did . . . so did Dad.'

A cold rage settles in my bones. Dominic is her father, he's supposed to listen to her, to defend her, to keep her safe from the world. I'd do all of those things if she was living with me. I wouldn't side with the bullies. I'd stand up for her. I'd do whatever it took to make her happy again. It's all I can do not to drive my fist into the landing wall.

'He was so angry with me,' Grace continues. 'He's always angry these days. He's on the phone now, shouting at someone.' She pauses and, sure enough, I hear Dominic's voice, raised in anger, ranting about having everything in hand. 'I heard him say my name,' Grace comes back on the phone, 'so I came out onto the landing to find out what he was talking about. I think it might be Mrs Hargreaves. She's probably going to exclude me and I haven't done anything wrong.'

I memorise the name. I might be banned from contacting Dominic but my probation officer didn't say anything about contacting the school.

'I know you haven't done anything wrong, Gracie. I believe you. I believe you, love.'

'I don't want to be here anymore. Can you come and get me? Please? I could share the sofa with you at Ayesha's. If you ask her, I'm sure she'll say yes.'

My heart aches, hearing the desperation in her voice. 'I'm sorry, sweetheart. I can't. I'm not allowed. I'm on something called a licence for the next five years. Because of the . . . because of the crime they think I've committed . . . I'm not allowed to live with you for a while. I have to stick to the rules about only having supervised visits. My social worker said they'll review the situation regularly, and ask you what you want, and maybe then we can live together. But I don't know when that will be. I'm sorry. We've got another visit coming up soon, sweetheart. I'll give you the biggest hug then.'

'No one will help me, not even you.' She bursts into loud angry tears. Between the sobs I hear the words that send a shiver down my spine: 'I'd rather be dead.'

'Grace! Don't say that. Please don't say that. I'm doing everything I can so that you can live with me again and when that happens we'll change your school. We can even move out of London if you want.'

'When?' The question is so plaintive, so loaded with desperation, it breaks my heart. I can't bear to tell her that she might not be able to live with me until she's sixteen and can decide for herself who she wants to live with. 'When, Mum? When?'

'I don't know, Grace, but I'm doing everything I can to make it happen. I promise you. You've got to be strong.'

'Oh for god's sake. The neighbour's cat has got in again. Petal! Go home!'

I hear a soft flumping noise, like the phone hitting the carpet, and the sound of footsteps grows fainter as, presumably, Grace runs after the cat. Without my daughter's voice in my ear I hear snatches of Dominic's conversation again. I turn up the volume on my handset.

'She was in the house today . . . Olivia was. Who else do you think I'm talking about?'

Who's he talking to? His lawyer? The police? Dani?

When I wasn't rereading Jack's email last night I was staring out of the window of Ayesha's place, waiting for the police to turn up. We'd outrun Dani but it wouldn't be hard for her to find out where I lived. I opened a bottle of wine and drank it as I paced around the small flat. It was a stupid idea, breaking into my old house. I'd risked everything and gained nothing. How long would I get for breaking and entering while I was on probation? Two years? Three? Grace would be almost an adult by the time I got out.

Only the police never showed up and when I woke up this morning, a Joker's smile stained around my lips in red wine, I cried with relief. But the fear's back now. Maybe Dani's telling him what she saw. By the time I leave work there could be a squad car outside.

'No,' Dom raises his voice. 'I'm not going to the police . . . I haven't got any evidence but I know she was here . . . Stuff was out of place in the office.'

He's lying. We were careful not to disturb anything.

'I don't know what they were looking for . . .' He's irritated now. I can hear it in his voice. 'No, she can't know about that.'

His shoes click on the tiles in the hall. He's pacing back and forth.

'Look, it's in a safe place . . . No, I'm not telling you where.'

More pacing. Tap, tap, tap, tap.

'Jesus Christ! It's in a safe at work. All right?' There's a pause then. 'You can't have it. We've already had this discussion.'

He continues to pace.

'Oh for god's sake. How many times do I have to tell you? I haven't got anything on you. I just want it where I can keep an eye on it. Now will you chill the fuck out?'

'Olivia?' The door to the stairwell swings open with a bang, flooding the top steps with light. My supervisor Noreen, a weighty woman from Northern Ireland, faces me with her hands on her hips. 'No phone calls at work. Turn it off.'

'I'm sorry. It was an emergency. My daughter rang me because—'

'Put the phone away and go back to work.'

'But I haven't said goodbye. My daughter will think that I've hung up on her.'

Noreen takes several steps towards me and I frantically jab at my phone, ending the call as the door closes and the stairwell is plunged into darkness again.

'You've a verbal warning,' she says. 'Step out of line again and it's a written one. If this was my company I wouldn't employ people like you.'

'What do you mean . . . people like me?'

I hear her footsteps on the tiled floor and the squeak of the door as she pulls it open. 'Just get back to work.'

The minibus that shuttles us between offices crawls through the dark streets of London and the sense of injustice that's been building since Noreen referred to 'people like you' has become unbearable. Is this how it's going to be for the rest of my life? Am I going to be talked down to, berated and patronised forever? Am I going to struggle to get – and keep – jobs? To find a home for me and my daughter? Am I going to spend the rest of my life paying for a crime I didn't commit? Grace needs me. I have to get her away from Dominic as soon as I can and it's people like Noreen who'll make that harder than it has to be.

We turn left onto Tooley Street and a building I recognise looms out of the gloom and lights up the sky. Just the sight of it makes me feel sick. It's The Radcliffe Building where Dominic works as a chartered surveyor. A broadsheet newspaper takes up three of the floors of the sixteen-storey building and a publishing house uses two. I can't remember which companies use the other floors but on the fifth floor, behind one of the brightly lit windows, is Dom's office, and inside that is his safe.

'Excuse me.' I lean across the aisle and wave at a woman with short dark hair in the same cleaning company polo shirt as me. I think her name's Jo.

She looks up from her phone, startled. 'Yes?'

'I thought we were being taken back to C&C Cleaning? Isn't it the end of our shift? We just missed our turning.'

'For you maybe.' She laughs softly. 'I've got another one to do.'

'There?' I gesture out of the window as we pull up outside The Radcliffe Building and Noreen stands up, clutching a clipboard.

'Yes,' Jo says as she gets to her feet.

'Debbie, Temi, Dawn,' Noreen reads from her list. 'Jakub, Corrina, Jo, Nas.'

'How do I get on the rota to clean it?'

'I can't help, sorry.' Jo shrugs, keen to be on her way. Half the minibus are on their feet now, all making their way to the front. 'Ask Noreen.'

I take one look at our supervisor, standing beside the driver with her pinched mouth and her cold eyes, and I sink back into my seat. That's not a conversation either of us want to have right now. My colleagues file out of the bus, one by one, and make their way towards The Radcliffe Building, a navy blue stream snaking towards the revolving glass doors, with Noreen, the rattle at the end.

The driver starts up the engine, the minibus shudders and we pull away. I twist around, my eyes fixed on the fifth floor until the skyscraper disappears from view.

Chapter 20

DANI

It's Dani's day off and she's wasted three hours of it sitting in her car outside Kelly Smith's flat. On the upside she's got the money she needs to get Casey into rehab in an envelope tucked under her seat. Dom's text last night was brief – Borough Market, by Elsey and Bent, 7am tomorrow – and her reply – Ok – was even briefer. She fist-pumped the air after she sent the text. He was going to give her the cash. Why else would he want to meet up?

However, when she turned up at Borough Market Dominic didn't give her the cash straight away. He wanted photos, he said, and daily updates: where Olivia was and what she was up to. Dani shook her head. There was no way she could agree to that. She wasn't a bloody private detective. She had a job to do and there were only so many hours of the day. Dominic said he wouldn't pay for sightings of Liv in the pub or out to dinner. He wanted to know what she was planning, not what she had to drink.

Dani was irritated. What he wanted was a mind-reader, or

for her to become Olivia's best friend. The thought made a muscle in her cheek twitch. There had been a time when she'd considered Liv a friend. She was good company, despite their age difference, and she was one of the few clients she looked forward to seeing because she made the session fun.

But Dani's not one of Liv's favourite people anymore and mind-reading isn't in her job description so she's going to have to do the next best thing: tap up someone who knows Liv well. Only Kelly Smith is taking her sweet time getting out of bed. There's a possibility she might not leave the flat at all, but Dani knows her well enough to discount that. From the way Smith fidgeted throughout every interview Dani ever sat in, she's pretty sure she'll be up and out of the front door as soon as she's awake. People like Smithy have to keep moving. She'll be itching to find her next target or go on a shoplifting spree. Dani's not the only one who gets her kicks from the thrill of the chase.

Growing bored, she reaches under her seat and pulls out the envelope Dom gave her. She counts out the wrapped piles of notes and indignation catches in her throat. A grand? A solitary grand? She can't even buy a month in rehab with that. She taps at her phone, sending him a text:

One grand? Are you taking the piss?

A couple of seconds later a reply appears:

I told you. I can't get hold of that kind of money right now. But if you keep watching her I'll give you the rest in a week.

Dani grinds her teeth, her thumbs poised to tap out another message. What's Dom playing at? He genuinely looked like he was shitting it when she showed him the photos of Olivia and Smith in his front garden, and he agreed to pay her to keep an eye on them, so why take the piss and only give her a grand? She doesn't believe for one second that he can't find another twenty-nine. Maybe he thinks if he gives her more she'll take the money and then sit on her arse? Or is it about control? Is he getting a thrill out of making her work for it? She tosses the phone onto the passenger seat. The last time she lost her temper with Dom she stormed off empty-handed. She needs to keep it together. Four more grand and at least Casey will be safe for a month and—

She slips down in her seat, pulling the lip of her baseball cap low over her eyes as a slight figure in an oversized puffer jacket walks out of the door next to the antique shop.

'Hello, Kelly,' Dani breathes.

Dani has trailed Kelly Smith all the way from her flat to Elephant and Castle shopping centre and now she's keeping a close eye on her as she casually drifts in and out of the various shops. Smith's destination isn't a huge surprise – where there are crowds and shops, there are rich pickings for a thief. She'll probably be stealing to order – a packet of razors here, a designer handbag there, booze, clothing, jewellery, even baby formula – anything that can easily be sold on.

As Kelly walks out of Boots, Dani follows her at a distance. She's not going to approach her in a shop where store detectives are milling around, and she's going to leave her alone in the open spaces where CCTV is tracking their every move. What she wants is to get Kelly on her own, where they won't be seen or overheard.

She can't tell what Smith is smuggling out of each store beneath the massive bulk of her coat but she's pretty sure she'll have nabbed at least a couple of hundred quid's worth of stuff already and she's only been in the shopping centre for half an hour.

Get in, get out, be quick.

Dani quickens her pace, matching Smith's as they approach the escalator that leads to the exit. She needs to get to her before anyone else does. She glances around, checking the location of the CCTV cameras, then pauses to glance at a map. The ladies' loos are just before the exit. Perfect. There won't be any cameras in there.

She carries on towards the escalator. Smith's already on it and she's drifting out of sight. Dani lets a woman with a buggy step onto it first then ducks down behind her. If Smith sees her she'll panic and run.

She waits until Kelly gets off and is halfway to the exit before she squeezes past buggy woman and hurries down the last few steps. One of the security guards, radio to his ear, is heading in Kelly's direction. They must have picked her up on the CCTV. If he gets to her first he'll haul her up to the office and ring it in. Smith will get nicked and any chance Dani had of getting Olivia intel from her will be gone.

She swears under her breath. Kelly's clocked the security guard and she's speeding up, preparing to run. 'Shit, shit, shit.'

Dani makes a split-second decision.

'Police.' She flashes her badge at the guard. 'Don't get involved.' She peels off before he can reply but his startled expression reassures her. He won't be going anywhere. He froze the moment he saw the badge.

Smith's nearly at the doors to the exit. Any hope Dani had of bundling her into the toilets out of sight of the CCTV cameras and the public is long gone. She's going to have to grab her outside instead. She breaks into a run. The automatic doors have opened and Kelly's sprinting through them.

'Shit.' Dani pushes harder. Smith's a fast runner – it's not the first time she's chased after her – but all those hours of training in the gym have paid off and she's closing the gap. There's no way Kelly can outrun her with all the crap she's got stuffed into her coat. Kelly rounds the corner of the shopping centre. Dani follows. Kelly darts across the car park, oblivious to the cars that have to screech to a halt to avoid hitting her. Dani chases. There's less than two metres between them now and she can hear Kelly gasping for air.

'Stop!' she shouts. 'Police.'

Her warning seems to give Kelly a burst of energy because she pulls away again and charges into a verge of trees and bushes that separates the car park from a main road. Dani grits her teeth. Being seen by a dozen people in the car park is one thing but there's going to be an audience once they reach the main road. The last thing she needs is for a squad car to get involved.

'Kelly! Stop!'

Smith pitches forward. She's caught her foot on a tree root or a branch. She lands heavily, hands outstretched to break her fall. Dani's on her before she can get to her feet.

'Kelly Smith,' she pants as she twists the shoplifter's arms behind her back. 'I'm arresting you on suspicion of theft. You do not have to say anything. But, it may harm your defence if you do not mention when questioned something which you later rely on in court.' She takes a breath as she fastens handcuffs around Smith's wrists. 'Anything you do say may be—'

'Yeah, yeah. I know the speech.'

'So why do it?' Dani pulls her to her feet although neither of them can stand up straight, surrounded by all the branches and leaves. 'You got out less than two weeks ago and now you're going back in.'

Smith laughs; it's the husky crackle of a woman at least thirty years older. 'Maybe I like the attention. I dunno. Ask my therapist.'

'With a charge of breaking and entering added to your rap sheet you're looking at at least another two years.'

Kelly's laughter dries up. 'What are you talking about? Breaking and entering?'

'Don't bullshit me, Smith. I saw you last Friday, in a house on Oakfield Road. And I know you saw me.'

'You stalking me, miss?'

'I've got a photo, of you and Olivia Sutherland, evidence that you broke in. You might not give two shits about going back inside but I bet she does.'

Kelly shifts under her bulky coat. 'I wouldn't know.'

'Wouldn't you? She's got a daughter. Grace. Twelve years old. She hasn't seen her for a while. I think you're a good enough friend to help her break into her ex-husband's house and I know you lifted the key from the cleaner.'

'I don't know what you're talking about.'

Dani crouches down so they're eye to eye. 'I think you do.'

Kelly shrugs. 'No comment. Are you gonna take me down the station or what?'

'That depends.'

'On what?'

'If you can be a good friend to me.'

'You what?' There's the husky laugh again.

'Have you got a phone, Kelly?'

'Course I have.'

'Good. So here's the deal. I let you walk, but I need to know what Olivia's up to.'

Kelly's expression hardens. 'I'm not grassing anyone up.'

'I'm not asking you to. And I'm pretty sure Olivia's not in any hurry to break the law again. I just want to know what the two of you chat about and where she goes day to day. I need to know where her head's at.'

A mischievous light enters Kelly's eyes. 'I got it wrong, miss. You're not stalking me. You're stalking her.'

'I'm not stalking anyone. I'm just trying to keep people safe.'

'Safe, eh? What's it worth?'

Dani's face remains expressionless but there's a spark of jubilation in her chest. She knew Smith would mention money eventually. It's all solidarity and not grassing your mates up until money is involved.

'Well you won't go to prison for one.'

'That's not what I meant.'

'I know exactly what you meant.'

'I'm not helping you stalk Liv.'

'You sure about that?' Dani says. 'Because I'll be nicking her next and she's on probation. She'll be back inside before she knows it. I wonder how many more of her daughter's birthdays she'll miss. Shame you don't want to save her from that, Smith.'

The defiance in Kelly's eyes softens, ever so slightly. She might not care about going back to prison, but she doesn't want her mate to miss out on any more of her daughter's life.

'I just want the occasional text,' Dani says, 'that's all I'm asking.'

'You're covering your back, aren't ya?' Kelly says, a smile pricking at her lips. 'She's got you worried.'

That's part of it, Dani thinks but doesn't say. If Olivia is sniffing around to prove she was framed then it won't just be Dom she takes down.

'Like I said,' she says. 'I'm just keeping people safe. So, are you going to do it or am I going to take you both down the station now?'

Smith searches her eyes. She's still suspicious, and with good reason. 'What's to say you won't nick us anyway?'

'That depends if you commit another crime.'

'Or if you catch me.'

'I'll catch you, believe you me. And if you tell Olivia about this, or if I get the slightest inkling that you've lied to me or omitted to tell me something, it won't just be a breaking and entering charge you'll both be facing. I'll make sure you're both sent down for a very, very long time.'

Kelly stares back at her, disgust twisting her face as she shakes her head slowly from side to side. 'You're a piece of shit.'

Dani raises her eyebrows. 'Takes one to know one, Smith.' She thinks about the envelope in her car, stuffed with twenty-pound notes. It's nowhere near enough to get Casey to rehab but it's more than enough to seal this deal. She can't trust Smith not to tell Olivia everything. The threat of prison isn't enough. But cash might be. She can see it in Kelly's eyes – she's tired and she's hungry. She's grubby too, and shivering under her cheap bomber jacket.

'I'll give you fifty quid now,' Dani says, 'to buy yourself something to eat.'

Kelly remains defiant. 'I don't need anything to eat.'

'No? But you'd like a shower, wouldn't you? And a warm flat? Fifty quid will feed the electricity meter for a while.' She holds up a hand as the other woman attempts to interject. 'Yeah, yeah, you could nick well over fifty quid's worth of stuff in half an hour and sell it on, but how long is that going to take you? How many pubs and flats are you going to have to visit to shift it all? Assuming you don't get caught first. The security guards in that shopping centre will be on the lookout for you now. You'll have to "shop" somewhere else. Fifty quid, Smith. Now, in your hand. And another fifty at the end of the week if you do what you're told. And if you don't do what you're—'

'A hundred,' Smith counters.

Dani pulls on her arms, still twisted up behind her back. 'Forget it. Let's go down the station. We can pick Olivia up en route. Let her know that you had the chance to save her and you screwed her over.'

'All right, all right.' Kelly whimpers in pain as Dani pulls on her arms again. 'I'll do it. I'll do it, okay?'

Chapter 21

Ayesha drops into the armchair, puts her feet up on the foot-stool and sighs with satisfaction.

'Thanks.' She takes the mug I'm holding out and shoots me a grateful smile. She blows on the tea then takes a sip. 'God, I needed that. Remind me how much it knackers me out, the next time I volunteer to arrange a team retreat.'

I take a seat on the sofa, nursing my mug of tea. 'Was it that bad?'

'No. It was all right, quite good fun, but I didn't stop the whole time.' She casts an appraising eye over the flat. Thank god I went on a massive cleaning spree the other day. 'How are you anyway? You look tired.'

'Yeah, I struggled to get to sleep last night. I did my first cleaning shift and . . . well, a lot's happened since I last saw you.'

Ayesha listens, sipping her tea as I tell her everything – from meeting up with Smithy, to breaking into Dominic's

112

house, to Grace's teary phone call and the conversation I overheard.

'Hold on.' Ayesha makes a rewind motion with her hand. 'What were you doing in your ex-husband's house? Liv, there's a restraining order against you and—'

'I know, I know. It was risky—'

'Risky?' She puts down her tea and shifts onto the edge of her seat. 'Liv, the police officer who testified against you in court knew what you were doing!' She pauses, a frown creasing her brow. 'If she was outside why didn't she arrest you? Why aren't you in a cell right now?'

'I'm not sure. We outran her and—'

'You're not sure? That woman knows where you live. Here,' she jabs a painted fingernail into the arm of her chair, 'in my flat. It'll be my block they'll park outside, with the lights flashing, when they come to arrest you. My door they bang on. A black woman's door! Seriously, Olivia? You'd do that to me? When you know how hard it's been for me to get where I am and how many obstacles have been thrown in my path?'

A wave of horrified shame courses through me as Ayesha stares at me, waiting for my reply. But there's nothing I can say that can justify the choice I made because she's right. I didn't give a single thought to how my actions would impact her life. She's right to be angry with me. There's no justification for what I did. None at all.

'I'm sorry.' I stand up on shaky legs and gather up the few possessions I own. 'I am really, really sorry. I screwed up. I'll move out and hand myself in. I'll make sure they don't turn up here. I'm so sorry, Ayesha. You've been such a good friend and I've been so thoughtless. I honestly don't know what to—'

'Sit down.' She waves a hand in the direction of the sofa. 'Just sit down.'

I do as I'm told.

'If the police come here,' Ayesha says, 'then they come. We can't undo that now. But I won't let you hand yourself in. You've spent enough time in jail already and Grace has suffered enough.'

Tears prick at my eyes. I'm such an arsehole. I don't deserve a friend like her.

'I should have known you wouldn't behave yourself after you got me to drive you to see Grace. I never should have gone away and left you alone.'

'Aysh, it's really not your—'

'Of course it's not my fault!' She cuts me off. 'I'm kidding. Sort of. Look, Liv, I understand your motivations. In your shoes I'd be doing exactly the same thing but you have to keep me in the loop. I don't want to find out what you've been up to when the police turn up at my door, especially when I've just got back from Birmingham.' Her expression softens into a smile. 'Now, let's go through the bit about your phone conversation with Grace.'

'There's something else,' I tell her. 'Something that happened while you were away.'

She shifts in her seat. 'Am I going to need something stronger than tea?'

'Jack sent me an email, saying he was sorry.'

'Okay.' She makes a flicking motion with her hand. 'Now you need to open the wine.'

I sit down with my glass and reach for my phone. It's been bleeping intermittently all day with messages from Grace. I had hoped that speaking to me on the phone, and a good night's sleep, would have made her a little happier but, if anything, she's even more fraught than she was last night. She's hanging everything on the promise I made her about moving out of London and living with me.

'Is that Jack?' Ayesha asks.

I shake my head. 'No, it's Grace. I did receive a second email from Jack this morning though.'

'Go on.'

'He's in hiding. He said he's too scared to tell me where, and that sending the emails was risky enough.'

She raises an eyebrow. 'Do you believe him?'

'It explains a few things. I'd have gone into hiding too if I'd got wind of the arrest.'

'No you wouldn't. You were certain you could prove your innocence.'

'True.'

'Why didn't he phone you?'

'Maybe he tried. I haven't got the same phone number anymore.'

Ayesha takes a sip of her wine and looks thoughtful. 'You need to send him your new number; talk to him properly, find out what's going on. Assuming you do want to talk to him. I think it's strange that he's waited until now to get in touch.'

That's something that's been bugging me too. Why dump me and then wait five years before he got in touch again? He must know that I'm out of jail.

'I think he wants something,' Ayesha says. 'And he's building up to ask you.'

'Wants what though?'

She runs a hand over her hair. 'Who knows? But I think he's bad news. He's a coward and he let you down when you needed him most. I think you should tell the police about the emails and let their tech guys deal with it. I'm sure they can trace his IP.'

'Why would I want to do that? He'd end up in prison for a crime he didn't commit.'

'Are you sure about that?'

'What?' My wine slops in my glass.

'Well. You said Dominic was on the phone to someone last night. It can't have been Dani because she already knew you broke into the house. What if it was Jack? What if he had something to do with you getting framed?'

I laugh at the absurdity of the suggestion but it's a thin sound that fades quickly. 'Why would he do that? The police had an arrest warrant for him too. He wouldn't have framed himself.'

Ayesha swirls her wine around her glass, looking thoughtful. 'Okay. But something about this doesn't ring true. I can understand Jack going on the run to avoid being arrested. What I don't understand is why he's got back in touch.'

'Maybe he . . . maybe he heard I was out and he wants to find out if the coast is clear? Maybe he wants to . . . I don't know . . . start things up with me again?'

'Hell no!' Ayesha fixes me with a stern look. 'You wouldn't say yes, would you? Please tell me you've got more self-respect.'

'Of course I wouldn't. But what if Jack knows something that can help clear us both? We're assuming he's hiding from the police but what if he's hiding from Dom?'

Ayesha sighs loudly and gives me a despairing look. 'I'm not going to talk you out of this, am I? You're going to try and meet up with him?'

'I can't do that if he won't tell me where he is.'

'So ask someone.'

I laugh, confused. 'Like who?'

'I dunno. Has he got family? Parents? Siblings? Someone has to know where he is.'

THE GUILTY COUPLE

I take a sip of my wine and mull over what she just said.
Jack didn't open up much about his family but he did mention
a sister called Sonia who lives in Essex; Audley End, I think.
He never introduced us but one night, a week after he'd
ghosted me, I looked Sonia up on Facebook and asked her
if she could please tell Jack to contact me. Her response, the
next morning, was brief: It's been a long time since Jack did
anything I asked him to do. I'm sorry but I can't help you. I
was too embarrassed to contact her again.

'He's got a sister,' I tell Ayesha. 'I found her on Facebook
once. She wouldn't talk to me then but she might now.'

'Go on then. Get it out of your system. I know you're not
going to let this drop.'

'You know I love you.' I shoot her a smile before I tap the
Facebook icon on my phone.

'Yeah, yeah. Read me what you write before you hit send.'

She gets up and potters around the kitchen, unstacking
the dishwasher and putting things away as I write, and
rewrite, my message to Sonia.

'Okay.' I twist round to share it with her. 'This is what I've
got . . .'

Hello, Sonia, it's Olivia Sutherland, Jack's ex-girlfriend. I
was released from prison a little over two weeks ago and
I've been trying to pick up the remnants of my life.

As you know, Jack and I were falsely accused of a
crime we didn't commit and I want to clear both of our
names. I've recently received some information about
him that you might be interested in hearing. If you are,
we need to talk face to face. Sooner rather than later
ideally.

I hope you're well.

All the best, Liv.

117

'Well?' I ask.

Ayesha shrugs. 'It sounds mysterious enough to make her curious. If someone sent me a message like that about my brother I'd answer.'

'That's good enough for me.' I hit send.

Chapter 22

DOMINIC

A tendon pulses in Dom's jaw as he taps out a message on his daughter's pink iPhone:

Grace isn't allowed to use this phone anymore because she's been bullying another child on social media. She has been lying a lot recently – to me, to her teachers and to her friends – and I'd be very wary of accepting anything she says as the truth. If you try and contact her again I will call the police. Dominic.

He presses send on the message to his ex-wife then hurls the phone away, sending it scuttling across his desk before it drops onto the carpeted office floor. He had no idea that Olivia and Grace were in touch until earlier that morning when the ping, ping, ping of Grace's phone at the breakfast table nearly drove him insane. He snatched it out of her hands, sure that he'd find messages from her, bullying another child. Instead he found a string of texts from her mother.

How the hell had Olivia got hold of Grace's number? They'd only had one supervised visit so it must have happened at the zoo. He's going to have to ask his mother to up her game the next time the two meet.

He found only one phone call between Grace and Olivia – at 10.45 p.m. two days earlier. That was the day he'd met Dani in the car park after he'd discussed the bullying issue with Grace's head of year. Had Grace called her mother as a result of that conversation? According to Mrs Hargreaves the physical bullying had stopped but the harassment had gone online instead. Grace had claimed that she was the one being bullied but the evidence was damning: cruel message after cruel message, all in her name.

When he took his daughter home after the meeting she refused to talk or even look at him. She threw down her school bag and ran up the stairs. He was about to go after her but then his burner phone rang. As he took the call in the hall he could hear his daughter upstairs, banging around on the landing, screaming at next door's cat and repeatedly slamming her bedroom door. He blew a gasket then. He stormed up the stairs, threw open her door and threatened to confiscate her phone unless she stopped bullying other children. She jumped off her bed and attacked him as he made a grab for her mobile. She scratched at his arms and called him every name under the sun. He relented and let her keep the phone and, as he made his way back downstairs, he heard the sound of wretched sobbing from behind her closed bedroom door.

Still, he's got her phone now which kills two birds. No more bullying and no more contact with her mum. Any conversations they have now will be confined to supervised visits with Esther and George, and Olivia won't be able to do so much as sneeze without Dani telling him about it.

After their conversation in the car park he panicked and sent a frantic text on his burner phone, saying he urgently needed to find thirty grand. The reply, when it came, was as measured as ever. Making an enemy of Dani would be foolish and an insight into Olivia's movements would be useful. Dom should withdraw a thousand pounds on his credit card and give it to Dani, promising to pay her the rest in seven days. In the meantime he should string her along. By the time she started making noises about the other twenty-nine thousand, she wouldn't be a problem anymore.

Now Dominic rounds his desk, picks up Grace's pink mobile phone and chucks it into his safe. He sighs with relief as he closes the door and the electronic display bleeps that it's locked. In six days' time he'll be millions of pounds richer, Dani will be out of his life, and Olivia will never see her daughter again.

Chapter 23

OLIVIA

When I woke up this morning and checked my phone I was convinced that Sonia hadn't replied. There was every chance she was in touch with Jack and had no need to have a conversation with me. Or perhaps my message had scared her – I had been convicted for conspiracy to murder and for all she knew I could be the psychopath everyone else believed me to be. I'd slept fitfully and my head was foggy from too much wine but I wasn't dreaming Sonia's reply:

> Hello, Olivia, I would very much like to talk to you. We've all been hugely worried about Jack. I am happy to chat to you over the phone or, if you'd like to pop in for a coffee, I'll be in all day (between football runs) if you're able to travel to Audley End. Here's my phone number and address . . .

I was surprised that she'd invited me into her home but I wasn't about to give her reason to change her mind. I messaged her back, telling her I'd be over around 2 p.m.

It's a half-hour walk from Audley End train station to Sonia's house on Freshwell Street and I'm hot and sweaty when I arrive. The house is a terraced cottage with a tiled roof, overgrown with moss, a wooden front door with shrubs in pots on either side and sash windows made up of lots of little panes of glass. A quick peek in one of the windows reveals a living room with beams running along the ceiling, a brick fireplace and wood burner, and soft squishy sofas. It looks cosy, warm and lived-in, the kind of home I could imagine sharing with Grace. I could kill Dominic for taking her phone away from her. It was the one lifeline I had to check she was okay. I'm not going to see her again until Monday and I'm terrified she might do something silly between now and then. But what can I do? It's Saturday so I can't turn up at school and if I go round to the house Dominic will have me arrested. *Please*, I will her, *please stay strong*.

I raise a hand to rattle the knocker on Sonia's door. It opens before I can touch it and I jolt in alarm.

'Olivia?' says a tall, middle-aged woman with jaw-length brown curly hair, glasses and a wide warm smile. 'Sorry, I didn't mean to make you jump. I saw you approaching from the kitchen.' She steps back into the hallway and I follow her inside. 'Can I take your coat?'

I'm so stunned at how similar she looks to her brother that it takes me a second to register what she just asked. She's got the same broad nose, pinched at the tip, deep brown eyes and identical lines either side of her mouth when she smiles. I didn't have a mental image of her on the train down here. Her Facebook photo was of a couple of dogs and the banner was of a beach somewhere. All her other photos were locked down.

'Sorry, yes, of course.' I shrug off my coat and hand it to

123

her. There's a line of wellies and trainers on a shoe rack along one of the walls. 'Should I take off my shoes too?'

'No need. We've got a golden retriever and a corgi. Mud on the rugs is the least of our problems!' She spots me glancing around for the dogs and adds, 'They're in the garden. Don't worry. We've got the house to ourselves.'

'Your children . . .' I search around for their names. Jack definitely mentioned a nephew and niece.

'Elsie's out with her friends and Dylan's got a football match.'

The conversation's so easy-going and cordial that I feel completely disarmed. I'd expected her to be brusque or reserved.

'Should I?' I gesture towards the living room.

'Yes of course, take a seat.' She glances at her watch. 'We've got about an hour until I need to collect Dylan. Would you like a tea? Coffee? Some water perhaps?'

I shake my head even though my throat is parched. I can't put this conversation off a moment longer, I need to know what she knows.

'No problem.' She takes a seat on the sofa and her eyes flick over my face, my hair and my body. She's judging me, I can tell. 'Don't take this the wrong way,' she says. 'But you look very different from the photos that were shown on the news.'

I prickle, prepared to defend myself. 'In what way?'

'You're softer in person. You looked hard-faced on the TV.'

'Oh.' I'm not sure how to respond. 'I was scared. I'd never gone to court before.'

Her expression changes – from curiosity to a cold detachment – as though a shutter has come down behind her eyes. 'Of course, yes, I completely understand.'

If she closes down I won't be able to get anything out of

124

her. I need her to be as warm and open as she was when I came in.

'I loved Jack very much,' I say. 'We'd planned to start a new life together.'

'Right, yes. Jack's very good at making promises that he can't keep.'

I say nothing, willing her to say more.

'The children,' she says. 'My children. I've lost track of the times he's promised them something, a trip or a present or day out. They're always disappointed and I'm the one left to pick up the pieces, to mop up the tears. It's not fair on them, especially since their dad died.' She catches herself and her cheeks flush, as though she's said too much.

'Anyway,' she sits forward, her body language primed for bad news. 'Let's get to the reason you're here. What's this important information about Jack? What has he done now?'

'He hasn't done anything. Not that I know about anyway.'

Sonia slumps back on the sofa, takes off her glasses and rubs her hands over her face. 'Thank god for that. I thought he'd . . .' she tails off. 'He's alive then? You know that much?'

'Yes. He's alive. He sent me an email, saying sorry and telling me that he missed me. He said he was hiding but he couldn't tell me where. I don't know if he's still on the run from the police or if something else is going on. I was hoping you might be able to tell me.'

'Me?' Laughing, she puts her glasses back on. 'Whatever gave you that idea? I haven't seen Jack for years. I don't know what he told you about me but we're not exactly close.'

I didn't know that, and I'm starting to wonder how much I knew him at all.

'Can I see the emails?' Sonia asks.

'Of course.' I dig out my phone and show it to her. She

clicks through the emails, her brow furrowing as she scrolls down the screen.

'What is it?' I ask.

'Are you quite sure it's him?'

'Yes of course. He always signed off his texts like that – a J and a kiss.'

Sonia hands the phone back to me. 'Strange that he didn't give you a phone number.'

'I assume he hasn't got a signal wherever he is, or he doesn't want the police to trace the calls.' Even a burner phone can be triangulated. I had enough conversations in prison to know that that's true.

Sonia raises an eyebrow. 'You know the police can trace emails too?'

This conversation is strangely similar to the one I had with Ayesha last night. They're both suspicious about the messages. Ayesha questioned Jack's motive for sending them and it sounds like Sonia doesn't even believe that they're from him.

'Can't you ask him something?' Sonia says. 'To check it's him? Ask him what his nickname was for Dylan? If it really is Jack he'll know.'

I tap reply on Jack's message then look back at Sonia, suddenly unsure. 'He'll know I've been to see you if I do that. If he really is hiding he might panic about me telling too many people. I don't want him to stop contacting me. I need to find out what he knows.'

Sonia looks at me questioningly. 'What about?'

'The people who framed us.'

Her gaze becomes flinty. She thinks we did it. She thinks her own brother would try and have someone killed.

'Sonia, do you—'

She cuts me off. 'Ask him something only the two of you know. Did he have a pet name for you? Or was there

126

somewhere you went that only the two of you would know about?'

I feel like an idiot that she's had to suggest this. The first thing I should have done was verify that the email was actually from Jack. For all I know this could be something to do with Dominic, or the police.

'Okay.' I tap a short email into my phone: I need to check that this is really you. We used to daydream about going on holiday together. Where did we say that we'd go?

I glance at Sonia, who nods her approval.

'Now we wait,' she says. 'Would you like that cup of tea?'

There's still no reply from Jack and, three cups of tea later, conversation with Sonia is starting to dry up. We've covered my relationship with Jack and how it ended and I've explained how I think Dominic and Dani framed us (Sonia was shocked to discover a police detective could be so corrupt). I also glossed over the five years I spent in jail after Sonia asked me what it was like. On the train down from London I had hoped that seeing his sister would give me more information about Jack, and fill in the gaps in his life that I know nothing about, but whenever I probe a bit deeper Sonia changes the subject and tells me something inane about her kids or switches the topic back to me.

There's ten minutes left until she has to leave to collect her son from football and it doesn't look as though Jack's going to reply any time soon.

'Could I use your loo?' I slip my mobile into my bag and move to stand up.

'Of course.' She points towards a wooden door, painted white, at the back of the room. 'If you go up the stairs the bathroom's the first door on your left.'

'Thanks.'

I hurry across the room, through the door and up the stairs to the loo. I use the toilet and wash my hands then make my way back down the stairs, casting an eye over the photographs that make up a gallery of faces along the stairwell wall. There are lots of photos of two children, presumably Dylan and Elsie, a few shots of Sonia and her late partner, and several of two elderly couples – the grandparents, I imagine. There are photos with friends, at parties and weddings, camping trips and holidays abroad. It's like their whole life has been catalogued on one stretch of wall. I search the photos for pictures of Jack and find a faded photograph of two curly-haired children – a boy and a girl – in a paddling pool. There's a framed photograph of a seventieth birthday celebration but I can't see Jack in the family snap. I make a mental note to ask Sonia about that and then I spot another photograph that makes me gasp. It's a photo of Jack, and two of his friends, in what looks like a student union or a bar. They've got upturned plastic beer glasses on their heads and Jack's wearing an oversized badge that says '21 Today!' But it's not Jack's drunken, smiling face that makes my heart stop, it's the two other men.

'Sonia!' I unhook the photograph from the wall and hurry down the stairs. 'Sonia, where was this photo taken?'

'Sorry?' She gives me a blank look then gets up to take a closer look at the framed photograph in my hands.

'That's Manchester, where Jack did his degree. That photo always makes me laugh, it's the pint hat and the silly look on his face. I took it from Jack's old room at Mum and Dad's years ago. Those were his best friends at uni, Ian something on the left, I can't remember his last name. But I do remember the guy on the right because his name rhymed. Matt Platt.' She glances at me and her smile slips. 'What is it? What's wrong?'

'That there,' I point to the young man on Jack's left, 'is Ian Ritchie as you say. He's my ex-husband's best friend. And that,' I point to the dark-haired guy on Jack's other side, 'is Dominic Sutherland, my ex-husband.'

'No.' She shakes her head. 'No, that's not right.'

I bring up a photo of Dominic from his company website and show it to her. 'Look, that's him.'

She looks at the photo for a few seconds then hands my phone back to me.

'Either they're different people or your ex-husband has changed his name. That boy,' she taps the glass of the photograph, 'was called Matt Platt. I know because I was there, at Jack's twenty-first birthday party.'

I don't understand what's going on. I would put my house – if I had one – on the fact Dominic is the young man with his arm around Jack's neck. Ian's there too and Sonia remembered his name. Dom and Ian have been best friends since they met at Manchester Uni in halls. It makes sense that they're in the same photo, I've seen others, in one of Dom's photo albums. I even recognise the Pet Shop Boys T-shirt he's wearing.

'Maybe they were playing a joke on you,' I say. 'Getting you to say Matt Platt and laughing at you behind their backs. Or maybe it was someone else's name and you've confused him with Dom?'

'No.' She shakes her head again. 'His name was definitely Matt. I know because I slept with him.'

Chapter 24

Dani's phone pings as she's processing an arrest for a burglary with Jess. Kelly Smith has sent her a text.

She senses someone's eyes on her – heavy, weighted – and looks up to find Reece Argent watching her from across the room. He looks away sharply, suddenly fascinated by something on his screen, then glances back and meets her gaze. *Go on then*, she wills him, jaw clenched, *say something. Make a little dig about me being at my desk for a change.* But Reece doesn't say a word. Instead, he raises his eyebrows and looks back at his screen. *Dick*, Dani thinks then turns back to Jess.

'Back in a sec,' Dani says, pocketing her phone as she gets up from her desk. Jess grunts, her attention so focused on the sheets of paper in front of her that she doesn't even glance up as Dani heads out of the office to the loos.

She enters an empty cubicle, locks the door, takes her phone out of her pocket, and sits down on the closed toilet lid.

Smith's text is a message forwarded from Olivia: Sorry I can't meet you later but I'm going to see Jack's sister, Sonia,

130

in Audley End. Long story. Will tell you everything next time I
see you.

Interesting. First Olivia breaks into Dom's house, then she
goes to see her ex-lover's sister. Maybe Olivia thinks the sister's
still in touch with him? Dani feels a prickle of excitement.
Intel on Jack Law's whereabouts could lead to a long overdue
arrest, and a nice pat on the back for her. She'd have to fudge
where she got the intel, obviously, but that wouldn't be hard.
She opens the Maps app on her phone and calculates the
distance between New Scotland Yard to Audley End. It's only
an hour and a half in the car. A quick database search should
reveal Sonia's address, assuming she shares the same surname
as her brother. Not the Police National Computer, though,
she doesn't want to leave an audit trail. She looks at her
watch. Three more hours of her shift left and then she can
take off. She texts Dominic, telling him to meet her in the
car park at 10.30 p.m. for an update, then returns her phone
to her pocket and strolls back towards the office. As she
reaches the stairwell Reece walks towards her. She moves to
step around him but he sidesteps in the same direction, cutting
her off. He looms over her, six foot three inches of fragile
male ego and simmering aggression – the most dangerous
kind of man.

A sneer lifts his lip. 'PT client, was it, that sent you scurrying
out of the office? Or was it your rich boyfriend asking for a
favour?'

The 'rich boyfriend' jibe jabs at her guts and she suppresses
a gasp of surprise. Has Argent been tracking her off-duty
movements as well as on shift? The whole team knows she
was the PT to a victim in an attempted murder case (and
testified as a witness) but there's no way Reece could know
she's been sleeping with Dominic Sutherland. She's always
been very careful. No. She catches herself before her thoughts

131

spiral out of control. Reece doesn't know anything. It's a stab in the dark and she's overreacting. No one's going to find out what she did, not as long as she keeps Dominic sweet. She'll get his money out of him first, then she'll get whatever it is he's holding over her.

'Cat got your tongue?' Argent says, leering at her like she's PornHub on a lonely Saturday night. 'Or are you saving it for your boyfriend for later?' His lascivious wink turns Dani's stomach.

'Actually,' she taps him on the cheek, 'I thought I'd take a lesson from you and stick it up the boss's arse in the next briefing. Now get out of the bloody way.'

Chapter 25

OLIVIA

As the train pulls out of Audley End station I dial Nancy's number. I'm so stunned by Sonia's revelation that I need help to make sense of it all. I wasn't able to get any more information out of Sonia as she was rushing to pick up her son but she did tell me that she slept with Dominic only once, on the night of Jack's twenty-first birthday. Her exact words were 'It was a drunken one-night stand and I never saw, or heard from him again.' Four months later the three boys finished their third year and Sonia and Jack lost touch. I tried to push her to tell me why but she was halfway to her car and she brushed me off with a 'Sorry, I really have to go.'

'Hello?' Nancy picks up after three rings. 'Liv! How are you?'

Her voice sounds loud and echoey as though she's in a tunnel or shopping mall.

I cut straight to the chase. 'Nance, I'm going to send you a photo. Tell me who you recognise. I'm sending it now.'

I hear piped music, the beep of a cash register and a child's

133

faint squeal, then, 'Wow!' Nancy's voice cuts through the noise. 'God Ian looks young. Where did you find that?'

'I'll tell you in a minute. Who else do you recognise?'

'Well, that's definitely Dom on the right and is that . . . no, it's can't be . . . that's not . . . is that Jack? In the middle? Your Jack?'

I wince as she says, 'Your Jack.'

'Yes, it's him. I found the photo in Sonia's house, that's his sister. She thought Dom was someone called Matt Platt. She said she slept with him after Jack's twenty-first birthday party.'

'Wait, what? Rewind a second. You went to see Jack's sister?'

'Yeah. He's been emailing me and I wanted to talk to Sonia about it.'

There's a pause then, 'Emailing you? Seriously? What the hell did he say?'

'That he was sorry, basically. I asked him where he was and he said he was hiding, that it was too dangerous to tell me where.'

'Wow.'

'I know.'

'So he's been hiding from the police for five years?'

'I assume so.'

'What does he want though? Why has he suddenly got in touch?'

'I don't know. I haven't asked him yet. I'm waiting for proof that it's really him.'

'What do you mean, "proof"?'

'I asked him a question, about us, that only he could answer.'

'And?'

'He hasn't replied yet.'

'Right. Sorry. Give me a sec, Liv. I need to get out of this shop. I'm struggling to hear you.'

134

The phone line becomes muffled for a minute or so then she says, 'Can you hear me? I'm at the entrance to the women's loos.'

'I can hear you. So, what do you think? About the photo? They obviously all know each other but Dom and Jack never mentioned each other. In fact . . .' a memory comes back to me '. . . when Jack and I were getting to know each other he told me he went to Manchester Uni and I asked him if he knew Dom. He said no. He didn't recognise Ian's name either.'

'That's so weird. Why would he lie?'

'I don't know. Has Ian ever mentioned knowing Jack?'

'Nope. Never. Even when you were arrested and there were photos of Jack in the paper he never said, "I know him."' She goes quiet for a few seconds. 'Maybe they were acquaintances or Dom and Ian just happened to be in the pub that night?'

'I thought that but why take a photo? And Sonia said they were best friends. Could you show Ian the photo when he gets home tonight and ask him . . . no, actually don't do that. I don't want him to talk to Dom.'

'Okay, I won't say anything.' She makes a quiet *hmm* sound. 'What did you say Jack's sister thought Dom was called?'

'Matt Platt. Why?'

'I'm just trying to work out if Ian's ever mentioned that name to me but it's not ringing any bells.' I hear Nancy apologising to someone and the sound of voices. 'Sorry, I'm getting in the way now, everyone's descended on the toilets at once. Give me one second.' The line becomes muffled for a moment, presumably as she moves away. 'Anyway, the Matt Platt thing, it's got to be mistaken identity, hasn't it?'

'Yeah, or some kind of joke. His name's on the marriage certificate, the mortgage and his passport. If that wasn't his real name I'm pretty sure I'd know about it.'

135

'Weird. Maybe it was a nickname? Is it rude, like Mike Hunt? Matt Platt. Mart Plart. Matthew . . . Platt . . . oh, god knows. Are you sure you don't want me to do a bit of digging with Ian? I can be subtle.'

That makes me laugh. Nancy's about as subtle as a sledgehammer.

'No. Keep it to yourself for now. Hang on, my phone just bleeped.' I take the phone from my ear and check the notifications. It's from Gmail, a new email from Jack.

'Liv?' I can faintly hear Nancy's voice as I tap on the notification and the email opens. I quickly read what he's written.

'Liv?' Nancy says again as I raise the phone to my ear. 'Is everything okay?'

'Jack got the answer right. I asked him where we talked about going together and he said Iceland, to see the Northern Lights. Nancy, it's definitely him.'

'Oh my god. What are you going to do?'

'Arrange to meet him.'

'And then what?'

'I really don't know.'

My conversation with Nancy ends with neither of us any closer to solving the mystery surrounding Dominic's fake name and I spend the rest of the train journey frantically googling for answers.

I try searching for 'Matt Platt' but all Google returns is page after page of footballing news about a player with the same name. I try combining Ian and Dominic's names with Jack's but all that throws up is stuff about my court case. I try combining Matt Platt with Dominic Sutherland but, again, there's nothing of interest. There are several Matt and Matthew Platts on Facebook but the only ones who were Manchester Uni alumni are too young to have been in the same year as Dominic and Ian. I message a few Matts who are around the same age as them and then I compose a message to Jack. I keep it short and succinct: We need to meet. Where and when?

By the time my train pulls into London Liverpool Street my head is spinning. I take two hundred pounds out of a cashpoint so I can go to Cash Converters tomorrow to buy Grace a second-hand phone then I pop into WH Smiths. I buy a notepad and pen then take myself off to the nearest bar and order a large glass of Rioja. As I sip my wine I scribble everything I know, and everything that's been bothering me, onto the page:

- Dom and Dani framed me and Jack
- Dom paid Dani (saw possible repayment schedule?)
- Dani saw me and Smithy in Dom's house but she didn't arrest us. Why?
- Dom has hidden something at work that might help me (repayment schedule?)
- Jack is still alive but hiding
- Dom and Ian know Jack
- Dom may have used a false name (Matt Platt) at uni

I read, and reread the list and then something jumps out at me: *Dom may have used a false name (Matt Platt) at uni.* What if Matt Platt was his real name? What if he changed it before he met me? I could try asking Esther and George but there's no way they'd tell me the truth.

I pick up my phone and google 'how do you find out if someone has changed their name?'

As I'm reading the National Archives page on how to search deed polls Sonia's name flashes up on my phone. I answer it immediately.

'Hi Olivia, it's Sonia.' She sounds breathless, as though she's just been for a run. 'Sorry, I'm hiding in my bedroom from the kids. I don't want them to overhear me but there's something I have to tell you. Something I'm not sure you know.'

I brace myself. 'Okay . . .'

'You asked why Jack and I lost touch and, um . . . it's not really something we talk about as a family . . . but he went to prison, shortly after he graduated university. He'd befriended an elderly man on his road and stolen thousands of pounds from his account. He's been in and out of prison ever since. I've lost track of the number of times. Whenever he lets the kids down I assume it's because he's been arrested again. Mostly for fraud, forgery, theft,' she adds quickly. 'He's never been convicted of anything violent. When he disappeared ahead of your trial I assumed he'd gone abroad and was ripping off tourists in Spain or something. There's no predicting what Jack will do from one day to the next.'

I'm suddenly aware of a man at another table, staring at me as I fight to control my breathing. 'I can't . . . I can't believe it . . .'

'Jack's capable of more than you know and I'm sorry you got caught up with him. There's something else you should know too: Jack wasn't the only one sent to prison for defrauding that poor man. They blamed each other when they were arrested. No honour amongst thieves and all that.'

All the hairs on my arms stand up. I already know what she's going to say.

'My brother isn't the only one who's been keeping things from you, Liv. Your ex-husband is too.'

Chapter 26

DANI

Dani pulls her coat tighter around her as she approaches the Hart and Hound pub, about half a mile from Sonia Law's house. It's after nine o'clock at night and there's a cold chill in the air. When she arrived at the house, twenty minutes earlier, she was greeted by a teenaged girl, sixteen or seventeen years old with waist-length brown hair and freckles across the bridge of her nose. The girl only opened the door far enough to peer out at Dani through the gap between the door and frame. Her wary expression was replaced by shock when Dani flashed her badge and told her who she was. They had a brief exchange during which Dani discovered the girl's name – Elsie – and that her mum was at the pub.

'You're not going to arrest her, are you?' the girl asked, a note of panic in her voice.

Dani reassured her that she wasn't, that she had a couple of questions to ask her mum about her brother Jack Law.

'He hasn't killed anyone, has he?' Elsie asked.

Dani frowned. 'Why would you think that?'

The girl stepped from foot to foot, her grip on the door tightening. 'I dunno.' She shrugged. 'Mum said ages ago that Uncle Jack was wanted for trying to kill someone. Has he? Killed someone?'

Dani shook her head. 'Not as far as I know.'

Ever since that conversation ended she's been picking over the bones of what Elsie said, wondering where it fits with Olivia's visit to Sonia Law earlier that day. It's no surprise that Olivia would want to meet up with her lover after five years inside. Was she arranging a meeting via Sonia? It would have to be covert, given the fact there's still an arrest warrant out in Jack's name. Maybe Jack was in the house, and he's still there. It would explain why Elsie only opened the door a crack.

Dani blows on her hands then shoves them deep into her pockets. There's something about Jack Law being back on the scene that makes her nervous. What she's read about him suggests he's wily, manipulative and cunning (although not clever enough not to get caught) and she doesn't believe for one second that he's popped back up to be reunited with his lover. There has to be more to it than that.

She approaches a group of smokers, two men and one woman, shivering and sucking on cigarettes to the left of the pub's heavy oak front door.

'Do any of you know Sonia Law?'

Both men immediately stare at the woman and, from the look of surprise on her face, Dani's pretty sure she's just struck gold.

'Sonia?' she asks.

'Yes.' The woman looks Dani up and down, just like her daughter did twenty minutes ago. 'Why?'

'Could I have a quick chat?' Dani inclines her head away from the pub. 'In private?'

One of Sonia's companions, a tall bearded man with ruddy cheeks, casts an appraising eye over her. 'Are you police? You've got that look.'

'What look is that?' Dani asks, but she doesn't wait for a reply. Instead, she shows Sonia her badge. 'DS Danielle Anderson, Met Police. It's nothing to worry about. Just an informal chat.' She tilts her head to the left again. 'Shall we?'

She hears the men whisper furtively as she leads Sonia into the near empty car park next to the pub. What just happened will be all around Audley End by the morning.

'This won't take long,' she says as Sonia drops her cigarette butt into the gravel and grinds it out under the heel of one of her brown leather boots. 'I'm aware that—'

'I haven't done anything wrong,' Sonia interrupts. 'I know Jack's been in prison but that doesn't mean I'm a criminal too.'

'I know, and I'm not accusing you of anything.' From the hard set of Sonia's face Dani knows to tread gently. 'I just want to know if you have any idea where Jack might be.'

The other woman's lips tighten into a hard line. 'No. No idea. I didn't know when I was asked five years ago and I don't know now.'

'He didn't arrange to meet Olivia in your house, earlier today?'

'What?' The shock and incredulity in her voice is matched by her expression. Either she's a brilliant actress or she's telling the truth. 'No. Olivia came to see me because Jack's been emailing her and—' She swears under her breath and runs a hand over her hair. 'I probably shouldn't have said that but it's out now.' She sighs heavily.

'Did she tell you what was in the emails?'

'Just that he was in hiding and it was too dangerous to tell her where. That's why she came to see me, to find out if

141

I knew where. And I don't.' She gives Dani a defiant look. 'I'm glad he's alive, and I'm glad he's not in prison. I've worried about him, not hearing from him for so long.'

'How long since you last heard from him?'

'Since the, um . . .' Sonia digs around in her pockets and lights another cigarette. 'It was before all that stuff about trying to have Matt killed.'

Dani frowns. 'You've lost me there. Who's Matt?'

Sonia blows out a stream of smoke. 'Sorry, he'll always be Matt Platt to me. That was what he called himself when I met him, when he was at uni with Jack.'

'Who was? Sorry, I'm really not following—'

'Dominic . . . what's his new surname? . . . Sutherland. Olivia's husband.' She blinks, then corrects herself. 'Ex-husband. I explained all this to Olivia earlier. Matt and Jack were flatmates, in Manchester, after uni . . . along with another guy, Ian. They both went to prison – my brother and Matt – for defrauding a man on their street. Look . . .' She stamps her feet against the gravel and shivers. 'Can we do this somewhere else? I'm really cold.'

'Yeah. No.' Dani feels as though her brain has frozen too, thanks to the tsunami of new information she's just acquired. 'I'll let you go but I need to check something first. How much of this did Olivia know?

'None of it.' Sonia takes another puff on her cigarette. 'She was as surprised as you.'

Dani turns the heaters in her car to full blast and cups her hands over the vents until the feeling returns to her fingers. It's been fifteen minutes since she returned Sonia to her smokers' huddle and she's still reeling from what she was told. No wonder nothing came up when she ran Dominic's details through the database five years earlier. If what Sonia said is correct then he must have changed his name when he got out of prison. And because he hasn't committed any crimes since, the two names aren't linked.

'Shit.' She steeples her fingers over her nose and mouth and exhales heavily. Jack Law wasn't some random bloke Olivia had an affair with. Dominic knew him, they shared a flat and served time together. Dani's mind whirrs through the information she's acquired and how it might fit with what she already knows. Dominic's going to have a lot of explaining to do when she meets him later. Unless . . . unless she doesn't mention it. Her instinct is telling her that this is a piece of information she should keep close to her chest for a while.

Her phone pings and she snatches it up. It's a message from her mother, Brenda:

Where are you? I just got home from book club and Casey's gone. She's taken my bank card from my purse.

Chapter 27

OLIVIA

Ayesha wasn't home when I got back and, several hours later, I'm still struggling to come to terms with what Sonia told me on the phone. Jack is a career criminal who's been in and out of prison? I can't believe it. I don't want to believe it. We were together for six months and we talked about our pasts, we talked about *everything*. He told me that, after school, he'd taken a gap year to volunteer as an English teacher at a Tibetan monastery in India, then had returned to the UK to do a degree in English Literature. He said he'd bummed about a bit afterwards, travelling and working in restaurant kitchens or behind bars, then he'd settled in Leeds where he'd worked as a copywriter for a while before switching to be a web editor and content manager, which eventually led to a senior project manager role at some tech company in London. He didn't stumble or pause as he told me about his life. He kept eye contact with me and didn't look shifty once. And he never asked me for money. He paid for dinners, cinema tickets and river boat cruises. His flat was on the small and cosy side but that's far from unusual in London. Maybe he was keeping his past from me because we were madly in love and he didn't want to risk bursting the bubble?

Or maybe he thought I had enough on my plate with a struggling business, a child, and a husband I was planning to leave. But that's making excuses for him. He should have told me about his past, he knew everything about me. Would I have continued our affair if I'd known the truth? No, definitely not. It takes a certain kind of cruelty to trick someone elderly into trusting you and then steal everything they have. I feel sick, just thinking about it, as though the ground is shifting under my feet. If Sonia is telling me the truth then I didn't fall in love with Jack at all, I fell in love with the man he was pretending to be. Was our whole relationship a lie?

What dark twist of fate led me to start relationships with two men who had committed the same crime? Unless it wasn't a twist of fate. Did Jack know whose wife I was when he turned up at my exhibition and casually charmed me? Had Dominic done something twenty years earlier that Jack was still quietly seething about? Did he seduce me for revenge?

Is that why Dom framed us? To punish us both in one go?

The more I think about it, the more it makes sense. When Dom asked me who I was sleeping with and I told him Jack's full name he didn't so much as flinch and I'm pretty sure that's because he already knew about him. How? Perhaps they didn't fall out after they left university and they've kept in touch this whole time. Maybe they forged a plan for Jack to seduce me because Dominic needed me out of the house more often, he wanted to keep me distracted. But why? And why go on to frame me for conspiracy to murder? And not just me, Jack too. Had he gone too far when he seduced me and angered Dominic? Had their plan failed at some point?

The restraining order means I can't confront Dom so Jack's

my only shot at the truth. If he ever replies. It's been two days since I asked to meet him. He replied to my previous email about Iceland within ten minutes but now he's gone suspiciously quiet.

Now, the minibus that's ferrying us between offices brakes sharply as a car cuts in front of us and the driver shouts an apology as we all jerk forward in our seats. No one's spoken a word since we got on. Everyone's tired and sweaty and the atmosphere is muted. The windows are misted with condensation and all I can see are the blurred lights of the shops and buildings outside, patches of colour in the London gloom. I rub a hole in the mist and peer out, into the night. As we drive over London Bridge I turn to the man sitting next to me. He's slight with hollowed cheeks, a side parting and circular metal glasses – we haven't spoken, but we nodded and smiled as we took our seats. His name badge says his name's Jakub.

'Are you cleaning The Radcliffe Building next?' I ask him.

He grunts a yes.

'Could I do your shift for you?'

A frown creases his brow. 'Sorry?'

'Can I do your shift for you at The Radcliffe Building? I could pay you.'

'Pay?' He looks confused.

'I'll pay you, if let me have your shift.' I reach into my bag for my purse. 'We could pretend you're sick and I'll offer to take your place?'

He leans, ever so slightly, away. He's not looking confused anymore. He's looking at me as though I'm crazy. 'I'm sorry,' he says, 'I'm sorry, I cannot. No.'

My heart gives a little lurch as the towering, haunting shape of The Radcliffe Building comes into view. If I could just get inside I could find out what Dom's hiding.

146

'How much?' Jakub says, making me jump. The light from outside is glinting off his glasses, making it impossible for me to see his eyes. He reaches into his pocket and holds out his pass. It says 'C&C Cleaning Services' along the top and 'Commercial Contractor' written underneath.

'How much to take my shift?' he asks again.

I rummage around in my purse. I've still got the two hundred pounds I took out at the station after I visited Sonia.

'One hundred?' I suggest. I could still get Grace another phone for a hundred pounds. It would probably be a pretty old iPhone or smartphone but at least she'd be able to install WhatsApp.

'No.' His eyes flit back to my purse. I should never have opened it. He can tell I'm desperate and he knows I've got more.

The minibus is slowing down. Any second now it's going to stop and Noreen is going to shout out the names of the people who need to get off.

'A hundred and ten,' I say. If he's getting the same wage as me he'll be on around nine pounds an hour. A hundred and ten pounds is nearly four times what he'd earn if he did the shift.

He shakes his head, his lips pressed tightly together. 'I have a good reputation here. If I pretend to be sick Noreen will think I am unreliable.'

'I can't give you any more. I need the rest for my daughter.'

'So go home.' He sits back in his chair and puts his pass back in his pocket. 'Give it to your daughter.'

I close my purse and put it back in my bag but I can't stop thinking about the pass he flashed at me. It's so close I could almost reach out and grab it but the thought makes me feel sick with nerves. We're sitting so close together that if he caught me digging around in his pocket . . . a shudder passes through me . . . it doesn't bear thinking about. I could wait until the minibus stops and follow him into the aisle. A little knock as I 'stumble', a hand on the shoulder to distract him and a 'I'm sorry, excuse me' should give me enough time to slip my hand into his pocket and slide out the pass. Smithy would do it in a heartbeat but my own pulse is rocketing. It's not me, it's not what I do. If I couldn't grab Rosa's key when it was sticking out of her back pocket how can I possibly do this?

You have to, says a little voice in the back of my head, *if you don't want people to think you're a criminal for the rest of your life.*

The irony doesn't escape me – that to prove my innocence I need to commit another crime. But this isn't just about me. This is about regaining custody of Grace and getting our lives back on track.

'Cleaning team for The Radcliffe Building.' Noreen is standing at the front of the bus, her hands on her hips. Several people get up from their seats and move forward.

My Polish 'friend' glances at me. 'Hundred and fifty.'

I meet his gaze. 'The offer was a hundred.'

'You said a hundred and ten?'

'Do you know what?' I say. 'I've changed my mind. I'm going to ask Noreen if they need someone else.'

'Good luck with that.' A smile pricks at the corner of Jakub's mouth.

As he gets up from his seat I get up too but I stumble as I rise and knock into him, grabbing hold of his shoulder for support. My free hand reaches for his pocket but before it can even make contact Jakub pushes me roughly away.

'What are you doing?'

'Sorry, sorry.' My face burns with horror. 'My foot went to sleep.'

148

He snorts irritably and turns away.

'A hundred and twenty,' I hiss and he slowly turns back.

'Why do you want the pass?'

'To . . . to . . .' I frantically search for a plausible explanation. 'To prove to Noreen that I'm reliable. I got told off during my first shift because I had to take a call. She said she'd give me a written warning if I did anything else wrong. I really need to keep this job.'

'We all need this job. We wouldn't be cleaning up other people's crap if we didn't.'

'Jakub!' Noreen calls from the front of the bus. 'Now please. This is your stop.'

He raises a hand in acknowledgement.

'One hundred and fifty!' I say desperately. I have to get into that building.

Jakub grins as I take the notes out of my purse and swap them for the pass that he's slipped out of his pocket. He folds the notes into his hand.

'Noreen,' he calls. 'I'm so sorry. I'm not feeling very well.'

We enter The Radcliffe Building through the revolving door at the front then sign in at reception where a bored-looking security guard is sitting alone behind the long stretch of desk that runs along the wall to our right. To our left is a long line of black leather chairs and, beyond them, is an airport-style X-ray machine. Separating the foyer from the escalators are the entry and exit turnstiles. The pass Jakub gave me as I climbed out of the minibus has his name and photograph printed on the shiny plastic card. Noreen initially kicked up a fuss about me covering for him, saying that one of the other cleaners would have to do his floor as well as their own. The collective groan that went up about a late finishing time convinced her otherwise.

As the others queue up to sign in I ask Jo, the stocky woman with short dark hair who I've spoken to before, if I'll get in trouble if someone asks to see my pass. She shakes her head dismissively. 'Nah. If you're wearing this polo shirt,' she taps the C&C Cleaning Services logo on her chest, 'and you've got a hoover or a duster in your hand, no one'll give you a second look.'

I nod my thanks but, when it's my turn to sign in, I scribble something indecipherable where it says 'Name', just in case.

'Okay, let's go.' Noreen shepherds us through the turnstiles then points us in the direction of the contractors' lift. As we stand outside she allocates each of us a different floor of the building. 'Debbie, floor one, Terri floor two, Dawn floor three, Corrina floor four . . .' A bead of sweat rolls between my shoulder blades as she pauses to consult her list. Floor five is where Dominic works. It's where I'll find his safe. 'Floor five Jo, floor six . . .' I zone out until my name is mentioned. I'm on floor ten, five offices higher than I wanted to be.

'Excuse me, sorry.' I try to edge around the group to reach Jo who's been allocated floor five but, before I can get anywhere near her, Noreen shouts my name. 'Olivia, I haven't finished speaking.'

Mortified, I freeze, as my colleagues all turn to stare. We listen as Noreen explains where the cleaning cupboards can be found on each floor, the tasks we must complete and the standard of cleaning expected. When she finally finishes speaking she waves a dismissive hand through the air.

'Debbie, Terri, Dawn, Corrina and Jo please take the lift.' I watch, heart sinking, as the doors close on Jo, and my plan.

Several minutes later I step out onto floor ten, with Noreen by my side. She stalks off to the cleaning cupboard, opens it with a swipe of her pass and hands me a hoover and a bucket of cleaning supplies.

'This is you.' She gestures towards the large glass door of a publishing company. 'Open the door with your pass, then clean, put everything away and return to the ground floor at ten o'clock. No phone calls, no unauthorised absences. If you abuse my trust you will receive a written warning and your probation officer will be informed.'

I tense at the mention of my probation officer. Do all the staff get threatened with written warnings or is it special treatment for 'ex-cons' like me?

'I understand,' I say, and tighten my grip on my pass.

'Good.' Noreen presses the button on the lift. 'I'll be back to check on you soon.'

I don't wait for the lift doors to close. Instead I touch my pass to the entry system and the office door swings open. Inside is a huge open-plan space with clusters of desks arranged along the side of the room nearest the floor-to-ceiling windows. On the other side are a number of glass offices and meeting rooms, many with blinds drawn. It's the same layout as Dom's office on floor five. He works in the first glass-walled room. I need to get down there but I've got no idea how I'm going to sneak away, not without Noreen noticing that I've gone.

I set to work scrubbing desks, taking in the minutiae of other people's lives: mugs with cringeworthy catchphrases, pen pots sprouting fake grass, stress toys, Post-It notes and the rictus grins of uniformed children in school photographs pinned next to memos and guides. I can hear the faint hum of hoovers above and below me as I squirt, wipe and clean. I glance at my watch. There's only an hour and ten minutes until I have to regroup with the others downstairs. I can't afford to pay Jakub another one hundred and fifty pounds to take his shift and if Noreen takes his pass off me later I'll never get this chance again. I need to sneak into Dom's office now, before I completely lose my nerve.

I abandon my antibac bottle and my cloth and make my way to the lift. I'll nip inside, jump out on floor five and sneak into Dom's office before Noreen comes back to check up on me. If Jo says anything I'll tell her I've been asked to look for a missing cleaning bucket.

Shit. The arrow above the lift is pointing downwards. Floor thirteen. Floor twelve. Floor eleven. I beat a hasty retreat back to the office door but it's already closed and locked. As I reach into my pocket for my pass Noreen steps out of the lift.

'Olivia.' Her mouth is a hard line, her eyes flinty and suspicious. 'What are you doing?'

'I was . . . I was going to use the toilet. Could you tell me where it is please?'

'Round there,' she gestures around the corner, beyond the lift, then her gaze returns to me. It flicks from my face to my hands. She's looking for my mobile.

'You have five minutes.' She taps her watch. 'One second late and it's a written warning. No phone calls.'

It's all I can do not to roll my eyes at her. Instead I say, 'Of course,' and hurry away in the direction of the toilets. As soon as I'm out of sight I glance at my watch: 10.53 p.m.. I've got until 10.58 p.m. to get down to Dom's office, open the safe and get back upstairs. I can't use the lift because Noreen's standing right next to it. There are stairs at the end of the corridor though, past the toilets. I'm mad to even attempt this but I have to at least try.

I set off at a run and speed down the stairs, my hand on the rail for balance. After three floors I'm breathing loudly and by floor five my heart is hammering.

10.53 p.m. and 52 seconds. I've got three minutes to get into the office, search it and get back to floor ten. I speed past the toilets, past the lift and pause by the glass doors to the office. No sign of another cleaner inside. A bead of sweat curves down the side of my face as I tap my pass against the lock and push at the door. Jo is partway down the room with her back to me. The hoover's going and she's got headphones on.

10.54 p.m. and 50 seconds.

I run lightly across the carpeted floor and pull open the glass door to Dom's office. His desk is clean and tidy with a leather-bound A4 notebook, a letter opener and a pot of pens arranged just so. But I'm not interested in what my ex-husband has on show. I want what he's hiding. I head for the bookcase and zero in on a small black safe that's nestled between a dozen thick, leather-bound hardbacks. I tap Dom's date of birth into the keypad on the front. Nothing. I try Grace's. Nothing. 123456? Again, nothing. There's a narrow gap between the door and the edge of the safe. Can I prise it open somehow?

I shuffle over to the desk on my knees and reach for the letter opener. As my fingers graze the metal handle I see a flash of navy outside and I snatch my hand back, sending the pen pot tumbling as Jo strolls past. I freeze, crouching beside the chair, as pens and pencils roll off the desk and fall to the floor. I risk a glance at the glass wall but Jo hasn't returned to see what's going on. I've got less than a minute and a half to get out of here and up five flights of stairs before Noreen starts wondering where I am. I scrabble to my feet, dart out of the door and sprint across the office. Out of the corner of my eye I see Jo turning to stare at me, a startled expression on her face.

'Sorry!' I raise a hand in apology. 'I got lost!' Then I'm out of the door.

I speed up the first two flights of stairs, arms pumping, then slow as I hit floor eight. I wasn't fit before I went to prison and I'm even more unfit now. Ninth floor. My thighs are burning, my lungs feel half their size and my body is screaming at me to please stop running. But I'm nearly there. Just one more floor. How long have I got? Thirty seconds? None?

I sprint on wobbling legs past the toilets then slow as I reach the corner. I take a shallow, shaky breath, run my hands over my hair and step around the corner to find Noreen waiting for me, looking at her watch.

'Ten seconds.' She raises an eyebrow.

'I'm sorry . . . I'll get back to work.' I move to pass her but she holds out a hand, forcing me to stop.

'You're sweating.' Her eyes sweep my face. 'And you're out of breath.'

I don't know what to say. How do I explain the fact my hairline is wet and beads of sweat are rolling down the sides of my face?

Silence stretches between us as I search for an explanation that she'll believe.

'I, um . . . I splashed water on my face. I had an asthma attack. Sometimes cold water helps. It . . . it helps calm me down.'

'You had an asthma attack . . . in the toilets?'

'Yes. Yes, I did.'

Before she can say another word I swerve past her, swipe my pass against the lock and slide into the office. My legs give way the moment I'm out of sight and I sink to the floor. I've kept my job but I'm no closer to proving my innocence. Now what am I supposed to do?

Chapter 28

DOMINIC

Dominic glances at his watch. It's so late he saw the cleaning company bus pull up as he drove into the car park. He hopes to god that Grace is still asleep at home, not walking from room to room, wondering where he is. He sits up taller. Another car has pulled into the car park, its headlights illuminating the dark corner where he's parked, but it's not a BMW. He slips down in his seat, heart pounding, as a white Mercedes cruises past. No one else ever uses the car park this late. Where the hell is Dani? He's been psyching himself up all day and she's thirty minutes late. After she texted earlier to say she had news, she's been unusually quiet since. It's unsettling. He knows where he is with a woman who rants and rages and makes a big noise. Silent women are different. They're the only kind of woman he fears.

He sends Dani a text.

Where are you? What's happened?

Five minutes pass without a reply, then ten. Dominic shifts in his seat. This isn't like her, she's never been late before and

155

certainly not when money is involved. He swipes a hand over his damp forehead and takes a swig from his water bottle. *Do not panic*, he tells himself. *There'll have been a crime – a murder or a drugs bust – and she'll text me in a few hours once things have calmed down.* But there's no reasoning with anxiety and the other voice in his head drowns out all logical thought. *Dani's not here because she's been arrested and they're coming for me next.* He grips the steering wheel and starts the engine. *Run*, screams the voice in his head. *Run and hide. Get the hell out of here before they find you.*

He starts the engine and puts the car into first gear. He's shaking so much that when he presses the accelerator, the car lurches forward and then stalls. At the end of the car park the Mercedes has turned around and it's heading back towards him.

'Fuck!' Dom shouts into the darkness, fumbling with the ignition as the Mercedes draws closer. 'Fuck!'

Chapter 29

DANI

There's no reply to Dani's 'Hello?' as she lets herself into her mother's house.

'Mum?' She walks down the hall, hoping to god that Brenda hasn't gone out in search of Casey. It's nearly midnight and anyone out on the streets on a Saturday night will either be drunk, high or up to no good, none of which she wants her fifty-eight-year-old mother to encounter.

But Brenda hasn't left the house. She's sitting at the kitchen table with her head in her hands and Radio Two burbling softly in the background. She looks up sharply as Dani walks into the room and plucks the earphones from her ears. Her mobile is on the table in front of her.

'I was looking through Casey's social media.'

'Why?' Dani picks up the kettle and weighs it in her hand to check there's enough water inside then sets it back down and flicks the switch.

'Trying to find out where she's gone.'

Dani laughs, a tired, dry little sound that makes her mother tut.

'She'll be at her dealer's house.' She pulls out a chair and drops into it. 'Or with some of her skag-head mates, smoking her way through your nine hundred quid.'

'Don't say that.' Brenda's mouth pinches into a tight circle. 'She's not a . . . she's not one of those.'

'She stole all the money in your account to buy drugs. I'd say that pretty much fits the description. How did she know your PIN number anyway?'

'I took her shopping, a couple of weeks ago. I thought some new clothes might cheer her up. She must have looked over my shoulder when I was at the cashpoint.'

Of course she looked. Casey's not interested in fashion or looking nice – not anymore. It's a minor miracle if she takes a shower. The only reason she'd have agreed to go shopping with Brenda would be to return the clothes later and pocket the cash. There was a time when Casey wouldn't have dreamed of peeking at their mother's PIN number, when she'd have been the one taking Brenda out for a treat and not the other way round. In the five years she'd been clean she'd retaken the GCSEs that she'd failed and completed several beauty therapy courses at college. As soon as she was qualified she began applying for jobs and was offered a junior position at a local salon. Hair or beauty was something she'd always wanted to do. As a child she spent hours plaiting and styling the hair of a doll that was cropped at the shoulders. It would creep Dani out, the way it stared at her from across their bedroom. Casey found that funny so she'd randomly move the doll around the house like some kind of decapitated elf on the shelf, making Dani jump whenever she walked into the toilet or the kitchen or the hall. From the age of about twelve Casey became

158

fixated by the idea of going to beauty college but four years later, when it came to taking her GCSEs, Brenda confided in Dani that she was worried Casey was going to fail them. She was unmotivated and disruptive in class – playing up to get attention and laughs. She'd go out with her friends in the evening and come home drunk and smelling of weed. Sure enough, she failed to get the grades required for college, leaving school with just two GCSEs, neither of them Maths or English.

No amount of cajoling and encouragement from Dani or Brenda could convince her to retake her exams. All her friends were at college or starting apprenticeships or jobs. What kind of loser had to retake her GCSEs? Instead she got a job at a fast-food outlet. It was supposed to be a stop-gap, a way of bringing in a bit of money while she decided what to do next. Whenever she wasn't working she was out, socialising. She met the boyfriend who introduced her to hard drugs at a party. He was twenty-three to her eighteen and she idolised him in the way only teenaged girls can. She stayed out late and ignored Brenda's texts asking where she was and what time she'd be home. Sometimes she'd go out after work and vanish for forty-eight hours. When she did eventually return home she'd swerve Brenda's questions and stomp up the stairs saying she was tired and needed to go to bed.

Dani searched her room. She found heroin paraphernalia hidden under the mattress and a small quantity of the drug tucked into a pair of socks. When confronted about it Casey claimed she'd been 'looking after it for a friend'. She continued to lie and deny that she had a problem, saying she didn't need to go to rehab because she could stop whenever she wanted. Dani and Brenda thought otherwise.

Now, as the kettle wheezes steam into the small kitchen, Brenda sighs loudly. 'I don't suppose you could lend me nine hundred, could you, Dan? That was supposed to be for the rent.'

Dani looks into her mother's tired lined eyes and she pounds the kitchen table with her fist, making Brenda jump. 'For fuck's sake!'

Her mother's startled gasp makes her want to cry with frustration. 'Sorry, Mum. That wasn't aimed at you. Here.' She reaches into her jacket and pulls out an envelope thick with banknotes: one thousand pounds minus the fifty she gave to Smithy. Her mother's eyes grow big and round as Dani eases the bundle out of the envelope and peels off fifty pounds.

'Where'd you get that much?' Brenda asks in awe.

'PT clients,' Dani lies.

She tucks fifty quid into her pocket and presses the rest into her mother's hands. The irony of the transaction isn't lost on her. She was supposed to use this to help Casey go to rehab again, instead she's paying for her drugs.

'Hide it,' she tells her mother, 'until you can get to the bank on Monday. Not in your sock drawer, not under the mattress, not in the biscuit tin. Hide it somewhere Casey could never find it even if she turns this whole house upside down.'

'I will. I promise. Thank you, love. I don't know what I'd do without you.' Brenda has tears in her eyes as she approaches Dani for a hug. She also has nine hundred pounds clutched in one hand; money Dani earned by sneaking off from work and spying on Olivia Sutherland. Money she risked her job for. Again.

'You could get me a glass of wine,' she says as her mother releases her from the hug. Sod tea. She needs something stronger. Not only has she spent her day off digging around in Olivia Sutherland's life, she's also discovered that the man she's taken money from, lied for, and slept with, is a convicted criminal. Matt Platt? Seriously? No wonder Dominic changed his name.

She did a lot of thinking about that on the drive from Audley End to London; not the name change specifically but the type of man she's dealing with. The type of person who'd befriend and then defraud an elderly man would be someone with very few scruples; someone superficially charming, manipulative and self-serving. Someone with very little guilt. Looking at her own situation five years ago an observer might say that Dominic identified her as a vulnerable victim (her sister was an addict who desperately needed help), groomed her (by giving her five thousand pounds as a gift) and then manipulated her (by getting her to lie in court for more money). And here she is, five years later, dancing to his tune again. Only this time he hasn't given her all the money in advance and she's got a creeping suspicion that when she asks for the remaining twenty-nine thousand in three days' time, she's not going to receive it. Well, two can play at that game.

She glances at her watch. She was supposed to meet Dom some time ago but headed home instead. Her phone pinged with a text – Where are you? What's happened? He was obviously panicking. Well, let him panic a bit more.

Brenda, digging around in a food cupboard, presumably to find somewhere to stash the money, shakes her head. 'Sorry, love. I took the bottle of Prosecco I had to book club.'

'Vodka then? Tequila? Terps?'

'I might have a bottle of Advocaat from last Christmas.'

'I'm not that desperate. By the way, that's a shit hiding place. It's the first place I'd look.'

The sound of keys in the front door makes both women turn sharply and stare towards the hallway.

'Casey?' Brenda shouts. 'Is that you?'

Only the stairs creak in response and Dani gets up from

her seat. She holds out a hand, telling Brenda to stay where she is. 'I'll deal with this.'

She steps into the hallway prepared to peg it up the stairs before her sister can lock herself in her bedroom but Casey hasn't made it more than halfway up. One hand is gripping the banister and she's swaying lightly and staring into the middle distance, a beatific smile playing on her lips. Her hair, once halfway down her back and glossy, is greasy, dirty and sticking up at strange angles. When she left Josh she had her hair cut into a cute elfin style. There's nothing cute about it now, or the red rash on her neck.

'Case?'

Her sister's eyes slowly swivel towards her. Her pupils are pinprick small. 'I'm going to bed.'

'No, you're not. You're talking to me. Where's Mum's money?'

'I don't know what you're talking about.' She lifts her left foot slowly, as though her leg weighs more than she does, and lowers it onto the next step. She does the same with her right foot. The movement is so tediously slow it makes Dani want to shake her or shove her up the rest of the stairs.

'I could arrest you,' she says. 'What you did is theft. You'll probably get arrested anyway. How are you getting the money for drugs? Shoplifting? Stealing? Turning tricks?'

Casey's soft chuckle ignites the fuse of the rage, fear and frustration that Dani's been feeling for months. She's put *everything* on the line for her sister – her reputation, job, self-worth and freedom – and for what? To be laughed at and mocked?

'Funny, is it?' she spits. 'Taking the piss out of me? Stealing from Mum? Have you got any idea how worried she is about you? How worried we both are? Do you think these new friends of yours will give you mouth-to-mouth and thump on your chest when you overdose? Will they fuck. They'll probably go through your pockets and see if you've got any smack left.'

She stares up at her sister. Casey's stopped climbing the stairs. Her eyes are closed, her breathing has slowed and her fingers are loosely curled around the banister.

'Look at me, Casey! If you keep this up, the money I'm saving for rehab will end up paying for your funeral. Do you understand?' Dani slips a hand through the bars and pulls on the denim of her sister's jeans. Casey doesn't respond. She's fallen asleep.

Chapter 30

DOMINIC

As Dominic steps out of London Bridge underground station a little after 8 a.m., his phone pings with a message. Dani's finally replied.

Was busy last night, the text reads. Olivia's been to see Sonia Law.

A bead of sweat forms on his brow as he swerves out of the crowd of suits and heels and steps into a doorway, his pulse gathering pace.

Why? he types back. What did they talk about?

Dani's reply arrives within seconds. I'll tell you on Thursday after you fulfil your side of the deal.

Shit. He swipes the palm of one hand over his forehead. She doesn't trust him to pay up. That's why she's withholding information. He can't threaten her because his recordings of their conversations before Olivia's trial prove his guilt as much as hers. And he can't give her money because he hasn't got any. Or maybe . . .

A thought hits him that makes him swear loudly enough

that a blonde woman turns sharply in his direction. Sonia knows who he is, who he *really* is. They didn't just chat at Jack's twenty-first birthday all those years ago – they slept together. It was a casual, drunken shag and they didn't see each other again. Well, not until he spotted her in the gallery when he and Jack were being sentenced at court. Has she told Olivia everything? And how much does Dani now know?

Dominic's breathing has become shallow and ragged and he fights to calm himself down. It's Monday. On Thursday it will all be over and he'll be able to sleep well for the first time in years. What damage could Olivia or Dani possibly do between now and then? Yes, he changed his name. Yes, he committed a crime when he was younger but who cares if his colleagues or the partners find out now? His reputation was destroyed the moment he filed his last valuation. He hasn't got a career to lose.

When he steps into his office at 8.16 a.m., Dominic keeps his head held high and his shoulders back. It's just a normal day, he tells himself as he shrugs off his jacket and hangs it on the back of his chair. He's completely in control. He glances at the floor. His pens and pencils are scattered all over the carpet and his pen pot's on its side on the desk. Strange. Did the cleaner knock it over? Why the hell didn't they pick them back up? Grunting, he crouches to gather the pens up, shoves them back into the pot then pulls out his chair and sits down. He gets up again, almost immediately, as the fear he quelled earlier threatens to erupt again. None of the stuff on his desk is straight. His notepad is skewwhiff and his letter opener isn't where he left it. He opens the door to his office and shouts down the room to Tom, one of the junior surveyors, alone in a cubicle.

'Hey, Tom! Has anyone been in my office?'

Tom swivels round in his chair and runs a hand over his dark quiff. 'Sorry, what?'

'Since you got in, has anyone been in my office?'

'No. Not that I've seen.' He shrugs. 'Why? Something wrong?'

'No, it's fine.'

Dom closes the door, pulls down the blinds and keys the code into his safe. His logical brain is telling him no one has been in his office but another, more paranoid part of him, is drowning it out.

He blows out his cheeks as he opens the door to the safe. Everything's still inside. Thank god. He closes the door, locks it, then sinks into his chair and groans. He's got to keep it together. Getting updates on Olivia's movements was supposed to make him feel in control but they're doing the opposite. Last night he freaked out when a random Mercedes drove into the car park (he realised only after it left that it belonged to one of the partners who'd gone out for dinner with a client). Then, when he got home, he barely slept for panicking about Dani's no-show. Now he's freaking out about the text she sent earlier and how much she knows.

He takes out his burner phone and taps out a message:

Have any of the loans come through yet?

A couple of seconds pass then a reply appears: First two have been approved. 10 mil total. The rest should be through soon.

Dom replies: Olivia is digging, asking questions.

She's not going to find anything.

He shakes his head, unconvinced: How do you know?

His phone buzzes: Hold your shit together. Three more days and she won't be a problem anymore.

Chapter 31

OLIVIA

The taxi drops me outside Esther and George's enormous detached house in Hampstead and I stare up at it in awe, just like I have every other time I've been here. My old house in Crouch End – correction, Esther and George's second home in Crouch End – must be worth 1.2 million but this place, with its private drive, seven bedrooms, five bathrooms and huge garden, is a palace in comparison.

The first time Dominic brought me to visit his parents I was so intimidated by the house that I refused to get out of the car. I was brought up in Brighton, in a narrow two-bedroom terraced house, miles from the sea. My parents separated when I was five and my mum paid the mortgage with her nurse's salary. I did well at school and got a place to study Art History at Exeter. I suppose that's where the 'posh' voice came from. I was trying to be accepted by the students whose parents were loaded. Lee and I gravitated towards each other, outsiders who didn't fit in. After we graduated we moved to London and rented a rundown house in Acton with damp patches on the walls and appliances that were at least twenty years old.

I met Dominic at the private showing of a play written by a friend of Lee's. I didn't know the playwright very well but he'd come round to our flat for a party once. Dominic sidled up to me during the interval and said, 'I'm guessing you're not one of the actors.' When I asked why he said, 'You shudder each time you take a sip of that godawful wine.'

He wasn't my normal type – he was too well dressed and far too posh – but he was handsome, funny and charming and we both liked the same sort of plays and films and admired the same artists so I chatted to him for a bit. Then I made my excuses and sloped off to find Lee.

The next day I received a text from Dominic saying he'd really enjoyed meeting me and would I like to see Matthew Bourne's *Swan Lake* the next week? It turned out he'd tracked down my number via a mutual contact, which I found singularly creepy and a little bit flattering. Lee thought Dominic was hot and somehow I let him talk me into going out on a date.

I don't know if it was the sinewy muscularity of the male dancers' bodies, the swell of emotion I felt as Prince Siegfried and Odette jumped into the lake, or the woody scent of Dominic's aftershave as I sobbed into his shoulder. Maybe it was a combination of all three, but when he leaned in for a kiss at the end of the evening I kissed him back. We went on another date – a tour of Highgate Cemetery. I laughed out loud when Dominic told me where we were going but, secretly, I was delighted. I thought I was the only weirdo who found cemeteries fascinating but it turned out Dom did too. On a visit to Paris he'd swerved the Eiffel Tower, Notre Dame and the typical tourist hangouts and had visited Père Lachaise, Montmartre and the Catacombs instead. To him romance lay, not in the present, but the past. Whether it was the music he listened to (Frank Sinatra, Tony Bennett, Nat King Cole), the black and white films he loved (*Laura, Vertigo, Criss Cross*) or the books he loved (*Jeeves and Wooster, The Picture of Dorian Gray, Brighton Rock*) he surrounded himself with echoes of times long gone. And I understood that kind of escapism, I felt it every time I looked at a painting from another era, swept with each brushstroke into another time, another world.

After our fourth or fifth date I no longer heard Dominic's plummy tones or commented on what he wore; those were superficial adornments and I knew the man beneath the tweed jackets and the well-spoken voice. Six months after our first date we moved in together. I could have moved into Dominic's one-bedroom flat in South London but we both felt we wanted somewhere new, somewhere where the only memories that existed were ours. One year after that we were married, a spontaneous decision that took us up to Gretna Green. When Grace was born some years later we both fell in love with her. Our life was complete, a little family of three.

My relationship with Dominic's parents swung from cordial to fractious. They were pleasant initially, prickly after our elopement and then coldly indifferent. Esther, Dominic's mother, made her opinions known after I gave birth to Grace. She didn't criticise me directly – she's too manipulative for that – but her 'advice' reached me via Dom who parroted the 'correct way' I should mother my daughter as I struggled with night feeds, sleep deprivation, colic and my eventual return to work.

George has always been harder to read. He largely keeps his own counsel but his sharp, analytical mind enabled him to make millions on the stock market in the mid to late eighties. He was always pleasant to me but I never had any idea what was going on behind those cool grey eyes. And now I'll be spending the next hour in his home because Esther has decided that public places are no longer suitable for my supervised visits with Grace.

My phone bleeps as I raise a finger to the doorbell and I dig around for it in my handbag. Has Jack finally replied? It's been nearly four days since I suggested we meet and I'm getting worried that something's happened to him. But there's no email notification on the screen. It's a number I haven't got stored in my phone.

Hello my love, the text message begins. You're out! Let's celebrate! It's Lee btw. I got your new number from Ayesha. I'm so sorry I haven't been in touch in forever but I'll make it up to you. I promise. Are you free tomorrow? A new gallery has opened in Shoreditch that I want to check out. Drinks on me afterwards. Xx

The sight of Lee's name makes my heart jolt. Of all the friends I've had and loved he was the biggest constant in my life. Until he wasn't. He all but abandoned me after I was sent to Bronzefield and I haven't heard from him for years. I tuck my phone back into my bag and ring the doorbell. I'll think about whether or not to meet Lee later, what matters most right now is seeing Grace. It's been two weeks since we met at London Zoo.

The door opens revealing George in beige chinos and a dark green jumper with a white shirt collar poking over the top.

'Good afternoon, Olivia.' He gives me a curt nod then opens the door wider. 'Grace is in the garden room. She's, er . . . she's not in the best of moods.'

'Okay, thank you.' I follow him into the house, closing the door behind me, and make my way down the hall. There are five ground-floor reception rooms – a kitchen with an attached laundry room, a study, a dining room, the family room at the front of the house and the 'garden room', with French doors that open onto the patio and manicured lawn, at the back.

'Cup of tea?' George asks, pausing at the entrance to the kitchen. His phone rings before I can answer and he turns away, abandoning me in the hall.

I hover, unsure whether I should wait for him to come back out or make my own way to the garden room, then I hear something that makes my heart miss a beat.

'Fifty-seven Oakfield Road,' George says from the kitchen, 'that's right. You've found new tenants, already? That's fantastic news. Hang on a moment.'

He pushes the door shut.

Fifty-seven Oakfield Road is my old house in Crouch End, where Dominic and Grace still live. Are they moving? I don't suppose anyone would think to tell me. I hurry away, before George discovers me listening, only to find that Esther is already in the garden room, sitting in a circular red velvet chair by the French doors, with a newspaper in her hands. She peers at me from above her reading glasses.

'You've got an hour,' she says. 'I will be here the whole time and there's to be no running off. Do you hear that, Grace?'

From behind the yellow sofa I hear a soft 'Urgh.'

'Thank you, Esther,' I say tightly and make my way across the room. Grace doesn't so much as glance at me from her supine position on the sofa. Her headphones are in her ears and a Nintendo Switch is inches from her face.

'Hi sweetheart.' I crouch on the floor beside her.

She continues to ignore me.

'Grace.' I touch her on the forearm. 'Are you okay?'

'Don't touch me.' She snatches her arm away and twists over to face the back of the sofa. There's a snort of amusement from Esther that makes my teeth clench.

171

'I'm sorry I haven't been in touch for a few days but when your dad took your phone off you I had no way of—'

'Just leave me alone.'

'What's happened? Talk to me, please.'

'No. Go away.'

'Grace. Just let me see your face.'

I don't understand what's happened. She was upset the last time I spoke to her but I managed to calm her down. She seemed quite hopeful about the future in the texts we exchanged before Dominic took her phone.

'Grace,' I drop my voice so Esther can't hear and dig around in my bag. I press the smartphone I bought into one of her hands. 'I bought you this. It's only cheap but I couldn't afford a better one. Hide it from Dad so we can stay in touch.'

My daughter flips over to look at me, her Switch abandoned, her fingers wrapped around the mobile. She mouths something I can't make out.

'Text me.' I gesture towards the phone. 'Wait,' I add before she can do anything. 'Don't send it. Show it to me then delete it.'

As Grace starts tapping at the phone Esther clears her throat. We've gone quiet and she's noticed. She's wondering what's going on.

'I had a text from Lee earlier,' I say, to fill the silence. 'Do you remember Lee, my friend from uni who owned the gallery with me?'

Grace looks at me, puzzled, and I gesture for her to continue typing.

'He wants to meet up tomorrow. To go to a new gallery in Shoreditch. It's been a long time since I've seen him but friends are so important. Don't you think?'

'I guess so.'

'I'm really looking forward to when we can do things like

that together. Maybe not an art gallery but the cinema, shopping, maybe a spa or to get our nails done. Would you like
that, sweetheart?'

'Uh-huh.' Grace holds her phone out to me.

I found something, she's typed. Right before Dad took my
phone off me.

As I watch she logs into her Google account and navigates
to her photos. She clicks on an image and hands me the
phone. It's a photograph of two printouts, one in Grace's
name, one in Dom's. I frown, unsure what I'm seeing. They're
British Airways boarding passes. Is Dom taking Grace abroad?
Can he even do that without my permission? The destination
is DXB. That's Dubai. Why would Dominic take her there?
He always used to call it a cultural wasteland, a soulless,
sandy preening ground for reality TV stars, and a tax haven
for thieves.

Grace types something else into the phone.

When I asked Dad about the tickets he said we're going on
holiday but I'm not to tell anyone. Not Granny, not Grandad,
not even my school friends. Is it because I'll be missing school?

I try not to show the horror I'm feeling on my face as I
slide the phone out of her hands, take another look at the
boarding pass photo and then tap out my reply: I don't know
sweetheart, but I'll find out.

The flight is on Thursday at 3.15 p.m. That's in three days'
time.

Chapter 32

Tooby Davies and Partners solicitors are based on Kilburn High Street, in a poky office squeezed between a kebab shop and a grocers. Unlike the law firm that represented me at court there are no glass partitions and expensive artworks on the wall but they're cheap and they were able to see me quickly and that's what matters most. I've arranged to meet Lee afterwards and I'm praying to god that it'll be a celebratory bottle of wine that we share, and not me crying with despair.

Yesterday, I was straight on my phone within minutes of leaving Esther and George's. I found 57 Oakfield Road on the third residential lettings website I checked. There was Grace's bedroom, Dominic's study, the living room, the kitchen. Fear flooded my body as I continued to scroll and I had to shove the phone back into my pocket to stop myself from hyperventilating.

I told myself to calm down and think clearly as I crossed the street and headed towards Crouch Hill overground. By the time I reached the station I'd come up with two possible explanations for the flight and the listing: one innocent and one that made me feel sick.

Explanation one: Dominic had decided to move house – possibly because he'd discovered that I'd broken in and he didn't want me to know where he lived. Either before, or after, that decision he changed his mind about Dubai and decided to take Grace out of school to get her away from the bullies and give her a nice holiday.

Explanation two: Dominic told his parents he was moving out of Oakfield Road but he lied about where he was going to live instead. That would explain why he told Grace not to tell them about the flight to Dubai. Because he's not taking her on holiday, they're moving there permanently and they're never coming back.

Explanation two is why I'm sitting in a lawyer's office. The only way to stop Dominic from taking my daughter out of the country is to pursue the legal route and I need to know exactly what rights I have.

Amir Ghavi, the family law solicitor sitting opposite me, is in his early forties with a neat beard, receding hairline, a slightly crumpled grey suit and thick-rimmed glasses. Behind the sheen of his spectacles his eyes wear the weary exhaustion of a man who's heard it all before. However, he listens intently, leaning forward in his seat as I explain my situation and the fact my ex-husband may be considering taking our daughter out of the country permanently.

'Okay.' He nods thoughtfully as I stop speaking, scribbles on his notepad for a few seconds then looks up. 'Did your daughter mention if the trip to Dubai would be a holiday or a more permanent move?'

'She thinks it's a holiday.'

'I see. And your ex-husband has confirmed this?'

'Well, no, I'm not allowed to contact him. My licence—'

'Yes of course. I understand. Well, as the law stands your husband doesn't require your permission to take your daughter on holiday, assuming it's for no more than twenty-eight days. But if he's planning on living abroad with your daughter he must consult you, regardless of the child arrangement order.'

'I don't think he will tell me. What would happen if I objected anyway, via you?'

'Your ex-husband could apply for a court order to be granted permission.'

A shiver passes through me as he says the word 'court'. The last time I stood before a judge I lost Grace for five years.

'Would I be able to fight it?' I've got just under two grand in my bank account but this conversation alone is going to cost me nearly two hundred pounds. I haven't got anywhere near enough to get my own team together and, after a quick google after I got home from seeing Grace, I know my chances of getting legal aid are slim.

'Yes. You can object to the application.'

'Okay. If I could get the money together, what do you think my chances of winning might be?'

Mr Ghavi opens his hands wide as though to say, 'your guess is as good as mine'. 'That would be for the judge to decide but, if I were representing you, I'd argue that a move abroad would damage your relationship with your child, a relationship that you are currently trying to rebuild. Also, as your daughter is twelve years old her wishes and feelings on the matter would have weight attached to them. If she didn't want to relocate abroad the judge would take that into account.'

'Really? Oh that's such a relief.' All the tension I've been holding in my body since I left Ayesha's flat this morning leaves in a rush and I slump back in my seat. Getting the money to fight Dominic is still an issue but I'll do whatever it takes to get it. I'll beg, borrow or steal.

'Do you have any other questions?' Mr Ghavi asks.

I'm about to say no but a thought needles at me, demanding an answer. 'The tickets I saw are for two days' time. If my . . . if my ex-husband were to pretend it's a holiday then I wouldn't be able to stop him, would I?'

Mr Ghavi presses his lips into a thin tight line. 'Legally, no.'

'Would I be able to get her back though, if that happened? Could the courts force him to return Grace to the UK?'

'Unfortunately, unlike many other countries, there is no possibility of enforcing English court orders concerning children in the UAE. The country is not a signatory to the Hague Convention on Child Abduction and, if your husband does take your daughter to Dubai without your consent, it will be very hard, if not impossible, to have her returned.'

Somehow I make it out of the solicitors' office dry-eyed and composed but, the moment I step into the street, angry, panicked tears start to flow. Dominic destroyed my life once and he's going to do it again. I'm as powerless as I was in prison. If he tricks Grace into permanently moving to Dubai with him there's nothing, legally, that I can do to get her back.

I lean against the small patch of wall between Tooby Davies and Partners and the kebab shop next door and watch as the world passes me by: a woman in a hijab laden with shopping bags, a man with a thick black beard and sunglasses holding hands with his young daughter in a pretty pink dress, two friends laughing and chatting, a road worker attacking the pavement with a drill. My gaze settles on a young man, no older than eighteen or nineteen, carrying a white bucket and mop, and an idea sparks in my mind. I dismiss it, but it returns a split second later, like a scene from a film.

Chapter 33

DANI

Dani is sitting in a window seat in a Costa coffee shop on Kilburn High Street. There's a lukewarm caffè latte on the table in front of her but she hasn't had more than a few sips until now. She's had to make it last, a placeholder to signal to the staff and the customers that she's a coffee lover like them, not a cop keeping an eye on the solicitors' across the road.

The text from Kelly Smith arrived as Dani and Brenda were listening at Casey's door. It was 7 a.m. and neither of them had had much sleep. After Casey had fallen asleep on the stairs they'd half carried, half dragged her up to her room and undressed her. When they put her to bed she was a ragdoll: limp, floppy and lifeless. completely out cold. She didn't so much as grunt or turn over as they whispered to each other and searched her underwear, jeans, hoodie, socks and trainers for any sign of money, or drugs. They found neither. God knows where all the money had gone; heroin was roughly ten pounds a bag.

179

It was Dani's idea to lock Casey in her room. She needed to talk to her sister when she was with it, not smacked off her head. Maybe she could convince her to see a doctor about getting methadone although she was pretty sure she knew what the answer would be. Casey was still in denial about her addiction, lying and doing god knows what to get hit after hit after hit. Dani's going to have a fight on her hands to get her sister to set foot in Carmichael House, never mind check in. That's if Dominic pays up. He didn't bite like she thought he would yesterday. He was certainly intrigued when she told him about Olivia going to see Sonia, and wanted to know more. But when she said she'd tell him more on Thursday, when he handed over the rest of the cash, he didn't object or try and convince her to tell him there and then. He simply replied 'fine'. Dominic Sutherland isn't a 'fine' kind of man and it only heightened her suspicion she was being played.

Smith's forwarded text that morning only added to her paranoia:

Found out yesterday that Dom might be moving to Dubai with Grace. Going to see a solicitor on Kilburn High St at 11.30. Want to meet at the Costa opposite for a catch-up before? 10.45?

Dominic was moving to Dubai with Grace? Interesting little detail that he hadn't mentioned before. Was he planning on leaving before, or after, he'd given her the twenty-nine grand? She messaged Smith back, telling her to make an excuse not to meet Olivia at 10.45 a.m., and to find out what date Dominic was flying to Dubai.

Now, she checks her phone for the time. It's been fifteen minutes since Olivia left Tooby Davies and Partners and there's been no text from Smith. Requesting passenger information from airlines for flight risks is something Dani's done dozens of times at work but it would be far too risky to put in a request for an individual who wasn't part of an active case. There's a paper trail for practically everything and it would almost certainly result in a request to have a chat with the boss. She's going to have to wait for Kelly Smith to do some digging instead.

She takes a sip of her tepid latte, grimaces and forwards the photo she took of Olivia opening the solicitors' black front door. She doesn't add a message. She wants to see what Dom will do.

Chapter 34

Colours and shapes leap from the walls as I walk into the gallery. They draw me in, each painting clamouring for my attention, but I'm struggling to take a step in any direction. It's been nearly five and a half years since I was last surrounded by art and it was my gallery I was standing in; each picture carefully curated by Lee or me. Our tastes couldn't have been more different. I was drawn to seascapes, to wild dark skies, fading light bouncing off water, waves churning, and the threat of a storm. Lee favoured bold, urban images crafted using stencils, spray paint and tape. The two styles shouldn't have worked, displayed in adjacent rooms, but somehow they did, just like our friendship. Lee was the loud and demonstrative counterpart to my quieter, more organised self.

I almost didn't come, after my conversation with Mr Ghavi earlier, but, right now, I need all the friends I can get.

I can see Lee now, standing with his back to me, looking at a powerful, loose portrait of a nude in a wide-legged pose. His bald head shines under the gallery lights and he's broad and strong in his black tailored jacket, dark denim jeans and black leather boots. The shape of him – still so familiar after all these years – makes me feel simultaneously excited and wary. Unlike Ayesha who visited me in prison every month, and Nancy who visited me every two or three months, Lee suddenly stopped coming after my first year in jail. I wrote to him, asking him if he was okay, and he didn't reply. I asked Ayesha and Nancy if they'd been in touch with him and whether everything was all right. They said they saw him occasionally but he seemed withdrawn and distracted. They didn't see each other very often either; without me as the glue that held their friendship together, they'd drifted apart. Lee's initial replies to my letters were brief – 'Sorry, so busy, will visit soon' – and then he stopped replying at all. There was a part of me that worried that maybe he thought I was guilty; that Dominic had said something damning to him when they sat side by side in the gallery at my trial. It would have been so easy to ignore his delighted text, to ghost him just like he ghosted me, but I've missed him, and I need answers.

I step closer and clear my throat. 'Hello, Lee.'

He spins round at the sound of my voice and his face sparks with joy.

'Olivia! Sweetheart!' He gathers me into his arms and hugs me so tightly I have to rise up on my toes. My hands flutter awkwardly at his waist. I'm too startled, too hurt, to return the embrace.

'Oh my god.' His hands move from my shoulders to my face and he brushes stray hairs from my skin, still damp from crying. 'I can't believe it. It's so good to see you, so, so good.'

'It's been a long time.' I feel a hundred years older than I did the last time we saw each other but Lee's barely aged. If anything he looks better than the last time we met. He's freshly shaved, his skin is glowing and his groomed eyebrows arch up to an unusually line-free forehead.

He follows my line of sight and smirks. 'Botox. Had to be done. Every time I met someone from Grindr they'd tell me I looked older in person.'

'You look very well.'

'So do you.' He lies effortlessly, just as he always did. He's the sort of person who will compliment you on the thing you feel most self-conscious about, almost as though he knows instinctively how to put a plaster over your Achilles heel. It's effortless, the way he makes whoever he spends time with – male or female – feel like the most enchanting creature in the room. Lee's company was always the panacea I needed after a horrible argument with Dominic or a stressful call with an artist who was upset that their work hadn't sold. He's not flawless, far from it. He can be stubborn, selfish and self-involved and we had plenty of arguments over the years, especially in the very early days of the business, but he was always such a positive light in my life for so long. That's why it hurt so much when his visits and letters tailed off.

'So.' He squeezes my hand. 'Want to have a look around then chat, or chat and then look?'

I return his smile. 'How about a little of both?'

'Wine for the lady.' The waiter places a glass of rosé in front of me. 'And a gin and tonic for the gentleman.' He sets a glass in front of Lee.

We've moved on to a little bistro around the corner from the gallery. We made short work of the exhibition, partly because we were underwhelmed by the work on show, mostly because we didn't stop talking for a single second. Just like Nancy and Ayesha, Lee wanted to know everything about prison – the routine, the other women, the showers, the fights and the relationships. I understand the fascination. I used to be the same. To those of us on the outside – housed, employed, lucky, law-abiding people who don't know a single person who's been to prison – it feels like an alien world. It's a planet we know about but that no one wants to visit. As planets go prison is grimy, broken and boring. I don't think Richard Branson will be booking his ticket any day soon.

We also talked about what Lee had been up to over the last five years: working in galleries and bars while he applied for Arts Council grants to start up a community-based arts project. And the state of his love life: a one-year relationship that broke his heart, a short-lived fling with a yoga instructor and various Grindr hook-ups which ranged from 'hot as hell' to 'I was scraping the barrel that night.' He listens intently, his eyes not leaving my face as I tell him everything that's happened since I left prison. When I reach the part about trying to break into Dominic's safe his jaw drops.

Neither of us have mentioned the way he ghosted me but I can't step around it much longer. I can't deny how deeply it hurt. I reach for my glass and take a sip.

'Wait, wait.' Lee holds out a hand to try and stop me. 'We haven't cheersed yet.'

'I know.' As I put my glass back on the table his expression changes. The smile slips from his lips and his posture, so loose and comfortable as we walked around the gallery, becomes tense and charged. 'I think there's something we need to talk about first.'

'Okay . . .' Now he takes a sip of his drink. He doesn't set it back down afterwards. Instead he nurses it, holding it in front of his chest like a barrier. 'I think I know what this is about.'

'Four years, Lee.'

'I know, I'm sorry.' The light dims in his eyes as he bows

his head. 'There's no excuse,' he risks a glance up at me from beneath his groomed eyebrows. 'I just . . . I guess . . . I went to a dark place, Liv. I could see how hard things were for you when I visited and how important it was to keep you optimistic and cheerful. You came alive whenever I mentioned the gallery and when I . . . when I had to tell that we'd failed, that I'd failed, I felt so guilty. It was your dream, our dream, for so many years and I'd run it into the ground.'

'That's not true, Lee. We'd been struggling for a long time. It was always touch and go – if we sell five paintings this week we'll stay afloat and if we don't, well, let's just hope that we do. It was like that for so long.'

'I know but . . .' He runs a hand over his head and inhales nosily through his nose.

'There's no but, Lee. You did what you could.'

'No.' He shakes his head, his gaze fixed on the little sprig of flowers in a vase in the centre of the table. 'I didn't. After you went to prison I fell apart. I didn't get out of bed. I didn't go to the gallery. I ignored phone calls and emails. I just . . . there didn't seem any point. And by the time I did drag myself into work I couldn't deal with how much there was to do just to keep it afloat. Without you there to talk to I was overwhelmed. Every time I had to make a decision I'd get paralysed by fear. So I did nothing. And I lied to you about how well we were doing, until I couldn't lie anymore.'

'You should have told me. I could have made suggestions. I could have helped.'

He sits back in his chair and gives me a long despairing look. 'I don't think you could.'

'And then? After it closed?'

He shrugs. 'Drinking heavily, drugs. Sex. Generally being an arsehole. Everyone I cared about fell away, like I was some kind of social pariah. I stopped going out, but I kept drinking.'

'You were depressed.'

He sighs heavily and looks away. 'It's no excuse. I abandoned you when you needed me most.'

Looking at him, so cowed, so ashamed, makes my heart ache. For us both.

I reach for his hand. He looks up sharply, meeting my gaze. 'What happened happened. We can't go back and fix it but we can move forward. I've missed you, Lee.'

'I've missed you too. You've got no idea how much.'

I pick up my glass and hold it across the table. 'Shall we do that cheers now?'

He clinks his glass against mine. 'To friendship and not fucking up again.'

'To friendship and not fucking up.'

I sense a change in his mood as he sets his glass back on the table.

'What is it?' I ask. 'What's wrong?'

'There's something I need to tell you, Liv. It's about Dom.'

I sit up taller. Just the mention of my ex-husband's name has put me on high alert. 'Go on.'

'He came to see me, Dom did, at the gallery. It was a couple of months before you were arrested. You were at an art fair, I think.' He takes a swig of gin. 'He wanted to see the accounts. He said he needed to check what kind of assets we had. I thought it was weird because it was our business and he was only a shareholder but he was really insistent.'

'Okay . . .'

'So I showed him the files and when he saw we were running at a deficit he couldn't get out of the gallery fast enough.'

'Why would he do that? He'd never shown any kind of interest in the business before.'

'Exactly. And he had this really panicky, paranoid vibe

about him. He told me to be careful, because you never knew who was out to screw you over. I thought maybe he was talking about you, that you'd asked him for a divorce.'

'I hadn't, not at that point.'

'Did he know about the affair?'

'I don't think so.' I pause to think. Jack and I met at the exhibition in the April, kissed for the first time two weeks later and I confessed the affair to Nancy about a month after that. If what Lee is saying is right then Dominic knew about the affair before I told anyone, even before I told Nancy. How is that even possible? We were very, very careful.

'I didn't mention it to you at the time,' Lee says, 'because I knew Dom was being a dick and I didn't want to stress you out even more. But after everything you've just said it feels like it's another part of the puzzle.'

'Maybe that's when he decided to frame me, and he was looking for money to give Dani? But why look at our accounts? Why not use his own money?'

'No idea. It's why I sat next to him at your trial. I was hoping he'd let something slip, but he didn't say anything useful. I feel like . . .' he clears his throat. 'I feel like I let you down, Liv. We all did. If there's anything I can do now, just say the word.'

I feel a spark of optimism, for the first time in a long time. 'I was hoping you'd say that.'

Chapter 35

DOMINIC

Dominic's feet pound the treadmill and a Spotify running playlist fills his ears. He's in the spare room at home, sweating heavily as Grace watches YouTube videos in the room next door. *Two days.* He says the words in his head like a mantra as he pumps his arms and kicks out each stride. *Two days. Two days. Two days.* It will all be over in just two days.

Earlier, shortly before lunch, Dani sent him a photograph of Olivia standing outside a solicitors'. Within seconds he was googling the name above the door. He discovered a kernel of information: Tooby Davies and Partners specialise in family law. Olivia had to have gone there to enquire about overturning the custody agreement in light of the information Sonia had shared. She would have felt full of hope as she turned up: Dominic wouldn't be in control anymore! She could get Grace back! They could go to a spa! He really wanted to see a photo of her disappointed expression as she left. His spent conviction didn't change a thing. She'd still

189

have to keep her distance from him and the house, and see Grace only when supervised by Esther and George.

He's tempted to message Dani back to ask if she took a photo of Liv leaving but he resists the urge. She's playing the same game that she started with the previous text, the one about Sonia; withholding information to make sure she gets her cash.

Two days. Two days. Two days. He ups the speed on the treadmill. He's got this. Nothing's going to go wrong.

Chapter 36

We are gathered in Ayesha's tiny living room – me, Lee, Smithy, Nancy and Ayesha – our knees touching as we sit cross-legged on the floor around her coffee table. As last-minute get-togethers go I'm amazed we could all make it. In my old life, the one that revolved around work, PTA meetings and Grace, I'd have to schedule social occasions months in advance to find a date that worked for everyone but here we are, glasses of red wine in our hands, the remains of a Deliveroo order piled up on the kitchen counter.

'To Olivia,' Lee says, raising his glass. 'And freedom!'

'To Olivia!' the others chorus, but only Smithy clinks her glass against Lee's. It's the fifth or sixth time someone has proposed a toast to me in the last two hours and the novelty is fast wearing off.

'I should probably go,' Nancy says, shifting awkwardly onto her knees. 'Ian's already sent me three texts asking when I'm coming home.'

'Not yet!' The words come out louder than I intended them to and all eyes turn to me. 'There's something important I need to talk to you all about first.'

'Okay . . .' Nancy drops back down onto her bum. Ayesha, sitting opposite me, raises an inquisitive eyebrow.

'Particularly you,' I tell her.

She places her elbows on the coffee table and leans towards me. 'Go on . . .'

'I need to get into the safe in Dom's office at work.' My gaze rests on each one of my friends. For my plan to work I need each of them to say they're onboard.

'A safe?' Nancy says. 'What's inside it?' Out of everyone here she's the least clued up. I haven't spoken to her since I got off the train from Audley End and we discussed Jack's email. He still hasn't replied but I've got more important things to worry about now.

'Evidence that proves my innocence. Six days ago Grace rang me when I was at work and I overheard a phone conversation Dominic was having. He was talking about me, breaking in. He said, "She can't know about that" then said it was in his safe at work.'

Nancy still looks confused. 'What is?'

'I think it's a repayment schedule that proves Dom paid Dani to frame me. Dani who, incidentally, he's also been sleeping with.'

Nancy clamps a hand to her mouth and Smithy reaches for the wine bottle. She tops up her glass, necks half, then tops it up again.

'Thirsty, are you, Kelly?' Lee comments, catching my eye.

Cracking open the wine before I shared all this was a mistake. Everyone's tipsy and Smithy's well on her way to being passed-out drunk.

'You need to talk to your lawyer,' Ayesha says, 'then go

over Dani's head to her superior. The police can get a warrant to search Dominic's office. Leave it to them.'

'Won't work.' Smithy tops up her glass again. I'm not sure what's going on but she's been weirdly twitchy since she arrived. Whenever I try and make eye contact she glances away.

'And you know that how?' Ayesha asks her.

'Because they all stick together, don't they?'

'Who? The police and the legal profession?' Lee rolls his eyes. 'Come on, Smithy. Just because Dani's bent it doesn't mean everyone else is.'

'Lee.' I know he doesn't trust Smithy but now's not the time for in-fighting. 'I can't risk going to the police in case Dani hears about it. If she manages to get a message to Dominic he'll move what's in the safe.'

'She wouldn't tell him though, would she?' Ayesha says. 'She'd try and take it.'

'Either way, I can't risk telling anyone outside of this room or . . .'

I'm distracted by Smithy who's shifted round to the side of the sofa where I keep my things.

'Smithy, what are you doing?'

'I found this!' She lifts the blue and white lanyard into the air and jiggles it so the keys clash together. 'We can break in.'

I've never seen her this drunk before and she's starting to annoy me. 'We don't need those.' I snatch the keys out of her hand and put them on the coffee table. 'I've still got Jakub's cleaning card. My boss didn't take it off me at the end of my shift. I'm hoping it'll get me into The Radcliffe Building again.'

'Hoping?' Smithy sighs dramatically. 'What did I tell you about that?'

'That it's never a good idea, but what can I do? Ring the office and ask? Because that's not going to look suspicious, is it?'

'All right. Keep your hair on. Have another drink and—'

'Moving on . . .' Nancy interrupts. 'Assuming you manage to get up to Dom's office, Liv . . . how are you going to open the safe? Unless . . .' She glances at Smithy who pulls a face.

'What are you looking at me for?'

'Smithy can't crack safes,' I tell Nancy. 'I've already asked her.'

'So, how are you going to do it?'

'With a diversion.'

Ayesha meets my eye. 'What kind of diversion?'

It seemed like a brilliant idea when I came up with it yesterday and Lee was totally on board when I shared it with him, so was Smithy. This is the first time Ayesha and Nancy have heard about it and Ayesha is the voice, or rather the face, of reason. Right now she's looking at me like I've gone insane.

'Excuse me a sec.' Lee levers himself up from the floor and heads for the bathroom.

I take a sip of wine, suddenly aware of the strained silence that's descended on the living room. 'You won't like the plan, Aysh. Which is why I've told my probation officer that I've moved house. From tomorrow I'll be living with Smithy.'

'Where?' Ayesha asks, watching as Smithy wanders around the room, picking up ornaments and turning them over in her hands.

'Elephant and Castle, above the junk shop antique shop,' Smithy mumbles.

'So if the police try to arrest me,' I tell Ayesha, 'they won't come here.'

She sighs heavily and rubs her hands over her face but says nothing.

'No one's going to get arrested,' Smithy interjects. 'Liv's a cleaner so she's allowed to be there.'

She's half right at least. I'm allowed into the building if I'm there to clean it. Officially I won't be on shift. I'll have to sign in, use Jakub's card on the gates, and hope that no one confronts me. There's that word again. Hope.

'And there's no reason why the rest of you can't be in the foyer. They don't know if you're visitors or not.' Smithy's got hold of Ayesha's water spray now and there's so much water on the fronds of the fern that it's dripping onto the floor. I mouth, 'Sorry,' to Ayesha, get up and take the water spray out of Smithy's hands.

'What are we doing in the foyer?' Nancy asks from the floor.

'Creating a diversion so she can slip in unnoticed,' Smithy says as Ayesha says, 'Olivia, this is ridiculous.'

'Okay, okay.' I hold out my hands. 'Nance, Ayesha, I get it. It is ridiculous but I haven't got any other option. Dominic's backed me into a corner. He's booked tickets for him and Grace to go to Dubai in two days' time. He's told her it's a holiday but I know he's lying. His parents are letting his house.'

'Is there nothing you can do to stop him?' Ayesha asks. 'Nothing legally?'

'No. Nothing. I saw a family solicitor earlier and Dominic can take Grace on holiday without my permission. But it's not a holiday. I know him and how his mind works. He hates Dubai. I used to suggest going there for a bit of winter sun when Grace was little and he shot me down every time. He thinks it's full of reality TV stars and footballers' wives. Something's spooked him into deciding to leave the country.

I don't know if it was me, getting out of prison and then breaking into his house, or the fact Grace and I are in touch but—'

'You could go back to prison if you get caught,' Ayesha says softly. 'You know that, don't you?'

'Yes.' I set the water spray back on the side. 'I do. But if Dom takes Grace to Dubai I'll never see her again. The UAE didn't sign the Hague Convention on Child Abduction and that means there's nothing anyone would be able to do to get her back. Not the police, not the courts, not even the Home Office.'

'I know you don't want to hear this,' Nancy says, 'but I think you're making a lot of assumptions and you've jumped to the worst possible conclusion. Just because Dominic's going to Dubai with Grace doesn't mean—'

'Maybe she is making assumptions.' Lee puts an arm around me and gives me a squeeze. 'But I trust her gut instinct and this is Dominic we're talking about. He framed her, we all know that, and I wouldn't put it past him to pull this kind of shit. If Liv needs our help then I'm in and the rest of you should be too.'

Smithy, who's peering outside through a gap in the blinds, raises a hand. 'I'm in.'

Nancy is deep in thought so I look at Ayesha.

She grimaces. 'I love you, Liv, but I'm not doing anything illegal.'

'You don't have to. You just have to send a text and meet me for lunch.'

'Okay then.' She sighs heavily. 'I'm in.'

'Nance?'

She looks up and smiles. 'Just tell me what you want me to do.'

'Um . . . Liv . . .' Smithy says from the window where she's staring outside. 'Before you get started, there's something I need to talk to you about. Can we go somewhere quiet?'

I have never seen Smithy look more shifty than she does right now. She's pacing around Ayesha's bedroom picking up her hair scarfs, combs, body creams and books, examining each item before she sets it back down.

'Smithy, could you sit down, you're doing my head in.'

She perches on the edge of the double bed, as far away from me as possible, then stands back up.

'Sorry, no, can't, sorry.' She sways on the spot, her hands dancing around at her sides. I hear a chorus of laughter from the living room, with Nancy's maniacal cackle cutting through Lee and Ayesha's lower-toned chortles. If I don't get back in there soon Smithy won't be the only one so drunk she can barely stand.

'What's going on, Smithy? What's this about?'

'That cop's outside. Dani Anderson.'

'What?' I run towards the window but Smithy stops me.

'She's out the front, parked up in her BMW. When we were in the living room I spotted the car from the window. She was on her phone and I saw her face.'

Fear shivers through me. I've been waiting for something to go wrong and it finally has. 'Do you think she's come to arrest us?'

'Nah.' She shakes her head. 'She's been there ages.'

'So what's she doing? Why is she here?'

'Because I fucked up.'

'What do you mean?' My stomach tightens. Now it's not just the wine and pizza that's making me feel sick. 'Smithy, what did you do?'

'I took money off her. Fifty quid but she said there'd be more.' She covers her face with her hands. 'She tried to arrest me outside Elephant and Castle shopping centre and said she'd nick us both unless I told her what you were up to. I've been forwarding her your texts and telling her what you've been up to. I'm sorry Liv, I shouldn't have done it but she really put the pressure on and I panicked.'

I drop onto the bed and crumple forward, my elbows on my knees and my head in my hands. If that's true, Dani knows almost everything I've done since I got out.

'Why didn't you tell me? We could have fed her false information.'

'Like I said, I panicked. I thought she'd know if we made shit up. She's a sneaky bitch. You know that. She said if I told you anything she'd fit us up for something that'd get us a long stretch. She said you wouldn't see Grace for years. And I knew how much you love your girl. I couldn't take that risk.'

'How much does she know?'

'Um . . .' Smithy clears her throat. 'That you went to see Sonia, and a lawyer.'

Oh god. I raise my head to look at her; her hands are still clamped to her face. 'Does she know Dominic's taking Grace to Dubai?'

'Yeah. I figured she already knew seeing as she's sleeping with the guy. I didn't tell her when, though. She wanted me to find out and I said you didn't know.'

I let out a low groan. 'This means Dominic knows that I know.'

'I'm sorry, Liv. Really I am. But I had to do it. If she'd nicked you for breaking and entering you would've broken the terms of your licence and gone back inside. I only took the money cos I needed it, for food and leccy for the meter and stuff. That's why I went out on the rob in the first place. To get some stuff to sell.' The bed sags beside me as Smithy sits down. 'It's been killing me not telling you but she didn't give me any choice.'

'I could have found fifty quid to give you.' I gave a hundred and fifty pounds to Jakub for his key card. I bought a second-hand phone for Grace with fifty. Ayesha's not going to let me starve while I stay with her. I could have found the money to help Smithy out.

'It wasn't about the money. It was about covering your arse. I would have told you eventually, I know I would, but I didn't want to stress you out when you were so worried about Grace. I thought I could handle it, pick and choose what I told her.'

'So why tell me now?'

'Because of what we've been planning tonight. The stakes just got a whole lot higher. You've been worrying about getting into the safe but what you really need to worry about is that bitch outside. I mean . . . she probably won't find out what we're up to, but if she does, you need to know that it didn't come from me. That's all.'

Her eyes are glassy and the base of her throat is pink. Behind the drunken sheen I can see how devastated she is. She thought she was protecting me by acquiescing to Dani's demands, but she took money from her too. Money I'd promised her when she got out of jail. Smithy isn't the only one to blame here. I am too.

'It's all right.' I reach for her hand. 'I'm not angry with you. I'm annoyed with myself. I should have checked up on you.'

'I can look after myself.'

'I know you can. But I promised to help you and I will. What happens tomorrow will change everything, assuming we pull it off.'

'It's still happening? After what I just said?'

'Of course it is. But I have to know that I can trust you, Smithy. No more secrets, okay?'

Her glazed eyes meet mine. 'None. I promise.'

'You swear you haven't told Dani about tomorrow?'

'I haven't. I swear I haven't.'

As she throws her arms around my neck and hugs me tightly I hope to god that she's telling the truth.

Chapter 37

DANI

Dani reaches into the glove box of her car and pulls out a pair of black leather gloves. She turned off the engine after she parked up outside the tower block and now it's bitterly cold. The curtains of apartment sixteen have been drawn for a while but at 8 p.m., when Dani arrived, they were wide open and she could see Olivia Sutherland and her flatmate moving around inside. Since then she's seen a number of people enter the building and then appear beyond the backlit window of number sixteen. She's spotted Kelly Smith, a woman in a faux-fur coat with striking red hair and a dapper bloke in a tailored jacket and a trilby hat. She assumes it's some kind of dinner party or a wine and cheese tasting or some other kind of middle-class crap. But she hasn't spent three hours freezing her arse off to pass judgement on Olivia's social life, she's waiting to make a move. Smithy still hasn't provided any intel on the details of Dominic's alleged emigration to Dubai and Dani's sick of waiting. Why speak to the monkey when the organ grinder knows the score? But getting any kind of information out of Olivia Sutherland will be tricky and she certainly won't be welcomed with open arms. She decided on her tactic while she drove over after work: *We've both been manipulated and lied to by Dominic. There are things we both want and if we work together there's more chance of us achieving them than if we fight him alone.* It's a compelling argument in theory but Olivia has good reason to distrust her. There's a strong possibility she'll be told to get fucked.

Dani had almost made up her mind to give it a go anyway when Kelly Smith turned up. She deliberated about calling her over to the car, but what would that achieve? If Smith really didn't know when Dominic was leaving then talking to her in person wouldn't make a difference and she'd probably alert Olivia to the fact Dani was sitting in her car outside. She'd wait it out, she decided. When Smith left she'd go up and talk to Olivia. But then the redhead and the trilby turned up and they're still stuffing their faces with cheese and wine.

Sighing, she reaches for her phone. She turned off the notifications during a meeting at work and she's missed a text from her mum.

Dani, I'm really sorry. Casey tricked me into unlocking her door, and now she's gone.

Dani closes her eyes and pulls the cold, car-scented air deep into her lungs. She holds her breath then exhales, opens her eyes and starts the engine.

'Fuck my fucking life,' she mutters as she drives off.

Chapter 38

OLIVIA

It's the day of the heist – Lee's term not mine – and, other than the day of my trial, I've never felt more scared. I didn't get more than two or three hours' sleep last night and, when I woke up, I made a coffee and went over the plan, reading it again and again to check there wasn't a massive great flaw I'd missed. The security at The Radcliffe Building is watertight. It's a stone's throw from Borough Market where eight people lost their lives during a terror attack in 2017. Any shiny sixteen-floor skyscraper in London employs fortress-like precautions against bombings and attacks.

Lee, Ayesha, Nancy and Smithy won't be able to get past the foyer without a pass. But as a cleaner, I can. All I need to do is sign in at reception as normal and touch my pass to the gates. My plan, should anyone stop me, is to say a clean-up is needed on floor five. And if they don't buy that? That's where Nancy and Lee come in.

They'll enter the building shortly before me, and, as I approach the reception desk to sign in, they'll launch into a loud and very public argument. With the receptionists and security guards distracted I'll scribble something unintelligible in the sign-in book and then swipe my pass through the gates.

The lift will take me to the fifth floor and, at 11 a.m. exactly, I'll send a text to Dom. I'll use Smithy's phone so he doesn't recognise the number. The text:

There are a lot of secrets in your safe.

should freak him out so much he'll open it to check that everything is still inside.

At 11.02 a.m. Ayesha will ring Dominic on her phone and pretend to be a member of office staff from Grace's school. She'll tell him that Grace has had an accident – a broken arm during a game of netball – and an ambulance has taken her to the Royal Free Hospital. She'll ask him to go straight to the hospital and, with any luck, he'll rush out of his office, forgetting to lock the safe. Then all I need to do is get in there, grab the evidence, run down the stairs so I don't bump into Dom by the lifts, then sneak out of the building. Smithy will be waiting outside and she'll take the evidence back to her flat. I was going to keep it with me but the others thought it would be safer to give it to Smithy, just in case I'm arrested later. Once I've given her the evidence I'll jump in a taxi and meet Ayesha at a restaurant near the Southbank – a public, if slightly shaky, alibi if Dominic reports the theft to the police. He'll realise the call from the school was a hoax fairly quickly once he arrives at the hospital but that won't matter as long as I've got whatever is in the safe.

Yesterday, as I pieced the plan together with Lee and Smithy, it seemed foolproof. Now, as the tube draws closer to London Bridge station, I'm obsessed with what could go wrong. And there are a *lot* of things that could. I messaged Grace before I left Ayesha's flat, to tell her I loved her. If I get caught it might be the last text I send her before I find myself back in prison. But it's not going to go wrong. It can't.

As the train pulls into the station I move closer to the doors, fighting the urge to scratch my scalp. My head is hot and irritated beneath a black baseball cap and Ayesha's shoulder-length auburn wig. I've got my plain black hoodie over my C&C Cleaning polo shirt and a cheap messenger bag slung across my body. There's CCTV monitoring every part of the tube station and I keep my head down and my eyes to the floor as I exit the train. Once I'm outside I take the escalator up to The Radcliffe Building. I'm so jittery that I nearly jump out of my skin when a man overtakes me and his shoulder brushes mine. When I step off the escalator I spot Smithy on a nearby bench, hugging a Costa coffee cup with her hands. There's no coffee inside. It's watered-down vegetable soup, so it looks like sick.

Smithy ignores me as I approach and take a seat on the adjacent bench. I try to steady myself, to push down the fear that's been building since I left Ayesha's flat an hour ago, but my feet betray me. The toes of my trainers tap-tap-tap on the concrete as The Radcliffe Building looms over us like a monolith. There's so much that could go wrong. If Dom sees me, I'm screwed.

'Liv, keep your bloody feet still,' Smithy hisses.

'I can't.' I press my palms to my jumping thighs and my feet into the ground. There are people everywhere, spilling out of the train station behind us, popping up from the escalator and strolling out of the tube exit that's just feet from the entrance to The Radcliffe Building. Busy is good. We decided on this time of day for a reason; I've got more of an opportunity to blend in and Dominic should be in his office to open the safe. *Should* being the operative word. When we were together his work schedule was always the same; he'd carry out his surveys in the afternoon and the next morning he'd write them up.

'You're a cleaner,' Smithy says in a low voice, 'and you're going to do your job. It's just a normal shift. All right? Get that in your head. If you don't stop looking so shifty you'll draw attention to yourself.'

It's good advice. I need to stride in there confidently as though it's something I do every day.

'Nancy and Lee are here.' Smithy nods in the direction of the tube exit and I spot them immediately – Nancy's long red hair cascading over the back of her pink faux-fur jacket and Lee in a hat and long dark coat. They look like a mobster and his moll.

'They'll certainly attract attention,' I say tightly.

Smithy makes an 'uh-huh' sound in her throat. 'That's exactly what you want.'

They stroll casually through the revolving doors of The Radcliffe Building and I see flashes of Nancy's hair and Lee's coat as they make their way into the foyer. They didn't tell me what they were going to argue about but I can tell they've started from Nancy's flailing arms.

'All right, Liv,' Smithy says, handing me her coffee and her phone. 'You're up.'

I pocket the phone, hold the coffee in one hand, take a slow deep breath and get up from the bench.

Chapter 39

DANI

Dani sits at Brenda's kitchen table, scrolling through her phone. Her mum's whittering on about something or other but Dani has completely zoned out. She didn't get more than four hours' sleep last night because her mum insisted they both stay up and wait until Casey came home. The hours ticked past as they sat side by side on the sofa watching quiz shows and nature programmes, reality TV and films. Somewhere around 4 a.m. Dani must have dropped off because she woke up with a start, and a crick in her neck, to the sound of Brenda clattering around in the kitchen a little after eight o'clock. Casey still wasn't home and Brenda had rung in sick at work so she'd be around when she eventually returned.

'We locked her in her room, Dan,' Brenda said as she handed her a cup of coffee. 'She probably hates me now.'

Dani tried to reassure her that Casey still loved her but the worry didn't shift from her mother's face.

'I've got a bad feeling, love. You'll spend your day off with me, won't you? You're not going home?'

Dani wanted to cry. She'd wasted one day off trailing Kelly Smith on a shoplifting spree and another one driving to Audley End and back. She couldn't remember the last time she'd spent some time alone, just chilling out.

It wasn't that she wasn't worried about Casey – she hated to think how much of Brenda's money her sister had drawn into her lungs in the last nine hours – but there was sod all she could do to bring her home. They'd combed through her social media the night before only to discover she hadn't updated it for months. They had no idea who she'd been hanging out with since her split with Josh and, even if they could track down where she'd gone, what were they supposed to do – drag her out and lock her back in her room?

Dani puts down her phone and reaches for the cup of tea that Brenda's just set in front of her. When Casey does come home, and she will return eventually, it'll be a rerun of the other night – she'll be too smacked up to talk and fall asleep on her feet. It's all going to be over soon, Dani tells herself as she sips at her tea. Dominic will give her the cash he owes her in a little over forty-eight hours (he texted her earlier to tell her where and when) and Casey will be locked up in a secure rehab unit for the next six months. *Over soon?* a small voice says in the back of her head. *What if, at 10.30 p.m. on Wednesday night, Dominic won't be in an underground car park in London Bridge? What if he's thirty thousand feet in the air?*

She tries to push the thought away but it refuses to be silenced. *He's played you, Dan, he's played you again.*

Feeling sick, she lowers the mug to the table. The tea's turned bitter in her mouth. What can she do? She can't stake out his house. Her mobile bleeps with a text notification and her heart leaps when she sees the sender's name. It has to be the Dubai info she's been waiting for. *Kelly Smith, you absolute star.*

Her jubilation turns to anger as she reads the message. Olivia Sutherland has just made the biggest mistake of her life.

Chapter 40

OLIVIA

When I step through the revolving doors of The Radcliffe Building, Lee and Nancy's argument is still in full flow. Being typically British, everyone in the foyer is pretending that they haven't noticed that a 'couple' are having a full-on marital dispute but their eyes are darting back and forth like they're watching the men's final at Wimbledon. There are three security guards on duty: a short, broad black guy outside the doors, a bespectacled, older white guy sitting behind the X-ray machine and a tall, bearded white guy with a barrel-like torso standing near the electronic gates. I swerve around Lee at the exact moment that Nancy decides to shove him, hard, in the chest. He stumbles backwards and I do a little skip and a jump to get out of the way. Nancy's push has attracted the attention of two of the security guards – the one from the entrance and one from the X-ray machine.

'All right you two,' the black guy says. 'You're going to have to take this outside.'

I've reached the reception desk nearest the gates but the

receptionist is so enthralled by the free entertainment that I have to cough to get her attention.

'C&C Cleaning.' I flash my pass at her, keeping my fingers over Jakub's photo and name.

She barely glances at me. Instead she pushes a clipboard in my direction, her gaze fixed on the scuffle behind me. I put Smithy's coffee cup down, scribble something unreadable on the sign-in sheet then pick the coffee back up and head for the gates. Out of the corner of my eye I see the bespectacled security guard returning to the X-ray machine a couple of metres to my left. A tall thin man in a suit hands him a tray containing a laptop case and a coat and he pushes it into the machine. The barrel-shaped guard hovers near the reception desk as I tap my pass against the gate sensor.

Nothing happens, the barriers don't move.

I tap it again. Still nothing. I can't get through.

The thin man passes through the gates without a problem and Barrel heads my way as the sensor flashes up red again.

'Is there a problem?' Barrel looks me up and down, his gaze resting on the logo on my shirt.

'My pass.' I tighten my grip on it so he can't see it's not mine. 'It's not working.'

'Show me.'

I tap it against the gate, keeping my hand curved over Jakub's face and name. Barrel snorts in amusement.

'You need to put it in the slot.' He slaps a meaty hand against the turnstile and I realise what I've done wrong. In my panic to get in I'd tapped it against the light on the top, like I was trying to get into the tube.

'Here, let me show you.' Barrel moves around me so he's on my right side, nearest the card.

'I can do it.' If he sees the pass there will be questions and a phone call to C&C Cleaning. Noreen would take great pleasure in telling him that she's got no idea why I've turned up to clean during the day.

'It's fine, honestly,' I add, but Barrel's not listening and his thumb and forefinger reach for the inch of plastic that's poking out of my clenched hand.

'Get your bloody hands off me!' Nancy's scream makes me jump and, as Barrel whips round to see what's going on, I thrust the pass into the slot and step through the gates. A bead of sweat rolls down my back as I head for the escalator. It's taking every ounce of willpower not to break into a run.

You're just a cleaner, I tell myself as the escalator carries me upwards. *You're just doing your job.*

I risk a glance at the foyer as I turn right, towards the lifts. Lee and Nancy are being ushered towards the revolving door, still ranting and raging. Everything that happens now is down to me.

I get a sideways look from a woman in her early twenties as I step into the lift and a quick glance at my reflection in a mirrored wall tells me why: my baseball cap and wig have slipped backwards and there's a band of blonde hair at my hairline where it should be auburn. I tug the cap forward and the wig slides into the correct position. The lift passes floor one, floor two and floor three. At floor four it stops and the young woman gets out. I steady my breathing as the doors close then glance at my watch as the lift continues to climb.

10.54 a.m.

The issue I had with my pass means I've only got six minutes to get into Dom's office, find an empty desk, surreptitiously spill the fake vomit, then send him a text as I pretend to clean up.

The doors open and I speed around the corner to the cleaning cupboard. My hand is shaking so much it takes two

212

taps of my pass to get the door open and I scrabble around
to find what I need. The coffee cup goes into the bottom of
a bucket and I plunge a mop into the space next to it to keep
it upright. I add an antibacterial spray and two cloths and
then glance at my watch.

10.56 a.m.

Shit, shit, shit.

I kick the door shut, hurry towards the glass doors of the
surveyors' office and tap my pass against the sensor. A wall
of noise hits me as I step inside. The last time I was here it
was empty apart from another cleaner. Now there are people
everywhere – bent over desks, tapping at keyboards and
talking into their phones. There's a desk directly opposite me
and a man in his early thirties in a shirt and tie lifts his head
from his work and looks at me quizzically. Before he can
speak I nod sharply and take off down the office. As I pass
Dom's office my stomach lurches. He's inside, leaning back
in his chair with his hands interlocked behind his head. An
image of him smirking at me from across the courtroom
almost stops me in my tracks but I keep going, head down,
bucket in hand. I've spotted an empty desk at the far end of
the room.

Eyes dart in my direction as I walk down a never ending
catwalk. *I am a cleaner*, I tell myself as I draw closer to the
empty desk, *I'm just doing my job*. I'm breathing so shal-
lowly that my head is swimming and when I reach the desk
I press my hand to its smooth surface, just long enough to
steady myself. Seconds later I'm under the desk, spilling
watery vegetable soup onto the cheap brown carpet. I place
the empty cup in the bin and reach for my antibac spray
and cloth.

'Excuse me.' The shirt and tie man from the desk at the
entrance looms over me. His gaze flicks from the tiny cubes

of vegetables to my quivering hand, reaching into the bucket. He's got a hard, angular face and there's suspicion glinting in his dark brown eyes. 'What's all this?'

My lips are so dry they're stuck to my teeth and I have to run my tongue over them before I can reply. 'I got asked to sort this out.'

'By whom?'

'My boss.'

'And who called her?'

'I don't know.' I look at him imploringly, willing him to leave me alone and just go away. I can't risk a glance at my watch but I can feel the seconds ticking away. If Ayesha rings Dominic before I text him he'll leave his office with the safe still locked. 'I was just told to come in.'

'First I've heard of it,' he arches a dark eyebrow, 'and I'm the office manager.'

'Rob,' a woman with greying curly hair leans around her monitor. I didn't even notice her as I walked past. 'Just leave her alone to get on with her job.'

I risk a glance at my watch. 10.59 a.m. I've got *one minute* to send Dom a text.

'Where is Tim anyway?' shirt and tie asks. 'And when the hell did he puke on the floor?'

I spot the jacket on the back of the chair and my chest constricts. Someone's been using this desk. When he comes back there will be a big discussion about whose vomit it is and I haven't got time for that crap.

'No idea. Some of us have got work to do.' The curly-haired woman gives Rob a pointed look.

His lips part, as though he's about to bite back, then he looks back down at me. 'Get it sorted, but I'm going to follow this up. If cleaning staff are required it's supposed to go via me.'

214

'I'll be very quick.' I reach for my antibac spray and squirt it onto the vomity mess.

I watch from beneath the desk until his shiny black shoes recede into the distance then I dig into my pocket for Smithy's phone and frantically tap out a message. I hit send at exactly 11 a.m. From this angle I can't see into Dom's office so I rise up onto my knees and rub over the surface of the desk with the dry cloth.

He's got the text. I can see him looking at his phone.

'Sorry about that,' the curly-headed woman leans around her monitor again. 'He wouldn't have done that if you were a bloke.'

'I appreciated you speaking up.' Dom's out of his chair and he's lowering the blinds in his window. He's about to open the safe.

Curly hair twists round in her chair. 'He won't come back,' she says, misinterpreting where I'm looking. 'I think he's scared of me.'

I fake a laugh and glance at my watch. 11.02 a.m. Ayesha should be ringing him any second now. I duck back under the desk and start putting everything back into the bucket, readying myself for the next stage of the heist. I reach for the vomit-sodden cloth and freeze. When Dom leaves his office how am I going to get in without being seen? Mr Jobsworth Office Manager isn't going to let me merrily stroll straight in there and I can't think of a single legitimate reason that he'd buy.

Can I get rid of him somehow? Ideally I need to get rid of everyone in the room. There's a 'Fire Door' sign above the door directly opposite me. I'm pretty certain it leads to the stairs. A fire alarm would get *everyone* out of the office, including Dom. There has to be a red box somewhere – one where you break the glass to set off the alarm. There isn't one in here that I can

215

see so it's got to be out there, at the top of the stairs. I scramble to my feet, bucket in hand.

'Have a nice day!' Curly hair calls after me as I head for the door.

I push it open and find myself in a stairwell. If I walk straight ahead and turn left I'll reach the toilet block. To the right are the stairs. And on the wall beside me is a small red box. Without pausing to think I lift the mop out of the bucket and jam the handle against the glass. As the fire alarm wails I take a left towards the toilet block and wait, out of sight, with my back to the wall.

Any second now staff will come pouring out of the stairwell door. Will Dominic come with them or will he lock the safe door first? If he does everything I've done today will be for nothing. Panic grips my chest as the sound of footsteps and voices fill the stairwell. I can't let him close that safe. I need to get there first. If I burst into his office he'll be so shocked I might buy myself enough time to grab what I can and make a run for it. It's the only chance I've got.

I set off before I can change my mind, past the toilets and the lift and back to the glass door entrance of Magna Lake Chartered Surveyors. The office manager has abandoned his desk and, from the looks of it, so has everyone else. I tap my pass against the sensor and poke my head around the door. The last few stragglers are filing out of the fire door at the far end. Am I too late? Has Dom already gone? As I step inside the office voices send me scurrying back to the door. I press my back against the glass, praying no one turns and looks in my direction as Rob shepherds Dom out of his office and towards the fire door.

My heart hammers against my ribs as the fire door closes behind them and I sprint across the room. The blinds are still down in Dom's office. If he didn't have time to open them maybe he didn't have time to lock the safe either.

My heart sinks as I burst into the room. The door to the safe is shut. He's locked it. It's over. He's going to take Grace to Dubai and I'm never going to see her again. I reach for the handle and twist it, just to make sure, and almost fall backwards as the door swings open.

Oh my god.

Grace's phone. A white iPhone. Two SIMs or SSD cards in a clear plastic bag. And a piece of paper. The same piece of paper I found wedged into a book at home. I shove everything into my pockets and head for the fire door. I've got everything I need but I'm not safe yet.

Chapter 41

DANI

Dani takes the corner faster than she should and, too late, spots a car travelling in the opposite direction. She slams her feet onto the clutch and the brake, forcing the car into a shuddering emergency stop, just as it clips the bumper of the other car.

'Shit!' She smashes her palms into the steering wheel then, without so much as a glance at the horrified expression on the other driver's face, reverses the car back around the corner. She hasn't got time for this. Every second she wastes is another second that's going to bring Olivia Sutherland closer to screwing up her life.

'Oi!' A burly bloke with tattoos on his neck and broken veins on his cheeks raps on her window as she puts the car into first gear. She considers ignoring him and pulling away but he could take down her registration and have her done for not swapping numbers. Irritated, she turns off the engine and winds her window down an inch.

'Are you blind or what?' the man bellows, nostrils flaring. 'You could have killed me there.'

Dani holds her badge to the window and smiles, showing her teeth. The man's expression changes in an instant and he jumps away from the car as though stung.

She rolls the window all the way down and leans out. 'Is there any damage?'

The man turns and looks at his car, then looks back at Dani, indecisiveness written all over his flushed face. Dani taps her foot impatiently as she waits for him to make a decision. Every second he spends thinking it over is taking her one step closer to jail. She touches the keys in the ignition, itching to turn them. Finally, just as she's about to shout out of the window that she hasn't got all day, the man shakes his head.

'I'll leave it.' The moment the words leave his mouth Dani starts the engine and she's off and driving down Horse Guards Road while he's still surveying his car.

She floors it the rest of the way, or as much as she can given London's congested streets, and fights to control her breathing as the large, imposing building comes into view, the windows glinting in the weak autumn sunlight. She parks up, sprints across the car park and hurries through the building's revolving glass doors, her heart ratcheting against her ribs as she flashes her badge at the woman behind the desk. Her shoes squeak on the shiny tiled floor as she speeds towards the lifts and a small part of her brain registers how quiet the place is but she doesn't give it more than a moment's thought.

'Come on,' she mutters as she watches the number on the LCD display decrease as the lift slowly descends to the ground floor. 'Come on, come on, come on.'

When the doors finally open she jumps in and taps the button for floor five. As the lift ascends she takes a tissue out of the pocket of her jacket and wipes it over her face and the hairline at the base of her ponytail. Her skin is slick with sweat. She shoves the damp tissue back into her pocket as the doors open and she steps onto the landing with her shoulders pulled back and her chin raised. Olivia Sutherland may think she's won but Dani's not going to go down without a fight. She strides into the room, her attention focused on the glass-walled room at one end, the blinds lowered. Is Olivia in there? Or is she already long gone? Dani raps three times on the door and straightens her jacket as she waits.

'Come!'

Detective Inspector Matthew Fielding looks up from his paperwork as she steps inside. 'I can give you five minutes.'

'Thanks boss.' Dani closes the door and takes the seat opposite him, her hands on her lap, the heels of her shoes pressed into the floor, her feet steady and still.

Fielding puts down his pen. 'Okay, what can I do you for?'

Dani searches his face, looking for tightness around his lips, a clench to his jaw or an angry glint in his eye, but finds nothing. Is he deliberately giving nothing away or was Smithy's text total bullshit? She can remember it word for word:

Liv is going to speak to your DI. She says she has evidence that can get you sent down.

'Dani?' Fielding says. He picks his pen back up and repeatedly clicks the button on the top. 'Everything okay?'

He raises his eyebrows, waiting for her to speak, and his expectant expression tells her everything she needs to know. She's been had. Kelly Smith's text was absolute bollocks, a diversion to stop her from finding out what Olivia is really up to. She could kill Smith. Stupid, time-wasting, sneaky little bitch.

'Yeah, sorry boss,' Dani says, fighting to keep her tone light as rage smoulders in the pit of her stomach. 'I just wanted to check that you're okay with the progress on the drugs case.'

Fielding looks confused. 'We talked about this the other day, didn't we?'

'Yeah, but I just . . . I heard rumours you weren't happy and wanted to check in with you. I've got a few more statements to—'

Fielding cuts her off with a wave of his hand. 'Ignore any rumours. I'm happy as long as you're doing your job and we're not falling behind.'

He puts down his pen, stands up and takes his jacket from the back of his chair and slips it on. 'Sorry, I've got somewhere to be.'

Dani stands up too and follows him out of the office. As he waits for the lift she takes the stairs. She moves down them at speed, anger fuelling each step. How dare Kelly Smith dick her around like that and waste her time. If she and Olivia Sutherland think they can take the piss out of her they've got another think coming. In less than a minute she's sprinting out of New Scotland Yard and heading for her car.

Chapter 42

OLIVIA

The fire alarm is still ringing, making my head pound, but I've made it down five flights of stairs. There are roughly a hundred people between me and freedom. I couldn't run for it if I tried. We're all packed into the foyer and we're shuffling slowly towards the doors at the far end. A security guard is standing in front of the revolving doors, preventing anyone from leaving that way. Instead we're being directed to exit through two glass doors either side. They were locked when I came in earlier but now they're wide open with people walking through them, two or three abreast. A couple of feet ahead of me the back of Dominic's head is visible in a crowd of shorter colleagues. There's a distinct grey peppering to his hair that wasn't there five years ago but I'd recognise the shape of his head and the set of his shoulders anywhere. There's a part of me that's desperate to see his expression when he returns to his office later and finds his safe empty. The other, more sensible part of me, wants to get as far away as I can. I won't be able to relax until I get the contents of my pockets into the hands of my lawyer.

Your turn to go to prison now, I silently tell Dominic then swiftly lower my chin to my chest, obscuring my face with the rim of my baseball cap as he turns, sensing he's being watched.

Shit, that was close.

I continue to keep my head down as we shuffle towards the doors. I feel like I've been trapped in the foyer for hours but it can't be more than a few minutes. Finally, I step outside, peel away from everyone else and take long, deep breaths of cool, city air as I weave through the groups that have formed outside. As I step onto the escalator that leads down to the street a heavy hand on my shoulder makes my blood freeze. I turn slowly and a thin woman with scraped-back hair pulls a face.

'Smithy! You *have* to stop doing that! You were supposed to meet me on the street.'

'Where's the fun in that? I'm guessing the fire alarm was down to you?'

'Yes, it was.'

'Well, did you get the stuff? Your wig's crooked by the way.'

'I've got it.' I tug on the rim of my baseball cap, keeping my voice low. 'I've got everything that was in the safe. Come on, let's move.'

I hurry down the last few steps, take a right and duck into a side street. I check for CCTV then dart into a doorway and gesture for Smithy to do the same. Only when I'm sure that no one can see us do I reach into my pockets.

'Here.' I press Dani's repayment schedule into Smithy's hand, feeling as though I'm handing her my life. I lost a lot of sleep last night, deliberating whether I could trust her with something so precious after she sold me out to Dani but I know she didn't do it to be malicious or for the money. She was trying to protect me. If she wanted to screw me over she wouldn't have confessed everything last night. She wants this to work as much as I do. We spent three years in our cell discussing how I was going to clear my name and get my daughter back. She's on my side. 'Don't get it wet whatever you do.'

She raises an eyebrow. 'I wasn't planning on going in the Thames for a dip.'

'I meant the rain. It's not in biro, it might smudge.'

'Righto.' She tucks it into the front pocket of her rucksack. 'What else have we got?'

'This phone.' I press the button on the side of the white iPhone but nothing happens; whatever charge it may once have held is long gone. I pop it into the pocket of her rucksack but keep the second phone in my hand. 'This one belongs to Grace. And this stuff . . .' I hold up the clear bag holding two SIM cards, '. . . I've got no idea what's on these. Is there a laptop where you're staying?'

'My mate's got a PC. Will that do?'

'It should, if it's not too old. I'll buy a converter for the SIM cards just in case. Can you ask your friend for the log-in details?'

'Sure.' Smithy tucks the plastic bag into the rucksack, zips it up and swings it onto her back. 'Bring it round to mine later and we'll find out exactly what your bastard ex has been up to.'

'Too right.' I give her a quick hug and turn to go. 'I'll see you later. Look after that stuff.'

'Will do.' She gives me a jokey salute.

*

'Table for two in the name of Ayesha Okoye.'

I nearly add, 'Sorry I'm late,' then stop myself. If I do end up being arrested I don't want any of the staff in the restaurant to remember that I turned up late. Our table is for 11 a.m. and that's what the police will see if they look at the bookings.

The bored-looking maître d' standing behind the counter glances at the clipboard in his hands. 'You're the first of your party to arrive. Follow me.'

'Sorry?' The word leaves my mouth before I can stop it but the maître d' is out of earshot, already halfway across the restaurant. I follow him, scanning the room for Ayesha's face. She was supposed to get here at 11 a.m. That was the plan.

'Your table.' The maître d' draws to a halt and gestures at a table in a dark corner of the restaurant. The cutlery is laid out and shining, the wine glasses are clean and sparkling, but there's no sign of Aysh.

I take a seat as the maître d' disappears off again and scan the street beyond the window. Where is she? I check my phone but she hasn't sent me a text. Did she go to the wrong restaurant? Did we cross wires somehow?

I tap out a text:

Aysh? Where are you?

What do I do now? Just wait? Sit here for an hour on my own? Will it still count as an alibi? Do I even need one? When Dominic returns to his office and his safe is open and empty he'll panic. He'll search for his stuff and then what? Call his lawyer? The police? But what would he say? 'The evidence I used to frame my ex-wife has been stolen'? He can't ring Dani because some of my haul incriminates her and, given the conversation Grace overheard, she'll be pleased if Dominic's bargaining chip has disappeared. Or will she? If she discovers that I'm behind the theft she'll definitely come knocking. And she knows where Smithy lives too.

'Shit.' My chair clatters to the floor as I stand up. I need to tell Smithy not to go back to the flat. But I've still got her phone. I forgot to give it back.

Chapter 43

DOMINIC

Dominic is furious that he spent forty minutes standing outside in the rain while the fire service checked The Radcliffe Building to find the source of the fire, only to discover that some arsehole deliberately smashed a fire alarm on the fifth floor. He's just spent thirty seconds crammed into a lift with half a dozen damp people who smell like wet dogs and he's pissed off with Rob for striding into his office earlier and ordering him out like a headteacher sending a recalcitrant child to detention. Rob Storey is a jumped-up little prick who should have been fired years ago and Dom's got a good mind to book a meeting with one of the partners to complain about him. Then there's the anonymous message on his phone that made him panic unnecessarily. There are three people who should be worried about the contents of his safe, and only one who knows it exists.

You can taunt me all you like, he thinks as he opens the door to his office, *but the second I get my share of the money I won't be the monkey dancing to your tune anymore.*

He strides across to his safe and touches a finger to the keypad, keying in the code to unlock it. His heart spasms in his chest – a double beat that makes him feel sick – as he opens the door and catches sight of what's inside. Or rather, what's not. Now he's not thinking about anything. He's trying not to throw up.

Chapter 44

OLIVIA

There's someone standing on the street outside Smithy's flat – a woman in a brown leather jacket and jeans with her dark hair pulled back into a ponytail. She's pushing at the door, oblivious to the curious glances of shoppers drifting up and down Walworth Road. The door gives way a little with each shove but there's resistance, as if someone standing behind the door is pushing back. A rush of fear passes through me. Smithy! Shit.

I sprint down the street, keeping to the edge of the pavement, out of leather jacket woman's eyeline, then I rush her from behind, knocking her away from the door. She tips sideways and falls heavily. Her forearm and elbow hit the pavement first before her hips follow suit.

'Smithy?' I turn the door handle and push lightly, leaving the woman still groaning on the concrete behind me. 'Smithy open up, it's me.'

When there's no reply I push harder. 'Smithy? It's Liv. Open the door!'

The door moves half an inch then catches on something and stops. There's a narrow band of space between the door and the frame but I can't see more than a thin strip of wall. Movement behind me makes me turn sharply. My blood runs cold as the woman I knocked down gets to her feet.

DS Danielle Anderson.

Confusion, then anger, flashes across her face and in an instant she's standing beside me, her lips pulled into a hard straight line.

'I could nick you for that.'

'Go on then.' I hold her stare. I'm breathing steadily even though my heart is pounding and my skin is tingling. All the frustration, hurt and anger I've felt over the last five years has risen to the surface. Inside Smithy's flat is the evidence that's going to send Dani Anderson to prison for a very long time.

A muscle twitches in her cheek. 'Take a step back, Sutherland. You're not in prison now.' There's a warning tone to her voice but I'm not afraid.

'What the hell are you doing?' I ask her.

'I don't think that's any of your business.'

'You bribed Smithy to keep tabs on me. Wasn't it enough to frame me once?'

'No one framed you, Liv.'

'We both know that's not true.'

'I know you're a very dangerous woman.'

'And I know you've been sleeping with Dom.'

'That's bullshit and you know it.' Her voice hasn't lost any of its power but, for the first time since she stood up, there's a hint of apprehension in her eyes.

'Missing a black bra, are you?'

She smirks. 'What? Did you break in again?'

'If I had you wouldn't report it. Why is that, Dani?'

'Again, none of your business, Liv.'

She's lost the polish she had in the gym. Her eye make-up has smudged, her hair is damp where it joins her forehead and there are beads of sweat above her top lip. 'You sold yourself too cheaply. In and out of the bedroom.'

To my satisfaction she bristles but she doesn't strike out at me, she's cleverer than that. She wouldn't do anything out here in front of witnesses and dash cams and CCTV trained on the street. If Dani retaliates she'll do it on the sly but she'll have to be quick because once I get inside Smithy's flat I'll have the evidence to send her away for a very long time. And then she'll have to watch her back for a completely different reason.

A low groan from behind the door makes me spin round.

'Smithy?' I call through the gap. 'Smithy is that you?'

There's another groan and this time I pinpoint the sound. I wasn't pushing against 'something' when I tried to get in, I was pushing against *someone*. That groan came from the ground. 'Are you hurt? Can you get up?'

There's a pause then a reply so faint I can barely hear it. 'It's gone.'

All the bravado I was feeling a few seconds ago evaporates. I don't have to ask what she means.

'Smithy, can you move away from the door?'

There's no reply. Even the groaning has stopped.

'Smithy!' The roar of traffic behind me is silenced by the rush of blood to my head.

'What have you done to her?' I spit the words into Dani's face. 'What the fuck have you done?'

She shakes her head lightly, a frown forming between her eyebrows. 'I don't know what you're talking about.'

She's lying. She stole the evidence and hurt Smithy and she's going to get away with it, just like she got away with framing me five years ago.

231

'What did you do to her?' The cold, dismissive look she gives me lifts the lid on my rage and I shove her, hard, in the chest. She stumbles backwards and I feel a rush of pleasure. How does it feel to be attacked when you least expect it, Dani? How does it feel to have no control over your fate? I push her again, before she can recover, and she takes another couple of steps back towards the road. She's only inches from the kerb now. There's a truck, about fifty feet to our right, travelling faster than it should on this stretch of road. I grab her jacket by the lapels. One more push and she'd be sprawled in its path.

She deserves this. She stole five years of my life. Of my daughter's life. She's stolen the evidence that proves I'm innocent and she's beaten up one of the few people in this world that I trust. Why should I play by the rules when she didn't? Why should I be a good person when everyone thinks that I'm not?

'You betrayed me, Dani.'

The truck rumbles closer – forty metres, thirty. Dani wrestles to get free, grabbing at my fingers then throwing her fists at my face. She lands a punch in my guts and one on the side of my head. Her knuckles connect with my cheekbone but I barely feel it. I'm not aware of anything other than the truck, drawing closer and closer with each ragged breath I take. Dani turns her head, following my line of sight, and the colour drains from her face.

'Don't do it!' she screams. 'Olivia, stop. I did it for my sister. She's ill. It saved her life.'

'And you stole mine!'

She's lying. She didn't frame me to help someone. She framed me because she's greedy and she's corrupt and she's—

The thought is knocked from my head as Dani's fist connects with my throat and a tsunami of pain crashes through my body. I press a hand to my neck as a strange, rasping sound creeps from my mouth. I drop to my knees, sucking in air in short, guttural gasps, only vaguely aware of the pedestrians who have stopped in their tracks either side of me, staring, their mouths agape.

'Police! Nothing to see here.' Dani's shout booms out from somewhere to my right and the gawkers and the rubberneckers begrudgingly disperse. I am vaguely aware of a phone ringing as I struggle to my feet, one hand pressed to my throat.

'Smithy . . .' I croak as I feel around in my pocket for my phone. I need to ring an ambulance.

But Dani's not listening. Her mobile is pressed to her ear and she's staring straight through me as though I'm a ghost.

It takes the firemen less than fifteen minutes to remove the door to Smithy's flat. The moment they step away the ambulance crew rush in and I catch a glimpse of her – lying crumpled on the ground at the foot of the stairs. Her skin is ashen and the hair on her crown is dark with blood. I rush forward but I'm intercepted before I can reach her.

'Miss,' a ruddy-cheeked uniformed policeman steps in front of me. 'Let the paramedics do their job.'

'But I know her. She's my friend.'

'What's her name?' He takes out a notebook and pen.

'Smith . . . Kelly Smith.'

Dani was long gone by the time the emergency services turned up. As I dialled 999 she sprinted in the direction of the tube station with her phone pressed to her ear. When the older of the two paramedics asked me what had happened I was shaking so violently I couldn't speak. What had I become? I'd almost thrown Dani into the road. If she reported me, I'd be arrested. I'd go back to prison. I'd lose everything, again.

I watch, helplessly, as the paramedics load Smithy onto a stretcher, her skin pallid beneath the oxygen mask, her eyes closed. She's alive, but I've never seen her so still.

'Are you a friend?' The policeman returns to my side as I follow the paramedics to the ambulance.

'Yes. We're really close.'

'What happened?'

'I was coming round to see her and I . . .' I tail off. Do I tell him about Dani? He's a constable and she's a detective. Until Smithy wakes up, or the police check the local CCTV footage, it's Dani's word against mine. A thought hits me. If there is CCTV footage they won't just see Dani barging her way into the flat, they'll see me almost pushing her into the road.

The police officer raises his eyebrows expectantly, waiting for me to continue.

'I tried to open the door,' I say, 'and it wouldn't open. I heard Kelly groaning and realised she was on the ground. When she stopped responding I rang for help.'

'Had she been drinking at all? Has she got any medical conditions that may have caused a fall?'

'No,' I say. 'She wasn't, she hasn't. I saw her earlier, she was fine.'

A frown furrows his brow. 'Is there something you're not telling me?'

'No. Nothing. I don't know what happened. Please, I need to ask the paramedics if I can go to the hospital with her. I need to check she's all right.'

'Okay, but I'm going to have to take some details first.'

I step from foot to foot, keeping an eye on the ambulance, as I answer his questions then leap away as one of the paramedics climbs into the cab. I wave desperately to get his attention.

'Please can I come? I'm Kelly's friend. She hasn't got anyone else.'

'Sure.' He gestures for me to approach. 'Get in.'

'She's not going to die, is she? Please tell me she's not going to die.'

Chapter 45

DOMINIC

Dominic is in the men's toilets on floor five of The Radcliffe Building. He's been sitting on a closed toilet lid for the last half an hour, fighting to catch his breath. Once the urge to throw up passed he felt a pain in his chest so intense, so constrictive, he was certain he was having a heart attack. Then his ears began to ring, his fingers tingled and he felt like he was choking. He could see Rob, staring at him from across the office, his eyebrows knitted together in concern. Instead of feeling reassured that someone had noticed what was happening to him, Dominic was gripped by paranoia. Was Rob staring at him because he was acting weirdly? He felt weird – worse than that, he felt terrified. It was as though he was outside of himself, no longer connected to his body. A wave of fear sent him running to the toilets with his phone in his hand. He splashed water onto his face and stared at his reflection in the mirror, his pupils dilated, his skin flushed and water dripping from his chin. With the safe empty any power he had has vanished, his destiny is no longer his own. If the SIM cards end up in the hands of the police he's going to prison for a very, very long time.

He taps out a message on his burner phone.

It's gone. The safe is empty.

There's no reply for a couple of minutes then,

What do you mean?

Beads of sweat form on his temples.

Exactly what I just said. EVERYTHING IS GONE. A fire alarm went off at work and when I got back the safe was empty. It has to be . . . he pauses. Liv's completely fucking clueless. It has to be Dani. He never told her about the safe but she knows he's got something on her. He bloody told her as much. Unless . . . he wipes his suit sleeve over his face as a new thought hits him. There's only one person who knows about the safe . . .

Did you take it? he asks.

The reply arrives within seconds.

Why the hell would I do that?

Because you don't trust me, Dom thinks but doesn't type. *And I don't trust you.*

His chest constricts and his breathing becomes shallow again. Was this the plan all along? To use him to get the loans and then stitch him up? Apparently they're 'in this together' but someone's been playing the long game, and now they've made their move.

If you take me down, Dominic types back then deletes it. Lashing out isn't going to work. He's already given too much away about his state of mind by throwing accusations around. What he wants is his share of the money and to get on with life with his daughter by his side. Dubai was never his idea. It was sold to him as a tax haven, somewhere he and Grace could be together and he wouldn't have to worry about the courts or the police. Before he could suggest anywhere else flights had been booked and the tickets emailed to him in his and Grace's names.

Of course you wouldn't empty the safe, he types back. Panicking here. Has to be the cop.

He really, really hopes it isn't Dani. Once she's deleted the recording of their conversation and shredded her repayment schedule there's nothing to stop her from destroying him. And she's got everything she needs to do it. He looks up from his phone, his vision swimming. The sides of the toilet cubicle are pulsing, closing in on him, squeezing him into a coffin-shaped space. He presses his left hand to the wall and taps at his phone with the thumb of his right hand.

We need to move the package.

– No.

But if Dani has the phone.

– That proves nothing.

She'll work it out.

– And we'll be long gone

I'm going to move the package.

Dom's phone rings, making him jump. He's never had a call on his burner before, not once. They're always very, very careful to avoid calls.

'I have the evidence,' says the voice in his ear.

'But . . . you . . .' Dom plucks at the collar of his shirt and fumbles with the button. It's so tight he can't breathe. '. . . You said . . .'

'Your ex-wife stole it from your safe. I took it back.'

'What . . .' his throat dries '. . . what are you going to do with it?'

'Look after it. Like you should have done.'

Dom rests the back of his head against the cool wall of

the cubicle, too relieved to care about the cistern digging into his back.

'You need to learn to trust me,' says the voice. 'How many times do I have to tell you that?'

Chapter 46

DANI

Dani walks through the labyrinthine corridors of the hospital, as though in a dream. An echo of the last conversation she had with her sister is the only thought in her brain:

If you keep this up, the money I'm saving for rehab will end up paying for your funeral. Do you understand?

Did she conjure this scenario just by mentioning it?

Logically she knows that this isn't her fault, that she didn't will it into being by forewarning her sister. But logic left her body the moment she heard her mother's anguished wail in her ear:

'Casey's overdosed. She's in the hospital. You need to get here now.'

Dani drove from Elephant and Castle to St Thomas' Hospital Emergency Department – stopping at red lights, indicating, tapping the brake – but she can't remember a single detail of the journey. There's a ten-minute hole in her memory that will never be filled. All she can remember is the tinny, desperate sound of her mother's voice as she explained what had happened. Not that she knew much. Paramedics had been dispatched to a flat in Bermondsey after a 999 call to report a drugs overdose. A young woman had led them to Casey who was slumped across the sofa with heroin paraphernalia strewn over the table beside her. Neither Dani nor her mother could think of anyone Casey knew who lived in Bermondsey, but then they knew so little about her life.

'Her organs are failing,' Brenda told Dani between sobs. 'The doctors don't think she'll make it through the night.'

Somehow Dani finds herself standing inside the entrance to the critical care ward. She has a conversation with a nurse that she won't remember later and follows the direction of the woman's outstretched arm.

Brenda, hollow-eyed and hunched, glances up from Casey's bedside as Dani pulls back the curtain that surrounds her sister's bed. The last time Dani saw her mother she looked every one of her fifty-eight years. Now she looks twenty years older. Her sister appears almost childlike in comparison, her tiny frame swamped by the hospital bed. Her terrible hair is dark spikes on the pillow and her long eyelashes are closed, resting on the deep circles under her eyes.

Dani grips the curtain, the cool material woven through her fingers. This isn't where Casey should be, in a white, metal bed in a ward that smells of cleaning fluid and death. She should be at home, tucked up beneath her duvet, watching a film. She should be sitting next to her on the sofa, crying with laughter at *I'm a Celebrity*. She should be out with her mates, throwing moves on the dancefloor. She should be walking and talking and pink-cheeked and healthy. She should be taking the piss and winding Dani up. She should be doing her head in and making her want to scream.

'Am I too . . .' The words fall away as Dani looks from her mother's heartbroken face to her sister's chest – so still beneath the starched, white sheet – to the heart monitor, plugged in but silent at the side of the bed.

Chapter 47

OLIVIA

The doctor who walks into the visiting room can't be more than thirty, but the weariness in her eyes makes her appear much older. I can't begin to imagine what she has to deal with, day in day out. If A&E is a hospital's front line then intensive care must be its field hospital with the sickest patients treading the line between life and death. That's where Smithy is now, having been poked and prodded, scanned and X-rayed. The nurse who ushered me here after Smithy was unloaded from the ambulance and rushed through the hospital told me she was still breathing but her pulse was weak and she remained unconscious. They needed to run a series of checks for head and spinal injuries, broken bones and internal bleeding and they'd come and get me when they'd run all their tests.

'Olivia?' the doctor says now.

I nod dumbly, too nervous to speak as she perches on the chair beside me. She presses her lips together in a manner that only ever suggests bad news and slides a box of tissues off the table and hands them to me as tears prick at my eyes.

'I'm afraid your friend Kelly is very unwell. She's suffering from an abdominal haemorrhage and she's been rushed to surgery to try and stop the bleeding.' She pauses to let it sink in. 'She's also suffered an edema – swelling – to her brain which will require another operation to drain the cerebro-spinal fluid to help relieve the pressure. Depending on the outcome of the first operation . . .'

She continues to talk but the words are running together in my head. If I hadn't given Smithy the contents of Dom's safe none of this would have happened. She'd be sitting in her flat with her feet up and a cup of tea in her hands watching reruns of *Frost* on ITV3.

'How . . . how do you think it happened?'

The doctor raises her shoulders in a small shrug. 'We can't say for sure but the brain injury could well have been caused by her falling down the stairs.'

'And the internal bleeding?'

'From the bruising on the stomach it seems likely that she was kicked, repeatedly.'

'Oh my god.' I cover my face with my hands. 'She's not . . . she won't die, will she?'

'We'll do everything we can,' the doctor says softly. 'Is there anyone else we should call? Parents, siblings?'

I shake my head. Smithy's dad has never been on the scene and her mum died of cancer when she was twelve. She doesn't have any siblings and, other than some of the girls on our wing, I couldn't name a single one of her friends.

'Kelly's going to be in surgery for several hours,' the doctor continues. 'We'll call you when she comes out but she probably won't be well enough to receive visitors until tomorrow. Is there anyone at home who can be with you while you wait?'

'Yes, I'm . . . I'm staying with a friend.'

'Okay, good.' She shifts in her chair. 'Have you got any questions you'd like to ask me?'

I've got a hundred questions – about the operations and Kelly's prognosis and whether there's any way of proving that she was pushed down the stairs – but I'm not sure I want to know the answers so I shake my head.

There's a flash of relief on the doctor's face. She's busy and she needs to get back to the ward.

'Thank you,' I stand up at the same time she does and awkwardly reach for her hand, 'for everything you do.'

She nods by way of reply then quickly steps out of the room. After a beat I follow her, my brain still cloudy from everything she told me and my heart aching with worry. Smithy has to get through this, she has to. My phone bleeps as I follow the signs to the exit. It's a text message from Ayesha.

Liv, I am SO SORRY. There was an emergency at work and I couldn't get away. I know how important today was to you and I hope everything went okay. Sorry again. I know I let you down. Xx

I'm still staring at the message when someone knocks my shoulder, sending my phone scuttling across the floor.

'Sorry.' A dark-haired woman ducks down to retrieve it. Our eyes meet as she stands back up but she doesn't say a word. Instead she holds out her hand, my phone balancing on her palm.

I drop it into my bag, not taking my eyes from hers.

The make-up under Dani's eyes is smudged and streaky and the end of her nose is swollen and red. She's looking at me the same way she did on the street, straight through me, to somewhere far, far away. There's no emotion in her eyes. She's a doll on a toyshop shelf, staring but not seeing, solid on the outside but hollow inside.

'It was all for nothing.' The words come out on a whisper, then she blinks and seems to see me again. 'You got it wrong, by the way. I didn't hurt your friend.'

'So, who did? Who took the stuff?'

'Stuff?'

'The evidence that Dominic paid you for your testimony. Someone took it from Smithy. If it wasn't you, who was it?'

'I don't know.' There's no fight in her dulled eyes, no tension in her body, no fight in her voice. She's telling the truth. She doesn't know and she doesn't care.

'Think! It can't have been Dominic because he doesn't know where Smithy lives. And she wouldn't have let him in.' A porter, pushing an empty wheelchair down the corridor, glances our way. I'm talking too loudly but I'm too desperate to care.

'Was it Ian? Did Nancy tell him about the plan? Was it him?' Deep in my bag my phone starts to ring but I ignore it.

'I don't know who you're talking about.'

She's so robotic, so devoid of emotion, I want to shake her. 'Dani, listen to me. Dominic is taking my daughter to Dubai tomorrow afternoon and he's never going to bring her back. Do you understand? I'll probably never see her again. If you admit that you lied in court you can still put this right. Please. It's not too late.'

'I don't know what you're talking about, Liv, and I really don't care.'

A cloud of despair engulfs me as she steps around me and walks away. There's nothing I can do now – legally or illegally – to stop Dom and Grace from getting on that plane. *You could run away*, a little voice calls from the back of my head. *You could take Grace and just go.* But where? Where could I go that I wouldn't be found?

I dig around in my bag for my phone, hoping for a miracle.

THE GUILTY COUPLE

An unknown number has rung me and there's a voicemail icon on the screen.

'Hello?' a voice says as I listen to the message – a voice I haven't heard for years.

Then the call cuts off.

'To listen to the message again press one,' says the pre-recorded message.

I press one, listening to the sound of Jack's voice in my ear, then I press one again and again and again.

Chapter 48

DOMINIC

Dominic wrenches open his wardrobe door and grabs the first suit he sees. He chucks it onto the bed then yanks at the bottom drawer of his chest of drawers and takes out a packet of shirts. He throws that onto the bed too, before adding underwear, socks, T-shirts, jeans and swimming trunks. He works his way around the room, eyeing each of his possessions, weighing up their usefulness. It's going to come as a shock to his parents to discover quite how much he's left behind. As far as they're concerned he's bought a beautiful but overpriced house in Clapham Common. If he told them he's actually moving to Dubai it would invite too many questions, questions he's only prepared to answer once he's safe and sound in Jumeirah. The other reason he hasn't told them what's really going on is because they might let something slip while his ex-wife is in earshot.

It was his idea that Esther should sit in on Olivia's last supervised visit with Grace. Although his mother raised her eyebrows at his suggestion that she record their meeting, she

248

did as he asked. He listened to the entire conversation but the only thing that made his ears prick up was Olivia's announcement that she was going to meet up with Lee. Then there was a load of crap about spa days and nail appointments with Grace. If Liv thought she had a future with their daughter she certainly didn't know about his plans.

Now, he grabs a bottle of aftershave, a hairbrush and some gel then moves into the en-suite where he picks up his toothbrush and toothpaste. He puts them back down again. He still needs to clean his teeth twice – tonight and tomorrow morning.

'Grace!' Still carrying his toiletries he walks across the landing and knocks on his daughter's door. 'Grace, are you packing?'

When there's no reply he turns the handle.

'Get out!' The door slams in his face. He takes a step back, startled.

'Grace?' He turns the handle again but his daughter's put the full force of her weight behind the door. 'Grace.' He adopts a softer tone and drops his toiletries onto the carpet. 'Please can we talk about this instead of shouting and slamming doors?'

'No!'

'If you won't talk to me how am I supposed to help?'

'I don't want your help. You're a liar.'

Dominic blows out his cheeks in an exasperated sigh. Can't one thing go right for him? Just one?

'What have I lied about, love?'

'Dubai,' she screams the word. 'It's not a holiday, is it? We're never going to come back.'

He stares at the white, painted wood of the door, stunned into silence. How the hell has she found out about that?

'Whoever told you that . . .' he says, fighting to keep his

voice calm and controlled '. . . must be confused because it's not true. It's just a lovely holiday, with shopping malls, water parks and aquariums. You'll love it.'

'No I won't because I'm not going.'

'Grace, just open the door please.'

'I want to live with Mum!'

'That's not going to happen.'

'I'll run away then.'

'No you bloody won't.' Dominic pushes at the door. Grace pushes back but he's almost twice the weight she is and one hefty shove is enough for the door to swing open.

'Get out of my room,' she screams up at him, hands clenched into fists at her sides, her blue eyes shining with angry tears.

Dominic steps around her and walks to the window. He pulls it shut then turns the key and slips it into his pocket.

'What are you doing?' Grace shoves past him to get a closer look. She stares at him in horror then turns and runs for the door.

'If you try and run away you won't get very far!' Dominic calls after her. 'Every door in the house is locked and I unplugged the landline. And don't even think about breaking a window because they're all double-glazed. You're coming with me tomorrow whether you like it or not.'

'I won't get on the plane. I'll scream and say you're abducting me and the police will stop you.'

He stares down at his daughter, imagining her screaming and shouting and drawing attention to them when that's the last thing he needs. 'Listen to me very carefully.' He lowers his voice and Grace stiffens, sensing the change in tone. 'We are going on holiday tomorrow and we'll be coming back in two weeks' time. If you behave yourself in the airport tomorrow I'll speak to the courts when we return to the UK and I'll request that you live with your mother every other week.'

'I don't believe—'

He raises a finger, silencing his daughter. 'However. If you cause a fuss at any point – in the airport or on the plane – I will ring my lawyer and tell him that your mother broke into this house while I was at work.'

'What?'

'Dani, my personal trainer, saw her breaking in and she took a photo. She's a police officer as well, by the way. I asked her not to report your mother because, believe it or not, I don't want her to go back to prison. I know how important it is that you get to know each other again.'

'Did you really do that?' His daughter's expression has softened and she looks like a little girl again, not a raging pre-teen.

'Yes, I did.'

'Mum said you're going to take me to Dubai and never bring me back.'

'That's because your mother is a very fearful person.' He reaches for his daughter's hand. 'She was in prison for a long time and she's scared she'll lose you again. She's not allowed to talk to me so she hasn't been able to ask me about our lovely holiday. Why don't I send her a message now, and let her know everything's going to be okay?'

Grace's chin bobs up and down as she nods enthusiastically, all traces of anger and mistrust gone.

'There we go then. All sorted.' He lets go of her hand and glances around the untidy room then frowns as he spots something nestling amongst the folds of the duvet.

It seems he's not the only one keeping secrets – his daughter is too.

Chapter 49

OLIVIA

I stumble, rather than walk, through Ayesha's front door, head straight for the sofa and check my phone, just as I've done a dozen times since I left the hospital, but there are no missed calls from Smithy's surgeon. She'll still be in surgery now, completely oblivious to what's going on. I pluck her book – *The Right Way to Do Wrong* by Harry Houdini – from the pile of my belongings on the floor and hug it to my chest. It's the book Smithy gave me on the day I was released from prison. It's her bible and her talisman. I wish there was something within the pages that I could use to rewind time, so I could have taken the evidence with me instead of giving it to her. None of this would have happened. She wouldn't be lying on a surgeon's table, fighting for her life.

Behind me, on the kitchen counter, are two glasses and an uncorked bottle of wine. I heave myself out of the chair, pour myself a large glass and drink half of it in one gulp. Smithy's surgeon isn't the only who hasn't contacted me. Jack hasn't tried to ring me again and Grace still hasn't replied to the text I sent before I got on the tube.

My new plan, the only plan left, is for her to run away with me. I texted her after I left the hospital to tell her the truth about her so-called holiday to Dubai, and that her father's been lying to her all along. I've told her I'll get a taxi to the house at 5 a.m. tomorrow and that she should sneak out to meet me without waking her dad. I don't know where we'll go once the taxi takes us to King's Cross, or how I'll support us, but she's not stepping foot on that plane. If the police track us down, I'll end up in prison so we'll have to keep moving around every few months but I'll do whatever it takes to keep her in my life.

'Liv!' Ayesha calls from the back of the flat. 'Is that you?'

'Yep!'

'I'm in the bathroom. Help yourself to wine. I'll be out in a bit.'

I raise the glass to my mouth again and I'm just about to take another sip when the fresh citrussy scent of Ayesha's bath oil wafts into the room. She strolls into the kitchen in a shower cap and a fluffy white dressing gown, takes one look at me and her face falls.

'Liv! What's happened? Did I screw everything up? I'm so sorry I didn't ring Dom or turn up to meet you. I had to—'

'It's okay.' I push a glass of wine across the counter towards her. 'It's not that. It's Smithy. Someone attacked her and she's in the hospital. The doctor said she's suffering from an abdominal haemorrhage and bleeding to the brain. They think she was pushed down the stairs of her flat and then kicked, repeatedly, in the stomach.'

'Oh my god, Liv.' Ayesha throws her arms around me and hugs me tightly then pulls away to look at my face. 'Is she going to be okay?'

'I don't know. The doctor said they'd do their best, which didn't exactly reassure me. She's gone into surgery. I won't find out how it went until tomorrow.'

'She'll get through it. She's a fighter.'

'Yeah.' I nod but I'm still gripped by the fear that I'll never see Smithy again.

'Who attacked her?' Ayesha asks. 'Are the police investigating?'

She listens intently, perched on the edge of the sofa, her wine untouched, as I tell her everything – about Nancy and Lee being thrown out of The Radcliffe Building, about the security guard that nearly rumbled me as I tried to get through the gates, and the fire alarm I had to set off in order to get into Dominic's office. I skip the part about the restaurant. Instead I tell her about Dani, the fight in the street, the police officer, the ambulance and everything the doctor told me in the visitors' room. By the time I reach the part about meeting Dani in the hospital corridor and the voicemail Jack left, she looks completely overwhelmed.

'Wait, what? Jack rang you?'

'Yeah. Listen.' I play her the voicemail on speakerphone.

'That's it?' she says as it finishes. 'Just hello? It could be anyone. It could be Dom. It could even be Lee.'

'It's not. I've listened to it dozens of times and it's definitely him. I'd know his voice anywhere. I've heard him say hello a hundred times.'

'Did you ring him back?'

I laugh, hollowly. 'Almost as many times as I listened to the message. He didn't pick up once.'

Ayesha sits back on the sofa and takes a sip of the wine. Her eyes drift to the window and she sighs softly. She can't make sense of this any more than I can.

'Do you think—' she stops herself.

'What?'

'No, you won't like it.'

'Just say it. Please.'

Her gaze flicks back towards me. 'Do you think Jack might have anything to do with this?'

'In what way?'

'I don't know. Don't you think the timing's a bit odd? That he ignores the email you sent asking him to meet up but when the evidence gets stolen and Smithy gets attacked he suddenly gets in touch.'

'You think he attacked her?'

'No.' She frowns, deep in thought. 'No, that wouldn't make sense because how would he know where she lived? And even if he did, why would he need to steal the evidence? It exonerates both of you and he wouldn't have to hide anymore. Unless . . .'

'What?'

'Unless he and Dom framed you. They know each other. Didn't his sister tell you they went to prison together?'

'Yes, for defrauding an old man. I've considered that, that they were in it together, but there's nothing either of them would have gained for framing me, not financially at least.'

'Maybe they gained something else?'

'Like what?'

She shakes her head. 'I don't know. I feel like there's a piece of the puzzle we haven't found yet.'

'Well,' I look at my watch and sigh. 'We've got less than sixteen hours to find it.'

We lapse into silence. It's dark outside, or as dark as London can get. Sirens wail in the distance and the rumble of a pounding bassline drifts through the ceiling.

'I don't think he did it,' I say. 'I don't think Jack fitted me up.'

Ayesha snorts in amusement.

'What?' I ask. 'What did I say?'

'Fitted me up.' She picks up my empty glass. 'That's not a phrase you would have used back in the day.'

'That's because I hadn't been fitted up then.'

I know what she means though. The last five years have changed me. I'm not the woman I was. I thought I could be. I thought I'd get out of prison, prove my innocence and everything would go back to normal. But even if I had the contents of Dominic's safe in my hands right now, there's no way I could rewind time and slip back into my old life. Too much has changed. I've changed.

'So what's the plan then?' Ayesha asks from the counter, topping up our glasses with the last of the wine.

I shift in my seat. This is a conversation I've been dreading.

'What's up?' She hands me a glass. 'Why are you looking at me like that?'

'Because I need to borrow some money.'

'What for?' She sits down and gathers a cushion to her chest.

'To go away with Grace. We're going to King's Cross, early tomorrow morning, and we're going to get on a train. I don't know where but I'll work it out. I can afford train tickets and maybe a month's rent but I'll need a deposit too and I haven't got enough. If you could help me out I'll pay you back as soon as I get a job.'

'Of course, I'd do anything to help you Liv, but . . . running away? There's got to be an alternative.'

'Then tell me because I've run out of options.'

'How about if—'

She's interrupted by my phone, pinging with a message. We share a look, both thinking the same thing. But the message isn't from Jack, it's from Grace.

256

Hi Mum. Guess what? I'm not going anywhere with you. I'm off to Dubai with Dad tomorrow and I CAN'T WAIT. I hated spending time with you but I had to do it to spy on you for Dad. How could I ever love someone who tried to have him killed? Ha ha. Turns out I am a liar after all.

I gasp so loudly that Ayesha leans over me to read the message. She clamps a hand over her mouth and looks up at me, disbelief clouding her eyes.

'I . . .' she shakes her head lightly. 'Liv, I don't know what to say.'

I don't bother with a text reply. I hit call, straight away, not caring that I told Grace we should never talk on the phone in case she's overheard. She doesn't pick up and the call goes to voicemail. I try again, and again, and again. With each call she fails to answer my panic increases. Why won't she pick up? The fifth time I call I leave a message:

'Grace, it's Mum. Please call me back.'

I send her a WhatsApp message, telling her to pick up the next time I call. Two ticks appear beside what I've written but when I ring again she doesn't answer.

'Do you believe her?' Ayesha asks. 'Do you really think she wants to go away with her dad?'

'No. I think he made her write that,' I say but I'm not as convinced as I sound. How well do I really know my daughter? I've only seen her three times, face to face, since I was released. Could she have been gathering information for Dominic the whole time? Was everything she told me about the bullying a lie?

I push the thought away. I know Grace. She might be older now but she's never been cruel or manipulative and I can tell when she's upset and in pain. Dominic has to have found the replacement phone that I bought her. Those were his words in the text – carefully arranged to cause maximum pain.

'What are you going to do?' Ayesha asks.

I don't know what to tell her because I don't know myself. I've run out of options. The only way to stop him is to go over there anyway and do whatever it takes to help my daughter escape. If I don't I'll spend the rest of my life trying, and failing, to get her back to the UK.

'I'm going over there.' I jump to my feet and pull a hoodie on over my top. 'I'll ring a cab and I'll—'

'Liv, wait. Think about it. If Dominic did send that text then he'll be waiting for you to—'

'I'm going to call an Uber.'

'No, don't.' She grabs at my sleeve as I swipe through the apps on my phone. 'This is what he wants. If you turn up, he'll call the police and you'll be arrested for breaking the conditions of your licence. You can't go anywhere near him, or the house. Not now, and not at five a.m. tomorrow.'

'I'll find a way to grab Grace without him spotting me. I've still got the key. I could—'

'Liv, listen to me.' She snatches the phone from my hands. 'This is exactly what he wants you to do. If that message was from Dominic then he's read the text you sent to Grace. He knows your plan and he'll be waiting for you to turn up.'

I slump forward and rest my head in my hands. She's right, of course she is. Dominic sent that message to make me panic, to make me act without thinking. If I turn up at the house I may as well walk myself straight into a cell.

'I'm sorry,' Ayesha says softly, 'if there was anything I could do, I would.'

There's nothing she can do, nothing anyone can. My only option now is to go to the airport tomorrow. If I get there in time for check-in the place will be buzzing with people and if Dom tries to stop me from taking Grace – which he will – I'll make enough noise to alert security. Then I'll tell them that he's removing my daughter from the country illegally and I want them to call the police. If Grace says she doesn't want to go with him and Dominic can't produce return tickets then it's abduction and they'll *have* to stop him from getting on the plane. He'll probably be allowed to take her back home but at least she'll still be in the country – until Dominic makes his next move . . .

'What are you doing?' Ayesha asks as I sit back up and reach for my phone.

'Finding out what time the check-in desks open for their flight.'

'You're not going to buy a ticket, are you?'

It's an idea, but hopefully it won't come to that.

'No,' I tell her. 'I'm going to intercept them, tomorrow.'

As plans go it's risky – there's every chance Dominic will use my criminal record against me if the police get involved – but, with no other avenues left open to me, it's all I've got.

Chapter 50

DANI

Dani smashes her fists into the punchbag, one after the other. Bang, bang, bang, bang, bang. The sound reverberates around the empty gym.

'No, Casey! No! No! No!' Each anguished cry matches a pounding jab, a twisting cross. Her thoughts are white noise. Her vision is blurred. It is as though grief has set off a bomb within her. It exploded in her chest the moment she saw her sister's lifeless body and now it's everywhere – in her stomach, in her guts, in her throat, in her head. Grief has filled her like dark smoke and with each punch she throws she feels it swell within her, filling her lungs and twisting, snake-like, around her heart. Bang, bang, bang, bang. She can't get rid of it, no matter how many times the bag flinches beneath her fists or how loudly she screams.

'Why! Why, Casey? Why!'

Grief is under her skin now, crawling like ants. She wants to tear off her gloves and claw at her arms – if she scratches deeply enough the grief can escape – but she can't stop pounding the bag. If she does the gym will grow silent, the white noise in her head will quieten and she'll have to listen to thoughts that are circling her brain, grief's henchmen, waiting for their chance to join the assault. It's too late. They've already fired and now they're screaming at her: *You could have saved her, you should have taken the key after you locked her in her room, you should have searched for her when she escaped. You went after Smithy instead of saving your own sister. You took Dominic's money and destroyed your reputation. It was all for nothing. Casey's dead. You lied in court and destroyed another woman's life. You robbed a child of her mother. Casey's dead. It's all your fault, all your fault, all your fault.*

Dominic.

The ants stop crawling as rage displaces grief like a fiery backdraught that sweeps through her body.

Dominic.

She's going to make him pay for what he did and to hell with the consequences.

It's not her fault Casey's dead. It's his.

Chapter 51

OLIVIA

It's 6.30 a.m. and, other than a brief doze on the sofa between 3 and 4.30, I've barely slept. Smithy's surgeon rang me at around 1 a.m. Both operations had gone well, she said, and her condition was stable. The news was a bright light after Grace's text had plunged me into darkness and I burst into tears as the surgeon ended the call.

Watching Smithy's lifeless body being carried into the ambulance was one of the worst moments of my life. It was my fault she was unconscious and I was terrified she would die. What she did to me, betraying me to Dani, was nothing in comparison. She wouldn't have been attacked if she hadn't helped me and I owe her everything. Even if it takes me ten years, I'll scrimp and save to get her the money I promised her. I told her I'd help her turn her life around and I will.

After Ayesha went to bed I drained the dregs from both our wine glasses but I still couldn't settle. Sitting made me twitchy and the television irritated me. I considered going for a walk but it was dark and cold and I didn't know Wood Green well enough to feel safe. I paced the living room instead, walking back and forth over the same stretch of carpet like a caged tiger as I ran over everything that could possibly go wrong with my plan. What if my train to Heathrow was delayed? What if Dominic had changed the flight since Grace took a photo of the tickets? What if they'd already left? The thought made me breathless with panic, then I remembered the text – *I'm off to Dubai with Dad tomorrow* – and I breathed a little deeper. Dominic didn't know that Grace had shown me the flight times and I'd made her delete the photo from the Cloud once I'd memorised the details.

Another worrying thought hit me as I marched from the sofa to the window: why would Dominic type *I'm off to Dubai with Dad tomorrow* and give me the opportunity to look up the flights? He had to suspect that I'd do that and turn up? Or maybe Ayesha was right. He'd sent the text to panic me and make me slip up. My thoughts shuttled between the different possibilities until I was so exhausted that I slumped onto the sofa and fell asleep.

When my alarm woke me at 4.30 a.m. the urge to ring a taxi to Crouch End was unbearable. I was sure Dominic would have locked every window and door the moment he'd discovered my plan but what if Grace had read the text before he took her phone and she'd managed to leave? What if she ended up wandering the streets at 5 a.m., looking for me, afraid and alone? I couldn't ring her to tell her I wasn't coming because Dominic had taken her phone. I'd promised Ayesha I wouldn't go over there but with every minute that passed my chest grew tighter and my breathing shallower. At 4.34 a.m. I rang a taxi. I'd rather be sent to prison than let anything happen to Grace.

All the lights were out at 57 Oakfield Road as we drew

up outside. Dominic's car was parked in the driveway but the street was empty. I made the taxi driver circle around as I scanned every pavement and alleyway for any sign of my daughter but I couldn't see her anywhere. At 5.40 I told him to bring me back here. Back to Plan B, intercept them at check-in and cause a scene. If they hadn't already left.

Now, with a cup of hot coffee in my hands, I hear cupboards opening and closing in the bathroom, and the buzz of an electric toothbrush as Ayesha gets ready for work. The emergency that kept her from meeting me for lunch yesterday turned out to be a complaint from a member of staff against one of her male colleagues. The woman alleged that he sexually assaulted her in a lift and, as head of department, Ayesha has to go in for another meeting today. I'll be going to the airport alone, unless I can convince Nancy or Lee to come with me. I should probably text them now. My phone buzzes as I reach for it, making me jump.

It's a message from Jack:

I know where the evidence is that Dominic used to frame you.

My hands shake as I tap at the screen: CALL ME NOW.

The bathroom door opens, releasing a sweet, fruity scent that fills the whole flat. A second later Ayesha's bedroom door clicks shut.

I can't. Jack's reply flashes up on the screen. Too dangerous.

But you tried to call me yesterday?

I know, and I nearly gave away my location.

Another message arrives as I'm typing.

I will explain everything when I see you. I promise. Can you get Dom's key to the lock-up?

Dominic's motorbike lock-up? Is that where Jack's been hiding? Or is Dominic keeping him prisoner? Is that why Jack needs the keys, to get out? But why message me now?

Why not ask for help the first time he emailed? And, as Ayesha said, why email and then suddenly phone? Something's not adding up.

I don't reply immediately, instead I sort through what I know:

- Dom, Jack and Ian were friends at university but pretended not to know each other when I began my affair with Jack.
- Dom changed his name from Matt Platt to Dominic Sutherland after they were imprisoned while Jack went on to commit more crimes.
- Dom and Dani framed me and Jack.
- Jack went missing for over five years, only getting in contact when I came out of prison, and he switched from email to phone, almost at random.
- Someone, who wasn't Dani, took the evidence from Smithy and pushed her down the stairs. And now Jack knows where that evidence is. The only way he could know that is if he took it, or he knows who did. Could a third person be involved in all of this? Someone I'm not aware of. Someone who—

An image flashes up in my mind, then another, and another and I'm fighting to catch my breath again; only this time it's not panic that's making me light-headed. It's shock. I slip off the sofa and sort through my possessions. I discard clothes and toiletries and make-up, tossing them behind me in my desperation to find the lanyard and keys. Smithy picked them up when we were planning the heist but they're not here now. She can't have taken them with her because I took them off her and put them on the coffee table.

I search through my things again, tipping out my make-up

and toiletry bags and shaking out each piece of clothing. And then I remember. When everyone left I put the lanyard in my pocket and I was wearing this hoodie. There's nothing in the first pocket I try but my fingers close around ribbon and metal in the second and I slump against the arm of the sofa with the keys in my hand.

When we stole them from Rosa I explained to Smithy that one key was for the front door, the one was for the back door and the third one was probably for the shed. I was so hyped up that it didn't strike me as odd that Rosa would have a full set of keys. When she worked for me she only had a key to the front door; there was no need for her to have a key to anything else. Dominic always put a bit of black tape on the back door key to distinguish it from the front door key.

This is his lanyard, they're his spare keys.

He must have changed the locks after I was arrested and forgotten to get a key cut for Rosa. And, unless he's bought a padlock in the last five years, I'm pretty sure the smallest key is for his lock-up, not our tumbledown, rotting shed.

With my phone to my ear I walk out of the living room and into the small hallway that leads to the bathroom and Ayesha's bedroom. I'm ringing Jack's number and he's not picking up. When I reach the bedroom I lower the phone and listen carefully. When I put it back to my ear it's clicked through to an automated voicemail.

I end the call and tap out a text as I make my way back to the living room. Sorry. I know you said not to ring. I just wanted to hear your voice. I've got so many questions I don't know where to start.

And I'll answer them, comes the reply. I promise you. Can you meet me at the lock-up with the keys?

I need proof it's you, I type back.

I thought I'd already done that?

One more question. I pause, searching for the right one. What's the most stupid thing I've ever done whilst drunk?

There's a lot to pick from!

The worst thing. Something that makes me cringe every time I think about it. Something to do with my first proper boyfriend.

There's a pause, then. When you went for a meal with his parents, you drank too much and puked over his mum in the cab.

Normally that response would make me laugh or cringe with embarrassment. Instead an icy sensation passes over me – a single sentence has hollowed out my heart. I glance at my watch: 6.50 a.m. I've got about six hours until I need to be at the airport. I've still got plenty of time. I know if I ask Ayesha for advice she'll tell me not to meet Jack but it's the only way I'm ever going to get answers. There have been too many secrets, and too many lies.

I create a WhatsApp group chat with Lee and Nancy and send them both the same message:

Jack's been in touch. He claims to know where the evidence is and wants me to meet him. Would one or both of you come with me please? I need to go as soon as possible. I know it's early but I really, really need your help.

Nancy looks simultaneously bleary-eyed and alert as I slip into the passenger side seat of her car. Her red hair is pulled into a ponytail, she's wearing a sweatshirt over her pyjamas and there isn't a scrap of make-up on her face. My text woke her up but she rang me immediately, unlike Lee who still hasn't replied.

'Are you all right?' she asks as I pull on my seatbelt.

'Not really.'

'Have you called the police?'

'To say what?'

'That you know where Jack is. There's an arrest warrant out in his name, isn't there?'

I sigh, wishing she'd just start the engine so we can get this over and done with. The sun's coming up now, streaking the sky between the buildings with scarlet and gold light.

'He said not to get the police involved or he'd run.'

'Okay . . .' she considers what I've just said. 'But if he does run you could still search the lock-up, couldn't you? You've got the key.'

'You're assuming there's evidence in there.'

She makes a little 'ooh' of surprise but she doesn't push it. She can tell I'm not in the mood. 'He's not going to be . . . dangerous, is he?'

I turn to look at her. 'Your guess is as good as mine. We don't have to do this if you don't want to.'

'I do.' She meets my eye. 'I definitely do.'

'Okay then, let's go.'

As we drive out of Wood Green along Great Cambridge Road I stare out through the window, seeing, but not registering, the people strolling down the streets, stepping onto buses and scurrying into tube stations. All around me life is continuing as normal while mine is anything but. Six years ago Nancy and I would have been sitting side by side in this car, chatting excitedly as we headed down to Brighton for a girlie weekend, or to a spa to pamper ourselves. We might even be doing something as mundane as going to Ikea in Croydon to buy our own bodyweight in candles or plants, or heading off to some random address to pick up something bizarre and useless that one of us had drunk-ordered from eBay after a particularly boozy night out. Now we're driving to my ex-husband's lock-up in Enfield so I can get answers to the questions that have been plaguing me for so long. I'm not hopeful, I know this is a goose chase to divert me from discovering the truth, but what the architect of this game doesn't realise is that I'm one step ahead of them – I know who they are.

'I think this is it,' Nancy says twenty-six minutes later as Google Maps tells us we're approaching our destination. We're on the edge of an industrial estate, on a dead-end street made up of a line of garages. I've been here only once before and the place was deserted, I didn't see a single person the whole time we were here. From the dirty, rusty, cobwebbed state of some of the doors it looks like no one's been here since. I came because I'd inherited a few antique pieces of furniture after my grandmother died and Dominic deigned to let me keep them in his lock-up. The nicer pieces I incorporated into our home and the rest I planned to sell on eBay. I never did get round to it. The chances are they're still in the lock-up with Dominic's motorbike and god knows how many spiders and mice.

Nancy glances across at me as I take off my seatbelt. 'Are you okay? You're really quiet.'

'I've got a lot on my mind.'

I touch her shoulder as she moves to open her door. 'Don't get out yet. We need to wait for Jack.'

'Right, yeah.' She settles back in her seat. 'Has he sent any more messages while I was driving?'

I don't even have to check my phone to answer her. I've had it in my hands the whole time. 'No. None.'

The garages form a cul-de-sac. From where we're parked at one end we can see nine garages to our left, each with a corrugated roof in varying stages of decay. After the block of garages there's a fence protecting an electricity pylon, then another nine garages. To our right is a narrow pedestrian alleyway then eleven garages. There's a gap after the block of eleven, where we drove in, then another five garages. Anyone arriving on foot would probably enter via the alleyway and anyone driving would take the road further down. Other than jumping a couple of fences there's no other way in or out and no houses that overlook this small stretch of road.

Five minutes pass. Dominic's lock-up is the second from the top, to my left. My gaze flicks from its dirty white door to the alleyway, to the gap between the garages where we drove in.

Ten minutes pass. I reach into my pocket for the key and rub my thumb over the cool metal. I so hope that I'm wrong.

Fifteen minutes pass. No sign of Jack or anyone else. The cul-de-sac is as silent as it was when we drove in. Nancy shifts in her seat. She hasn't spoken in at least ten minutes but I can feel the anxiety radiating off her. She's never been very good at staying still, or staying quiet.

'Okay.' I open the passenger side door. 'Let's go and see what's in there.'

Nancy doesn't say a word. She just gets out of the car.

A bead of sweat rolls down my back as I insert the key into the lock but my hand is steady and the key slides in first time. As I twist the handle and yank open the door Nancy inhales sharply but there's nothing inside the garage I wasn't expecting to see. Dom's motorbike takes pride of place in the centre and there's a heavy metal shelving unit to the right. Boxes and tools are stacked up on its shelves, alongside the wind-up torch I bought Dominic as a stocking filler one year. He couldn't have looked less impressed. Against the back wall, bound in bubble wrap, is the antique furniture I inherited: a trio of 1950s stacking tables, a cupboard and drawers in pale green and a 1930s glazed bookcase, made of oak. Something catches my eye in the far left corner of the garage – something large and white and ugly – incongruous against the delicate shapes of my grandmother's furniture. I move past the motorbike and walk towards it, dust and damp catching in the back of my throat. A scratchy metallic sound cuts through the silence. The garage door is being pulled shut.

'Nancy?' She's already pulled the door halfway down by the time I turn round. 'What are you doing?'

She glances at me then tugs the door all the way down, shutting us both inside. I blink, too disorientated to move, as my eyes adapt to the gloom. The only source of light is a broken corner of the roof.

Nancy takes a step towards me, her hand outstretched. 'Give me the keys, Liv.'

'So you can lock me in?' A laugh I wasn't expecting punctuates my question. When I slid into her car forty minutes ago I was primed for a confrontation but, now it's happening, I can't quite believe that it's real. This feels like a wind-up, like everyone but me is in on the joke.

The emails, the phone call, the texts. Jack didn't wait five years to get in touch. He didn't contact me at all. It was Nancy, it was all Nancy, and it took me far too long to figure it out.

There were five people sitting around the table in Ayesha's living room when we discussed stealing the contents of Dominic's safe: me, Smithy, Ayesha, Nancy and Lee. All five of them saw the keys (including the key to the lock-up) that were attached to the lanyard when Smithy chucked them onto the table, but only four people were in the room when I told Ayesha where Smithy lives; Lee had excused himself to go to the loo.

Ayesha was on to something when she expressed suspicion

271

that Jack had switched from emailing to calling me. He'd said it wasn't safe to call because his phone could be traced but he changed his mind yesterday. Why risk being arrested just to say hello?

There were two phones in Dominic's safe. One belonged to Grace, the other one wouldn't turn on. It was an iPhone: white, slightly battered with no distinguishing features. It could have belonged to anyone.

But what if it belonged to Jack?

The phone call threw me. It was his voice, I was certain of that. I also knew, from overhearing lengthy conversations between inmates who'd been convicted of romance fraud, how easy it is to steal someone's identity and use their voice notes and videos to catfish someone else. If I'd answered that phone call, instead of letting it go to voicemail, there wouldn't have been a conversation, it would have cut off the moment Jack said hello.

That thought didn't occur to me then because I was still in shock about Smithy's assault and running into Dani. I wasn't thinking clearly. Since I got out of prison I haven't been thinking clearly at all – emotion, not logic, has fuelled every decision that I've made. When I went to Sonia's house I was so caught up in everything she told me that I didn't take the time to think about the best way to verify that it was really Jack behind the emails. I chose the holiday location question off the top of my head. But Jack wasn't the only person who knew the answer to that question – Ayesha and Nancy knew it too. I'd told them both that the first thing Jack and I were going to do when my divorce was finalised was book a holiday to Iceland to see the Northern Lights.

Whoever sent me the emails, pretending to be Jack, had also stolen his phone.

272

Nancy or Ayesha? Ayesha or Nancy? One of them had followed Smithy back to her flat, stolen the evidence and pushed her down the stairs. I didn't want to believe it was either of them but I had to know for sure. When I tried to ring 'Jack' from Ayesha's apartment this morning I listened at her bedroom door for the sound of a mobile ringing. I didn't hear anything. Either she'd turned the phone to silent or she had nothing to do with it. I had to check.

Only one person knew the answer to the question I'd texted to 'Jack' about my most embarrassing drunken incident. I really did throw up on my first boyfriend's mother in a cab, an experience so humiliating I've always kept it to myself. Dominic didn't know about it. Nor did Lee, Ayesha or Jack. But I told Nancy, because I told her everything. She was the only person I knew who wouldn't judge me or bring it up in conversation to get a laugh at my expense.

'Give me the keys, Liv.' She takes another step closer. In the half-light of the garage her face is all dips and shadows and her hair is stripped of its red. It looks dark, the same colour it was before I was arrested, the same colour as the strand I found twirled around the pillow on my side of the marital bed.

'How long have you been sleeping with Dominic?' It's a guess, the only reason for her actions that makes sense, but, from the expression on her face, I know I'm right.

A slow smirk twists her lips. 'Long enough.'

It hurts more than I thought it would, the stab of betrayal, aimed straight for my heart.

'Is that why you're doing this, for him?'

'No. It's for both of us.'

I can't believe we're having this conversation, that the person standing in front of me, smirking and gloating and looking at me like I'm shit, is the same person I'd have trusted with my life.

'Did you know?' I ask her. 'That he was going to frame me?'

She laughs softly. 'Of course I did.'

If her first confession was a stab to my heart, this one is a blow to my guts.

I stare at her, still reeling. 'But I thought. I thought Dani—'

'She played her part.' Nancy's demeanour changes, as though a cold wind has swept through her. It's Dani, the mention of her name.

'You didn't know, did you? That he was sleeping with you both? You only found out the other night when I mentioned it. That's why you gasped. And you're still doing this? When Dominic lied to you! When he was shagging someone else?'

Anger spikes through me and I head for the door. Screw the evidence and proving my innocence. Screw what happens to her, and to Dom, all that matters is getting my daughter back.

'Give me the key.' Nancy sidesteps me, blocking my path.

'Fuck you.' I shove both palms against her chest and she stumbles backwards but she doesn't fall. She regains her balance and charges at me, throwing me against one of the garage's cold brick walls. My hands take the brunt of the impact but before I can take a breath she's on me again, yanking at the lanyard strap that's poking out of my pocket. I grab her wrist but her other hand is free and her fist connects with my jaw. It stings but she's too close for the punch to wield any power and when she swings for me again I raise my arm to block her and bring up my knee. She jumps backwards before it makes contact and swipes at the lanyard strap. I knock her hand away and spring away from the wall. We face off again, both breathing heavily: Nancy with her back to the door and me shoving the lanyard strap deep into my pocket.

'You don't have to do this, Nancy.'

Her dry laughter echoes off the walls. 'Don't I?'

'Why didn't you just tell me you were sleeping with Dom? Why do all of this?'

'There's a lot you don't know.'

'So tell me! We can still put this right. You can have Dom but he's not having Grace.'

'She'll be fine. Kids are resilient.'

'She's my daughter, Nancy!'

Her expression hardens. 'She's his daughter too and if she doesn't come to Dubai with us then he won't go.'

'So stay here! Divorce Ian and move into the fucking house. Just let me have Grace.'

'Stay in his parents' house? Scrimping and saving when I could have ten million pounds?' She laughs. 'I've waited a long, long time to become rich, Olivia, and I've given Dominic everything you couldn't – love, support, money and a new start in life. Once we set foot in Dubai we'll just disappear. Me, Dom and Grace.'

I don't know what she's talking about – ten million pounds – but she's not taking my daughter with her.

'They'll find you,' I say. 'They'll bring you back. You'll go to prison for a very long time.'

'Won't happen. Why do you think so many criminals go to Dubai to disappear?'

I stare at her, waiting for the Nancy I knew and loved to tell me that this is some horrible game, that she's been black-mailed into doing this, or that Dom manipulated her, like he manipulated me, but she's still staring at me with the same cold eyes that took my breath away when we first walked in.

'Screw this, Nancy. I'm going to get my daughter.'

I head for the door again, keeping an eye on her, bracing myself for another fight, but she doesn't so much as blink. She's frozen to the spot, watching me but not really seeing me. Did I get through to her? Has she realised how insane she's acting? I crouch down by the closed metal door and reach for the catch. Out of the corner of my eye I see the blurred stripes of Nancy's pyjama bottoms and the straight, hard line of the crowbar in her hands. I lift a hand to defend myself but I'm too slow and the crowbar connects with the back of my head. My nose crunches against the garage door and Nancy hits me again, across my right shoulder, and I drop onto the cold, concrete floor. I swim in and out of consciousness as the door opens, flooding the small space with light, then Nancy is beside me again, her face close to mine.

'I hope you and Jack are happy together,' she breathes. Then the garage door closes and the key turns in the lock.

My head throbs and my shoulder aches as I gingerly ease myself up into a sitting position. The back of my head is wet and when I touch it my hand is slick with blood. The sensation of it between my fingers, thick and viscous and warm, makes me dry-heave and I drag my hand across the floor – leaving a deep red stripe against the pale grey concrete. As the nausea fades, I grip the door handle, knowing it will be locked.

It doesn't turn.

The only way to get out is through the door but with the lock on the other side only brute force will work. What I need is some kind of industrial saw that can cut through metal but any saws in this garage would probably struggle to cut wood. A crowbar might jimmy up the door, at least

276

enough for me to shout for help through the gap, but when I reach around it's not on the floor.

Slowly I get to my feet, resting my weight against the garage door until my head has stopped spinning and the black spots have disappeared from before my eyes. I search my pockets for my phone but it's gone. Nancy must have taken it before she left.

I pick my way around the garage until I reach the shelving unit and run my hands over the shelves, feeling for the torch I saw when I first came in. One of my hands slides over it and I fumble for the handle, praying that it works. A whirring sound fills the garage and a weak shaft of light illuminates the floor. I sweep the light around the garage as I step around the motorbike, still searching for the crowbar.

And then I find it, lying on a pile of oily rags beside the bike. Either Nancy was too stupid to assume I'd use it, or she thought I was dead. I wind the torch over and over again then rest it on the ground, angled towards the door. I jam the crowbar beneath the base, directly beneath the handle, and I lean my weight into it. Metal scrapes against metal and . . . nothing.

The door doesn't shift.

I try again, shifting the position of the crowbar but the door still doesn't move. I try a third time, moving it further away from the lock. The door creaks, but doesn't lift. Maybe Nancy wasn't stupid after all. What good is a crowbar against heavy steel? With it in one hand and the torch in the other I head towards the back corner of the garage where a thin chink of light has found a hole in the roof. The walls must be seven feet tall and the only way I can reach to the roof is to stand on something. I test the nest of tables with my hand, agitating them to see if they could hold my weight. There's no way, the legs are too delicate. They're already wobbling under the smallest amount of pressure. The shelving unit is bolted to the wall so that's no use. The cupboard is too tall to stand on and the glazed bookshelf is rickety. I consider wedging the nest of tables between two other pieces of furniture, or placing something beneath them. I sweep the torch over the garage, looking for something I can use, and my eyes rest on the large white object on the other side of the room. It's been partially covered with a tartan picnic blanket and there are barbells and weights piled on the top. Why would anyone keep a chest freezer in a garage with no plug points and no electricity? Unless . . .

My vision blurs and I fight to stay on my feet. The walls are closing in on me and I can't breathe.

'Help!' I smash the crowbar against the garage door. 'Help! Someone help! Please! Someone help!'

I hit it over and over and again, the small space ringing with each clang and clank of metal beating on metal, but no one comes and I sink to the floor.

I don't want to open the freezer but I drag myself back onto my feet, and cross the room. I work methodically, lifting the lightest items first – the weight plates and the dumbbells – and place them on the ground. By the time I get to the last, and heaviest weight, I'm sweating and breathing heavily. My hand shakes as I reach for the edge of the blanket and pull it to the floor.

I don't want to open the freezer.

I want Jack to be sitting on a beach in Spain, oblivious to the mayhem he's left behind. I want him to be hiding out in Sonia's attic, creeping out to play with the children when no one else is around. I want him to be curled up in a tent in the Lake District, listening to the sound of the rain.

I don't want to open the freezer.

I want to scream at Jack for abandoning me. I want to tell

278

him that he hurt me more than Dominic ever did. I want to pound my fists against his chest. I want him to tell me why. I want him to explain. I want him to gather me into his arms and tell me that he'll never leave me again.

I open the door to the freezer.

The smell hits me first.

Chapter 52

DOMINIC

Dominic glances around the study to see if there's anything he's missed. He's shredded every bank statement, every printout, every scrap piece of paper he could find and all that's left in his desk drawers are a handful of pens, some paperclips and some stationery. There's nothing incriminating in the bedroom or any other room of the house. The companies that provided Nancy with the house loans will have copies of his inflated valuations, which implicate him in the fraud, but no one will know a crime has been committed until she defaults on the mortgage payments and, by then, they'll both be long gone. Nancy's got balls, he'll give her that much. There aren't many women, many *people*, who'd have the guts to stroll into a bank, claim to be a South African heiress and demand four separate loans worth £10.5 million to buy four properties in London. She scares him sometimes, the way her mind works. He's never met anyone more manipulative or ruthless in his life and the sooner he gets his share of the cash and shakes her off the better.

He strolls out of his office and pauses at the bottom of the stairs, listening. From the noises coming from the first floor it sounds like Grace is smashing up her room. He locked her in there last night, after he read the message on her phone from Olivia. As his daughter pounded her bedroom door, alternately begging to be let out and calling him every name under the sun, he sent a message to his ex-wife, grinning as he laid it on thick. Olivia's reaction couldn't have been more frantic. Call after call, then text after text after text. After ten minutes he turned off the phone, and left it off all night, but he couldn't settle. He couldn't shake the feeling that Olivia would turn up, restraining order or not. He double-locked the front door, checked all the windows were still closed and sat in the living room with the lights off and the curtains open, watching the driveway. He dozed off at some point and woke in a panic. The house was too quiet and he couldn't hear a sound from behind Grace's bedroom door. He banged on it, terrified she'd done something stupid. Her expletive-laden scream convinced him she was perfectly fine.

Now, he walks from the hallway to the kitchen, retrieves the SIM from Grace's phone and cuts it in two. He drops it, and the phone, into the bin then he checks his watch and walks up the stairs to his daughter's room.

'I'm unlocking your door,' he says as he turns the key. 'Our lift will be here any minute to pick us up.'

He hasn't told her that Nancy will be going to Dubai with them because he doesn't want to answer her questions. Questions he'll have to deal with at some point, ideally once they're safely in the departure lounge. He's going to have to work out a way to repair his damaged relationship with her too, but he hasn't got the head space for that right now.

'I hope you've packed,' he says instead. Grace's screamed

281

response is unintelligible but, before Dominic can ask her to repeat what she said, there's a knock at the front door.

He hurries down the stairs, hoping that a) it is Nancy and not Olivia, Dani or the police, and b) that there hasn't been a terrible cock-up. His parents have put the house on the letting market, he's destroyed his professional reputation, his bank account has never looked so infirm and his daughter hates his guts. He needs this to happen. He needs the cash, and to escape.

'Nance.' He opens the door to an unusually dishevelled Nancy. Her hair is piled up on her head in a messy bun, she's make-up-free and she appears to be wearing her pyjama bottoms. 'What the hell?'

He ushers her in, his gaze darting from her oversized blue handbag to the black suitcase she's dragging behind her like a dead weight. Once she's in the hallway, with the front door shut behind her, she looks him up and down then glances at his suitcase, standing alone near the living room door, and the bag that contains his travel documents and wallet, wound around the handle.

'Where's Grace's case? Is she ready?'

'Yeah,' Dominic says absently. 'What happened to you? Where are your clothes?'

'Long story. Has Grace got a skirt or some trousers I could wear?'

'I don't know, you'll have to ask her.' He glances, again, at her suitcase. 'Why've you brought that in with you? Didn't you come in your car?'

'Yes, it's outside,' she smirks and taps the handle, 'but I'm not letting this out of my sight.'

He shakes his head, confused. Why borrow clothes from Grace when she's got her suitcase with her? Why not get changed and brush her hair before she left home? Even when they were sleeping together, which he's successfully managed to avoid for the last few weeks, Nancy never once looked anything other than utterly polished. He'd wake up to find her lying in bed next to him with a full face of make-up and hair so silky and smooth it had to have been brushed. She couldn't have been more different to Dani or, for that matter, Liv. Nancy's mask – make-up or otherwise – never slipped.

'What's happened?' he asks. 'Something's happened, hasn't it?'

Nancy passes a hand over her hair, suddenly aware of his scrutiny. 'I was just tying up a few loose ends.'

'Like what?'

'Like your ex-wife, although not literally tying her up.' She meets his gaze, her eyes steely. 'I wasn't going to risk a show-down at the airport.'

'What did you do to her?'

'I didn't *do* anything.' She turns her head in the direction of the stairs. 'Grace, have you got some trousers I could borrow please? Could you bring them down?'

'Nancy,' Dominic grips her wrist, his voice low. 'What did you do?'

'Trousers please, Grace! We need to go soon.' She yanks her arm away and hisses at him, 'Don't ever put your hands on me. Jack's been sending Olivia messages—'

'What?' Dom's blood runs cold. 'That's not possible.'

'They were from me, obviously. Someone had to stop her sniffing around.'

'What?' he says again, as he struggles to keep up. Nancy's been contacting Olivia, pretending to be Jack? What else has she been doing? She's completely out of control. 'How . . . since when?'

'Since she started making noises about finding him. I couldn't let her discover that he's dead.'

283

'But how could she? No one knows. No one but us.'

'She's not as stupid as you think. Plus, she's got the key to the lock-up. I saw it the other day and recognised the shape.'

'No, I've got . . .' Dom searches his pockets for his keys but Nancy interrupts him before he can find them.

'Your spare keys. You gave them to Rosa, remember? And then Olivia stole them.'

'Shit.' Dom presses a hand to the side of his face, it's damp with sweat. When Dani had told him about Olivia breaking into the house he got the locks changed, again, but he completely forgot about the key to the lock-up.

'Don't worry. I took care of it.' Nancy taps him, patronisingly, on the cheek. 'Now Jack's not the only one in the lock-up. Your ex-wife is too.'

Dominic looks towards the top of the stairs. Grace's door is still closed. 'Is she—'

'No. She was still breathing when I left but she can't get out and she can shout until she's hoarse and no one will hear her, not unless they happen to be visiting their own lock-up. Even if that happens, it'll take forever for them to get her out.'

'But what if she tells them what you've done? What if it's happening right now and she's told them to ring the police?' Dominic's hyperventilating and his mind is racing as he searches for an escape plan that won't end up with him spending the rest of his life in prison. 'What if they go to the airport? You should have—'

'Killed her?' Nancy tilts her head to one side and frowns at him. 'I'm not a complete monster, Dom. She was my best friend.'

Right, Dom thinks, but it was fine to sleep with her husband, hide the dead body of her lover and help to frame her. There's a very good reason why he's stayed on Nancy's good side. Not that he's had any other choice. If starting an affair with her was a mistake, then turning to her for help when he killed Jack was a life sentence. He'd effectively handcuffed his future to hers. The only control he had was the memory card he kept in his safe: a home CCTV recording of Nancy helping him load Jack's body into his car. If she threatened to expose what he'd done he'd take her to jail with him. But when she pushed Olivia's friend Kelly down the stairs and stole the phones and the SIM cards, she snatched back the last bit of power that he had.

Jack had turned up one evening when Grace was having a sleepover with a friend, Olivia was attending an art fair in Paris and Dom and Nancy were relaxing on the sofa with a bottle of red wine, having screwed for a good hour in Dom's marital bed. Jack had never been to the house before. He made first contact by ringing Dom at work. His voice sent shivers down Dominic's back, as though a ghost was saying hello on the phone, rather than a man he'd once classed as one of his very best friends.

'You owe me,' Jack told him. 'I've seen your house, your wife, your kid and your cushy office block. I've got nothing. I took beatings because of the shit you said when we were inside and it's about time I got compensation. Fifty grand should do it.'

Dom laughed and put the phone down. What kind of drugs was Jack on, thinking he could just ring him up, twenty-five years after they'd walked separately through the doors of Strangeways as enemies, and demand a ridiculous amount of money? Money, incidentally, that Dominic no longer had thanks to investments that had crashed and died.

Jack rang back and Dominic put the phone down again. And the five times after that. Then he took the phone off the hook. The next day he turned up at work to find Jack sitting in the foyer.

'Give me the money,' Jack said, sidling up to Dom before he could alert security, 'or I'll tell everyone who you really are and what you did. I hear you're trying to become a partner in this firm. How do you think the other partners will react when they find out who you really are?'

Dominic strode away without saying a word but his hand shook as he inserted his pass into the electronic gate. He'd worked hard to put what had happened in his early twenties behind him. It had taken some convincing to get his parents to accept his new name, and to hide any evidence of their real surname when he took Olivia to meet them, but they eventually accepted that he wanted to put what had happened behind him and start again, and agreed to support him. He wasn't going to let Jack Law destroy the life that he'd made, or the life he was going to have when he became a partner and he was earning significantly more. He wasn't going to pay Jack a penny – he couldn't afford to – but, after he left work, he went to Olivia's gallery and checked the company accounts, just in case it came to it. She didn't have fifty grand either.

For the next month or so there were no phone calls or unexpected visits from Jack, and Dominic breathed a little easier. Maybe Law had given up. Maybe he was chancing it with everyone he knew. And then Olivia told him she was leaving him. She was going to start a new life – her and Grace – with a man called Jack Law. It took every ounce of self-control Dominic had not to explode. For Jack to blackmail him was one thing, to sleep with his wife was another, but if that contemptuous bastard thought he was going to take his daughter as well then . . . well, the thought 'Over my dead body' flew through his mind. 'Over my dead body – or his.'

Dominic visited a family solicitor. He asked questions about his rights as a father, about whether a career criminal like Law could even have access to his child. Yes, came the answer. As long as he doesn't have convictions for offences against minors, yes he can.

'You'll probably get shared residency where Grace spends half her time with you and half her time with your ex-wife,' the solicitor told him.

The thought of Grace living under the same roof as Jack Law was more than Dominic could bear. He walked out of the solicitor's office and went straight to the nearest pub. He drank until his vision blurred and he fell onto a table on his way to the loo.

Three days after that, Jack turned up at his door. 'Fifty grand,' he said, 'and you'll never see me again.'

Nancy, who Dominic had been sleeping with for over eighteen months at that point, knew what was going on and pulled Dom to one side. 'You need to tell Ian. He can find that kind of money.'

Borrow fifty grand from Ian? Never. Dom would rather tell him he was sleeping with his wife than admit he was skint.

'Your parents then?' Nancy suggested.

Again. No. He'd shamed them enough. He was a thirty-nine-year-old man, not a troubled teen. This was his problem to sort, not theirs.

If he handed over the money he wouldn't be able to live with himself. And Law would only come back for more. No, there was only one solution to this problem, and that was to beat the shit out of the man so he never came back.

'Come in.' He stepped back from the door and ushered Jack into the hallway. 'We'll do this inside.'

Dominic landed the first blow the moment the front door

closed. Jack retaliated. He was strong and wiry but he was four inches shorter and lighter by several stone. Then there was the fact Dominic had been working out with Dani for almost a year. He could bench press 225 pounds.

Nancy watched silently from the sidelines as the two men fought, landing blow after blow after blow. They moved from the hallway to the living room, wrestling and punching, falling and getting up again. It felt to Dominic like it was never going to end, that the other man would never tire and give up, but then he landed an upper cut on Jack's jaw that sent him reeling backwards. His head connected with the metal corner of the wood burner and he lay still, blood pooling beneath his head, dripping off the fire surround and onto the rug.

Dom loomed over him, fists still clenched and raised, waiting for him to get back up, too buzzed on adrenaline to realise the severity of the situation. It had taken Nancy's 'Call an ambulance!' scream to bring him back into himself and he sped up the stairs to the bedroom to retrieve his mobile. It was on his bedside table, abandoned after he and Nancy had had sex.

His thumb hovered over the digits. There would be questions if Jack went to hospital, and a possible assault charge. Was he really so badly hurt? There was a part of Dominic that hoped Jack might still get up and limp out of his house and his life. He weighed up his options, standing by the bed with his phone in his hand, for what felt like forever. By the time he decided not to ring 999 and returned to the living room, Jack was dead.

Panic set in as he stared down at the body. Calling the police or an ambulance was no longer an option. He hadn't meant to kill Law but he'd be tried for manslaughter at least and he'd seen enough of prison to know he didn't ever want to return. He rushed around the house gathering bin bags and tape and the key to the lock-up as Nancy hovered beside the body, sliding her hands into the pockets of Jack's jeans. She'd been to Law's flat with Olivia, she confessed when Dominic asked her what she was doing, and she was looking for his key. They took two trips to the lock-up: one to move the body, the other to transport the freezer and then they visited Law's flat. They shoved his passport, laptop and a few other items into a bag to make it look like he'd fled in a hurry, then they dropped the bag into the Thames.

When Olivia returned from Paris a couple of days later Dominic answered her questions: why did they have a new freezer? (The old one had broken.) Where was the rug? (He'd spilled red wine on it and sent it to be dry cleaned.) It was almost too easy, and the plan's loop closed when he got Dani on board.

'Grace!' Dominic shouts up the stairs now. 'Come down with your suitcase, please. Don't make me come up there!'

He reaches for Nancy's suitcase so he can put it with his and grimaces as he lifts it. 'What the hell have you got in here?'

Nancy smiles. 'Half a million pounds.'

Startled, he puts the case back down. 'You're kidding.'

'No.' She shakes her head lightly. 'It's my insurance policy, in case they put a stop on the loans.'

'And you expect to get this onto a plane? When they X-ray all the cases?'

'The money's vacuum-packed and hidden inside some clothes and coffee – to mask the smell from sniffer dogs.'

'And you expect that to work?'

She shrugs. 'I don't see why not. I read about a woman who did something similar. The only reason she was stopped was because she took five cases and the customs official became suspicious. Who takes five cases on holiday? Stupid woman tried to smuggle nearly two million pounds.'

Dominic lays the suitcase flat on the ground and unzips it. 'And you think you'll get away with it?'

'I don't see why not. We'll look like a lovely blended family going on holiday to Dubai.'

'Without a return ticket!' He flips back the lid of the suitcase and lifts the carefully folded clothes. His jaw drops. Other than thirty or so perforated coffee pods scattered around, the rest of the case is filled with bundles of fifty-pound notes. He's never seen so much money in his life. He looks up at Nancy. 'How did you manage to withdraw so much?'

She waves a hand through the air. 'Does it really matter? Anyway, imagine the wedding dress I'll be able to buy with that little lot!'

Dominic suppresses a shudder. If she thinks he's marrying her she's delusional. He knew, from the very first time he met Nancy – when Ian introduced her to him and Olivia eighteen months after Helena died – that she was attracted to him. She'd be telling a funny story to Olivia but her eyes would rest on him. When he went to the bar she followed, her hand resting on his bare arm longer than was socially acceptable as she told him she hadn't expected Ian to have such an attractive friend. She was certainly beautiful, vivacious too, but he was still in love with Olivia, and loyal to Ian.

It had been a long time since Dominic had seen him so happy and there was no way he'd jeopardise a friendship that had endured for so long. Ian knew who he really was, and what he'd done, and he'd kept his mouth shut. That counted for a lot.

Later, when Dominic mentioned Nancy's flirtatiousness, Ian

laughed it off. 'Harmless fun,' he said. Dominic wasn't sure he agreed.

A year after that first meeting, at Ian and Nancy's wedding, a drunken Nancy begged a cigarette from Dominic and, hidden away from the other guests behind the marquee, told him she'd 'married the wrong man'.

He didn't tell Ian. It had always been just the two of them at uni, two 'bros' joined at the hip, drinking, laughing, a regular fixture in the student union bar. Then they'd met Jack. He was funny, charming, a risk-taker, like no one Dominic had ever met. He felt alive just being around the guy. Ian liked him too, for a while. He pulled away as Dominic and Jack grew closer. At the time Dom thought Ian was being antisocial, later he realised he was hurt. It took him eighteen months after his release from prison, and a lot of grovelling, to regain Ian's trust and respect.

Sleeping with Nancy was a mistake. She'd made a move on him when he felt like a failure. He was working out at the gym but he was also drinking and eating too much, which had given him a paunch. He and Liv were bickering and they hadn't slept together for months. Nancy made him feel alive, just like Jack had all those years earlier and, for the second time in Dominic's life, he blocked Ian from his mind.

'I think I should take half the money,' he says now.

'What?' Nancy looks horrified. 'No.'

'It'll be safer. If we split it the cash will be less noticeable in the X-ray machines.' He reaches into the case for a wad of fifties then yanks out his hand as the lid is slapped down on his wrist.

Nancy pushes her face close to his. 'That's . . . not . . . happening.' Anger flares in her eyes. 'I don't understand why still you don't trust me, Dominic. I have done nothing but support you. I haven't let you down or betrayed you once.

Who was there for you when you lost everything on the stock market and you were too scared to tell Olivia that you'd emptied your savings accounts? And what about when Jack blackmailed you? Who talked you down when he threatened to tell your CEO that Dominic Sutherland – upstanding chartered surveyor, desperate to become a partner – was actually Matt Platt, convicted fraudster and a congenital liar?' Her voice grows louder and shriller and her breath is hot on his face.

'Keep your voice down!' he hisses. 'Grace will hear you.'

He can't stand her screechy tone, the yellow crust of sleep in the inner corner of her eye or her taut lips pulled back from her teeth. He wants her to shut up, to vanish, to disappear in a puff of smoke, but Nancy keeps on talking, talking, talking.

'Oh, and who helped you hide his body?'

'Keep your fucking voice down.' Dom clamps a hand to her mouth. 'My daughter's upstairs.'

Incensed, Nancy grips his wrist and yanks his hand away. 'Trust, Dominic, appears to be something you are incapable of. I looked through the SIM cards you stashed in your safe. Was there a particular reason why you kept the CCTV footage of us moving the body?'

Dominic grits his teeth and says nothing. He can't, it's taking every ounce of self-control not to slam his fist into Nancy's pinched, vicious, snarling face. How dare she talk to him like he's a whipping boy? She's pulled his strings for long enough. But Nancy's not done talking yet.

'And when were you planning on telling me you were sleeping with that cop as well as me?' She jabs a finger into his chest. "*Olivia doesn't understand me, Nancy. I love you, Nancy. I want to make a life with you, Nancy. But we can't do it yet because of X, Y, Z.*" Did you feed her those lies too or did you craft them especially for me? I looked through everything Olivia took out of your safe. Do you know how close I was to sending the SIM of you and Dani discussing how you were going to frame her to Dani's boss? I'm going to overlook what happened as a slip of your dick but you're going to make it up to me. I haven't decided how yet, but you will.'

Still Dominic says nothing. He's looking at the oversized blue handbag, lying on the floor behind her. Has she got Jack's phone and the SIM cards in there? He'd bet his life on it. He moves quickly, rising up onto his knees, knocking Nancy out of the way as he reaches behind her for the bag.

'Grace!' he shouts as he gets to his feet and catches a glimpse of his daughter's legs as she darts across the landing upstairs. 'Come on we're—'

Nancy is on him before he can finish his sentence, snatching at the bag, calling him all the names under the sun. He swats her away – a backhand swipe that catches her under the jaw and sends her sprawling across the hallway tiles.

'You fucking bastard.' She holds a hand to her chin and tries to get to her feet. 'Give me my bag. I'm done. You can stay here and rot. You and your little bitch.'

As the last thread of Dominic's self-control snaps he launches himself across the hallway, grabs Nancy by the throat and hurls her into the wall. He hears a crunch, or a snapping sound, and Nancy drops to the floor and lies still. Sweating, with his pulse pounding in his ears, he drags her into the kitchen out of sight, then storms up the stairs and into his daughter's bedroom. Grace is curled up in a ball in the far corner of her bed, sobbing softly and shaking. Her suitcase, lying open on the floor, is empty. Dominic grabs random toiletries from the top of her chest of drawers and drops them into the suitcase, then he opens the drawers and randomly selects knickers, bras, T-shirts, a swimsuit, skirts and shorts. He throws them on top of the rest of the stuff then, almost in a trance, zips up the suitcase and taps his daughter on the arm.

'Come on Gracie, time to go.'

Grace doesn't argue. She doesn't shout, she doesn't beg. She uncurls and, without looking at him, picks up the suitcase. As she moves to walk past him he reaches out to give her shoulder a reassuring squeeze. She flinches as his hand moves towards her and he sees a flash of fear on her face. God knows what she saw from the top of the stairs but he'll make it up to her. He'll give her the best life he can.

Grace walks out of her bedroom and down the stairs to the hall. She stands silently by the front door, chin lowered, her blonde curls covering her face as Dominic tips out Nancy's handbag and places Jack's phone, Dani's repayment plan and the two SIM cards in his travel bag, then he clips the travel bag to Nancy's suitcase and wheels it to where Grace is standing. Taking his daughter by the hand he opens the front door. There's a stillness inside him that he hasn't felt for quite some time. Over five years in fact.

Chapter 53

OLIVIA

Bin bags. Masking tape. A person-shaped package, knees bent, the black shiny head resting against one corner of the freezer, the feet, bound together to make one foot-shaped parcel, in the other. I can still see it behind my closed eyes, my hands smothering my nose and my mouth. The lid of the freezer is closed. I slammed it shut as soon as I saw what was inside but the putrid, rotting, rancid smell is everywhere, around me, inside me, dissolving in my lungs and moving into my bloodstream, travelling around my body and into my heart. I can't stop gagging but there's no escape. Death has bound itself to me and there's nowhere to run.

I tremble uncontrollably as shock ebbs away, replaced by the gut-wrenching certainty that the decaying body, shrouded in bin bags, is Jack. My breath, already shallow and rapid beneath the warmth of my palms, is accompanied by a pounding of my heart, so frantic and powerful I fear it might stop. Dominic killed Jack. For what? For daring to love me? For trying to help me escape? My howl echoes off the four

295

walls of the garage. He killed Jack and framed me so no one would ever find out. Rage slices through my horror and I hurl my grandmother's bookcase onto the floor. The panels shatter and glass crunches underfoot as I push the recumbent book-case towards the corner of the room. I place the trio of tables on top of it and put an upturned metal toolbox underneath for support. I pick up the crowbar and step onto the table, holding onto the wall for support, then I drive the crowbar up and into the hole in the roof and yank it back towards me, hard. The crowbar slips back through the hole and I topple backwards. The air leaves my lungs as I hit the floor but I roll onto my side and get back up, retrieve the crowbar and clamber back onto the table.

This time, instead of pulling at the roof, I hack at the hole, then turn my head sharply as shards of rusty metal drop onto my face. I climb back down and search all the toolboxes until I find a pair of protective goggles. I find a rag in the same box and tie that over my nose and mouth and climb back onto the table. All the anger, all the frustration, all the pain I'm feeling is propelled out of my body and into the crowbar as I smash it against the roof over and over and over again.

I don't know how much time passes but I keep ramming the crowbar against the roof and slowly, slowly the hole gets larger. Cool air chills the sweat on my brow but there's no escaping the scent of death. I blink away sweat and tears as my arms and shoulders scream with each upwards thrust of the crowbar but I don't pause, and I don't stop. Dominic has stolen everything from me. I won't let him take Grace too.

By the time the hole is big enough for me to squeeze through I have almost no strength left in my arms and I try once, twice, three times to lift myself up and out into the cool North London air, only to drop back into the garage again and tumble to the floor. I pile weights onto the tables to give me a few extra inches in height. It sways precariously as I step onto it but I get my fingers through the hole and manage to stabilise myself then, taking one last look at the freezer, I pull myself through.

It's starting to rain as I scrabble across the roof, twist onto my stomach and drop to the floor. It grows heavier as I run out of the cul-de-sac and find myself on a main road with houses on either side of the street. Cars zoom back and forth but there are no people around apart from a young, dark-haired woman in black boots, a black jacket and khaki trousers, holding a red umbrella. I run to catch up with her.

'Excuse me?' I touch her on the shoulder when she doesn't respond. 'Excuse me! Please, I need help!'

She jolts and twists round, pulling the ear pods from her ears. Her eyes flick from my head to my feet and she takes a step back, startled by what she sees.

'Please.' I press a hand to my chest as I try to catch enough breath to speak. 'What time is it?'

She takes a phone from her pocket. 'Just after one p.m.' As she turns to continue walking I follow alongside her.

'I need to get to Heathrow. Is there a taxi rank nearby?'

She looks annoyed that I'm still bothering her but she stops walking and points down the street. 'Enfield Lock's just down there. You could take a train.'

'Does it take long? To get to Heathrow?'

She shrugs. 'Dunno. Depends if the trains are running.'

It's too risky. I could end up anywhere and I haven't got any money to buy a ticket. I could jump the ticket barriers but the last thing I need is for a guard to chase me down. A taxi wouldn't ask for the money until I arrived. We're near the M25 here. If the traffic's not too bad it might even be quicker.

297

'Is there a cab firm?' I ask. 'Nearby?'

She raises an eyebrow. 'The nearest one's about twenty-five, thirty minutes away if you walk fast.'

'Can I borrow your phone? To ring one instead?'

She eyes me dubiously.

'Please. You have no idea how important it is that I get to Heathrow.'

'Okay.' She visibly tenses as she hands the phone over. She thinks I'm going to take off.

As the rain soaks through my hoodie, I call for a cab.

The taxi driver, a thin, balding man in his late fifties, nearly refused to take me. He took one look at me – soaking wet, red-faced, bloodied and breathing heavily whilst frantically explaining that I didn't have the money on me to pay for the fare upfront but someone would pay for it at Heathrow – and the expression on his face said it all. It was only when I burst into tears and told him that my daughter was leaving for Dubai, and I needed to say goodbye because I didn't know when I'd see her again, that he finally took pity on me and unlocked the doors. He glanced at me as I got in and started the engine before I'd clipped in my seatbelt.

I waited a full five minutes before I asked if I could use his mobile. He wasn't keen but I convinced him it was an emergency and he reluctantly handed me his iPhone. I dialled 999, watching out of the corner of my eye as the taxi driver's eyebrows twitched upwards when I asked to be connected to the police. I told the operator my name and that I'd just escaped from a garage on Bridle Road, Enfield, after I'd been locked inside by Nancy Ritchie. I said I'd discovered the body of Jack Law who had been murdered by Dominic Sutherland and that they'd find it in the only garage in the row with a broken roof. I told her Dominic was about to leave for Dubai on a one-way ticket and they had to stop him before he left the country for good.

There was a sharp intake of breath from the cabbie then but he was either too stunned, or too scared, to ask me any questions as I handed back his phone.

For the last forty-five minutes Radio Five Live has been blaring out sports news, filling the space between us. The driver's silence suits me and the incessant drone of the radio is helping to drown out thoughts about Jack and how I'm never going to see him again.

I shift in my seat. Watching the minutes tick by as the cars in front of us draw to a halt, yet again, is more than I can bear.

'How much longer do you think?'

'Nearly there.' He inclines his head to one side. 'That's the sign for Terminal Five.'

The clock on the dashboard says 2.55 p.m. My aim was to arrive two hours before check-in so I could wait for Dominic and Grace to arrive but it took me so long to get out of the garage there's only twenty minutes until check-in closes. They might have passed through security hours ago for all I know. I might already be too late.

'Here we are,' the taxi driver says as we pull into the drop-off place and I unclip my seatbelt. 'That'll be a hundred quid please.'

I open the passenger side door. 'I'll just go and get it. My friend's waiting for me inside with the cash.'

'You've got sixty seconds. I don't want to get towed.'

I leap out of the car and run across the zebra crossing and through the revolving doors to Terminal Five. Frantically, I search the suspended electronic board for the check-in zone for a British Airways flight to Dubai but the yellow and white lettering blurs as I look from one flight to the next. I can't find it. It's not here. Did Dominic change the flights? Have they already left? My heart leaps as I spot it – British Airways, Dubai, Zone B – and I frantically search the signs. Where's B? Which way is B? And then I'm off again, running as fast as I can, weaving between idling couples pulling trolleys and noisy families trying to keep hold of their suitcases as they corral their wayward kids.

Zone B. I'm here, and it's so busy I don't know where to look. There are hundreds of people, queuing up in zigzag lines, loaded with luggage, shuffling slowly towards the check-in desks. Where's Grace? Please don't say I'm too late. There are dozens of blonde teenaged girls but none of them are mine. None of the red-haired women are Nancy either. None of the six-foot-two men are Dom. Chatter, laughter, shouts, announcements and the thunder of hundreds of suitcases being pulled across lino; the noise fills my ears as I ricochet from one queue to another, searching faces, analysing height, trying to identify the backs of people's heads. I can't find them. I've missed them. They're not here, but they might still be at security. If they haven't passed through it yet, I could shout Grace's name. She could slip Dom's hand and come running. It's the only hope I've got.

I speed up the nearest escalator and run until I reach the tables where travellers empty their toiletries into clear plastic bags. There's no sign of Dominic, Grace or Nancy so I approach the boarding pass gates and step from left to right, desperately trying to see beyond the archway to the lines of people queuing up for the X-ray machines, shuffling forwards as they remove their coats, belts and boots. I can't see Grace but I know there are dozens of other queues, all out of sight.

As I rise up on my tiptoes to get a better view a security guard, in black trousers and a blue shirt with epaulettes on his shoulders, approaches me. 'Everything okay, madam?'

'My . . . my husband and daughter are going through security.' I gesture beyond the gates. I don't imagine for one second that he'll let me through but I have to try. 'And my daughter's got my boarding pass. It's in my handbag. I gave it to her to hold when I popped to the toilet. Could you let me through? I'll come back to show you the pass.'

The guard's face is steely. 'I can't let you through without a boarding pass I'm afraid. Have you tried ringing your husband?'

'My . . . my phone's in the bag too. Please, if you could just—'

'You need to go to the information desk . . .' he points back towards the escalator '. . . on the ground floor and ask for assistance there.'

He moves away before I can reply and I feel myself slump. If I do as he suggests, I'll have to tell them the truth: that I think my ex-husband is attempting to abduct our daughter. Even if they take me seriously what can they do? They can't drag Dominic and Grace out of the departure lounge unless the police are involved and I've got no idea if, or when, they'll arrive. They might not even be at the lock-up, searching for Jack's body. They might think my call was a hoax.

The only option left to me is to buy a ticket to Dubai and get myself on the plane. But what with? I haven't got my purse.

In tears, I head for the escalator. As it slowly descends I scan the ground floor for any sign of the police then jolt as someone overtakes me, knocking my shoulder and grazing the backs of my legs with her bag. She carries on down the escalator without so much as a backward glance.

'Hey . . .' I shout after her but the admonishment dries on my tongue. Running through the airport, hand in hand and dragging their suitcases behind them, are Dominic and

Grace. I race down the remainder of the steps and sprint towards them.

'Grace! Grace! GRACE!'

My daughter's pale, tear-stained face twists in my direction and, as our eyes meet, her expression switches from empty despair to shock.

'Mum!' She wrenches her hand from Dominic's, abandons her suitcase and sprints towards me. 'Mum! Mum!'

She is on me in an instant, long slim arms gripping my waist, her head buried under my chin.

'I couldn't get out,' she says into my chest. 'He took my phone. He locked me in.' She looks up at me and her eyes widen with fear. 'Mum! You're bleeding!'

'It's okay. I'm fine. I'll explain everything—'

Dominic descends on us before I can finish my sentence. He keeps one hand firmly locked around his and Grace's suitcases, and pulls at her shoulder with the other. His eyes flick towards me and a frown settles between his eyebrows. It's the first time we've been face to face in over five years and he's aged: his skin is rugged and lined and his hair is flecked with grey, but his eyes are as cold as ever. They have the same sheen of anger and disgust I saw when I told him our marriage was over because I'd fallen in love with another man.

'Come on, Grace. We've only got ten minutes to check in.'

I tighten my grip on her. 'She's not going anywhere.'

'You should leave,' he says tautly, 'before I call the police.'

'Funny you should say that.' I match his cold, controlled tone. 'Because I'm waiting for them to turn up too. They know you murdered Jack.' I glance behind him, expecting to see Nancy's mane of red hair, but there's no sign of her. Why isn't she here? She gloated about leaving with Dom.

'Dad murdered someone?' Grace stares up at me, her eyes

wide with fear. 'Mum, back at the house, Nancy turned up and—'

'Of course I haven't murdered anyone.' Dominic yanks Grace towards him and grips her arm. 'Your mother's lying, just like she lied about trying to have me killed.'

'Excuse me, mate.' The taxi driver taps Dom on the shoulder. 'You owe me a hundred quid.'

Dom lets go of Grace and fronts up to him. 'I don't know what you're talking about.'

'Enfield to Terminal Five,' the taxi driver holds out his hand. 'Hundred quid. Lady said you'd pay up.'

I sidestep to my left, out of both of their eyelines, and slide a hand into Dominic's jacket pocket. If Nancy stole the evidence from Smithy, she will have given it back to Dom, I'm sure of it. As my ex-husband continues to argue with the taxi driver I carefully lift out what I find and push it into my jeans pocket. It's not what I was looking for and I'm standing at the wrong angle to be able to reach the inner pockets of his jacket without being caught.

'Mum,' Grace hisses in my ear. 'What are you doing?'

'Looking for something that Nancy stole.'

'Dad took something from her handbag after . . . after he . . . he put it in there.' She gestures at the travel bag, clipped around the handle of his suitcase. He's let go of the handle to gesticulate at the cabbie. I reach for the strap at the exact moment Dominic's hand falls back to his side and his fingers splay, searching for the handle of the suitcase. I snatch my hand away a split second before he finds it and folds his fingers over the clip.

Shit. The only way I can retrieve what's inside now is to open the bag but I need to be careful. He mustn't feel a tug on the strap as I reach inside.

I crouch down and pluck at the zip, steadying the bag with

my other hand. Dominic's curled hand with its broad knuckles and thick fingers is just inches from my face and I hold my breath as I tug on the zip. Slowly, carefully, I slide it to the right and open the bag. I exhale slowly then dip my hand inside.

'She is not my friend. She's my EX-wife.' Dominic's voice booms above me as my fingers graze paper and plastic. I hold myself very, very still, trying to anticipate whether this is the moment he'll drag me back into the conversation. 'She has nothing to do with me. If you want your money, ask her.' My breath catches in my throat as he turns to look behind him and I whip my hand out of the bag.

'Daddy!' Grace leaps forward and grabs his arm, twisting him away before he can spot me, crouching behind him. 'I'm hungry. Can we get something to eat?'

In an instant my hand's in the travel bag again and I pull out what's inside: a clear plastic bag containing two SIM cards, a handwritten note and a phone.

'I'll have those please.' A voice behind me makes me jump.

'Olivia.' Dani holds out a hand for my spoils as I straighten up. Her skin is still as puffy and red as it was when I ran into her in the hospital corridor but the hollows under her eyes look darker and deeper, as though she hasn't slept since.

Dominic turns sharply, the colour draining from his skin as his eyes meet Dani's. He grabs at my hand but I snatch it back. Grace darts to my side.

'Oh no you don't.' Dani slaps his arm away as he reaches for me. 'Olivia, give that to me.'

'No.' I twist my arm behind my back and take several steps away.

'I'll let you walk away with your daughter,' Dani says steadily as she matches me pace for pace, 'if you give that to me.'

'She's not taking her anywhere!' Dominic's indignant cry

is so loud that several people in the check-in queues turn to stare. A security guard in the corner of the room cranes his neck for a better look at what's going on.

'Hey!' the cabbie interjects. 'You still owe me—'

Dani flashes her badge at him. 'Take a walk. And you,' she looks at Dominic, 'I'd keep my mouth shut if I were you. Well, Liv. What's it to be?'

Indecision gnaws at my brain. If I hand the evidence over she'll get away with framing me. There'll be nothing left that connects her to Dominic and I'll spend the rest of my life being treated as an ex-con. I'll never get a decent job again. I'll never be trusted. I'll always be 'that posh blonde woman who tried to have her husband killed'.

'Mum.' Grace pulls on my sleeve. 'Mum, please. Can we go?'

The pleading expression in her eyes is more than I can bear. I can't put her through this. She's already been through so much.

'Here.' I hold out the travel bag to Dani then look away sharply as she slings it across her body. I can't stand the triumphant look on her face. 'Come on, love.' I reach for Grace's hand. 'Let's go.'

'No!' Dom bellows.

'Leave it, Dom,' Dani snaps. 'Or should I say, Matt?'

Dominic jolts and takes a step backwards, repelled by the mention of his real name. I don't wait for his response, instead I quicken my pace, certain that one or both of them will come sprinting after us and rip Grace away. We're fifty feet away from the glass doors of the exit. I don't know where we'll go or what we'll do once we step outside but I'll figure that out when I get there. All I care about now is getting my daughter as far away from her father as I can.

'Oh, wait!' Grace slips her hand out of mine and dashes back towards Dom.

'No, Grace. Come back!' I run after her, terrified she's changed her mind and she's decided to stay with him instead. But she doesn't break up the argument he's having with Dani so she can throw herself into his arms. She grabs the handle of a suitcase and hauls it back in my direction.

Dom moves to run after her but Dani grabs his wrist, lightning fast, and twists it behind his back.

'Dominic Sutherland.' Her voice rings out, clear and loud. 'I am arresting you for the murder of Jack Law . . .'

I feel hollowed out and empty as the cab carries us out of Heathrow and back towards the M25. The cabbie I owed money to was long gone when we left the airport but a friendly older woman, travelling to Cape Town to see her daughter, lent me her phone so I could look up the number of Ayesha's university and give her a call. Ayesha booked us an Uber and she's left work to meet us at her flat. After I told her what had happened in the garage she insisted I get the cab to a hospital so I could be checked over but I can't face sitting in A&E for the next however many hours. I'll go later. Right now I just need to be somewhere safe.

I should feel happy, with Grace sitting beside me – her heavy suitcase on her knees because she wouldn't let the driver put it in the back – and the knowledge that Dominic will be going to prison for a very long time, but I'm broken inside. Jack is dead, murdered for loving me, and Smithy's in hospital, beaten up and broken for being my friend. Grace has told me everything she saw and heard back in the house and if Dominic didn't kill Nancy when he threw her across the hall she'll be arrested too. Knowing they'll both end up in prison won't bring Jack back and it won't heal Smithy's wounds. Without that travel bag no one will ever know what Dani did and I'll never prove that I didn't commit a crime. But I have my daughter back, and that's all that matters – assuming Social Services let her live with me, that is. Relief and grief crash over me like a wave and exhausted tears prick at my eyes. I reach into my pocket in the slim hope that I tucked a tissue in there at some point last night.

'Mum!' Grace nudges me, as my fingers close over something smooth and solid. 'Mum, look!'

'What is it, love?' I watch as she unzips the suitcase on her lap, expecting her to show me a gadget or a fashionable item of clothing she owns. I'll feign interest in it, whatever it is.

'Dad and Nancy had a fight,' she says quietly, keeping one eye on the driver in the front of the cab. 'They didn't realise, but I was watching from upstairs.' She lifts the lid of the case a couple of inches, just enough for me to see what's inside. She looks at me expectantly, waiting for my reaction.

'Half a million pounds,' she breathes.

Chapter 54

DOMINIC

Five Months Later

The shirt Esther provided for Dominic to wear to court is a half an inch too small around the collar and, with the button done up, he feels like he's being throttled. It's also a viscose-mix fabric and his armpits and back are slick with sweat under his heavy suit jacket. He runs a finger around the collar, then, suddenly aware of the jury filing back into the court-room, drops his hand to his side. Only a guilty man would feel hot under the collar and if there's the smallest chance of him walking out the courtroom as a free man he doesn't want one of the journalists in the viewing gallery to write about how shifty he looked as the verdict came in.

He isn't hopeful. Not in the slightest. The prosecution barrister painted Dominic to be a desperate man, a man who'd lost his savings, lost his wife and then lost his temper when confronted by the man who had been blackmailing him. Dominic, the barrister said, was a man living a fantasy life he'd become so embedded in that he'd been prepared to go to any lengths to protect it, even if that meant killing a man. The forensics were damning. Dom's DNA was all over the body and his fingerprints were on the masking tape. Minuscule amounts of Jack's blood were found on the skirting board in the hallway and on the living room carpet and the fireplace surround.

Olivia's testimony slammed the last nail into the coffin of his defence. She openly sobbed on the witness stand as she told the court the terror she'd felt at being locked in the garage and how traumatised she'd been to discover the body of the man she'd loved. She didn't mention the fact that Dominic had framed her to stop her questioning Jack's disappearance, which Dominic found strange. If their roles had been reversed he'd have shouted his innocence from the rooftops, taken down everyone who had framed him, and then fleeced the government for miscarriage of justice. Not Liv, though. She was as weak and guileless as she'd ever been. She'd got Grace back. She probably accepted that as her win.

Dani, on the other hand, lied through her teeth when she appeared as a witness for the prosecution and gave an account of his arrest. She happened to be near Heathrow, she told the court, when the call came through about a potential murder suspect at the airport. She said she recognised the name as he was the victim in another crime she'd brought to court. Dominic knew that was absolute bullshit. Somehow she'd worked out that he was leaving, and what flight he was on, and she'd turned up at the airport to snatch the phone recording and the repayment schedule before he could leave. It was pure luck on Dani's part that the call to arrest him had come through. As he sat in the back of a squad car, handcuffed and humiliated, he was determined that, if he was sent to prison, he'd take her down with him.

His solicitor had talked him out of it. Given the fact Jack's body had been found in a freezer in his garage, it would be foolhardy for him to deny he was responsible for the man's death. Either he'd killed Jack in self-defence after he'd discovering that Jack and Olivia had arranged to have him murdered, panicked at what he'd done, and hidden the body. Or, he'd killed Jack in anger, hidden his body and framed Jack and Olivia to disguise what he'd done.

'Which option,' his solicitor asked him, 'would allow a jury to see you in the most favourable light?'

Dominic had to concede that she had a point but inwardly he raged. There was no way he could take Dani down too, not without weakening his own case.

As for the fraud charge, his solicitor said he wouldn't be tried for it before the manslaughter case had been heard. If he was found guilty of manslaughter he wouldn't be charged with fraud at all. It wasn't win-win, it was lose-lose.

Now, a trapped nerve twitches under Dominic's right eye as the jury take their seats. It's Nancy's fault he's standing in the dock. He could be on a beach in Dubai now, sipping cocktails under a flaming-hot sun if she hadn't done what she did. Nancy isn't standing beside him, not because she isn't also on trial, but because her wheelchair doesn't fit in the dock so she's been parked up beside it. Dom hasn't given her more than a passing glance during the two weeks of the trial. According to the detective who interviewed him, Nancy suffered a broken neck when he threw her against the wall. He should have thrown her harder.

He stands up taller as the judge beckons the court usher to approach. Her low heels clack on the wooden floorboards as she crosses the room and the judge speaks to her in a low voice as she approaches the podium.

The usher turns to the jury. 'Would the foreman please stand.'

THE GUILTY COUPLE

A short man with a beard levers his heft out of his seat and stands up.

'Mr Foreman,' the usher's voice rings out through the wood-panelled courtroom. 'On this indictment have the jury reached a verdict upon which you are all agreed?'

Beardy man nods. 'Yes, we have.'

'On count one,' the usher says. Dominic grips the dock. If Nancy is found guilty of preventing a lawful burial, he will be, too. 'Do you find the defendant Nancy Ritchie guilty or not guilty?'

'Guilty.' The foreman's voice rings out loud and clear.

Dominic's vision swims. The maximum sentence for preventing a lawful burial is life. They're both going to prison for a very, very long time. 'On count two,' the usher says. It's the kidnap charge now, for locking Olivia in the garage. 'Do you find the defendant Nancy Ritchie guilty or not guilty?'

'Guilty.'

The nerve twitches again below Dominic's right eye. He looks down at the ground, willing it to stop. It's his manslaughter charge now and he's struggling to breathe.

'On count one,' the usher says, 'do you find the defendant Dominic Sutherland guilty or not guilty?'

'Guilty.'

'On count two,' the usher says, 'do you find the defendant Dominic Sutherland guilty or not guilty?'

'Guilty.'

Dominic raises his chin and looks across the court to where Olivia is sitting in the raised viewing gallery, with Lee on one side of her and Ayesha on the other. His eyes meet Liv's and she smirks.

Chapter 55

OLIVIA

Two Months After The Trial

The choices we make can be small and insignificant – a prawn mayo sandwich for lunch or a tray of sushi rolls? – or they can be so big, so monumental they can change the course of our lives forever. I was a biddable child and I played by the rules. I wouldn't go so far as to tell another child off but if they put the drawing pencils in the coloured pencil pot I'd wait for them to walk away and then swap them around. Wherever I went – ballet class, Exeter Uni, Sotheby's – I tried to fit in. I didn't want to stand out, I didn't want to be noticed and, given the decision between a risky choice with a high reward or a safe choice without, I'd always go for safe. I believed that by playing by the rules the world would see me as a good person. And, if I worked hard enough and stuck at something for long enough, I'd earn my recompense. I liked my life – mother, art gallery owner, wife – at least that was the official line. I'd been unhappily married for years but hadn't admitted it to myself because to admit that would be to admit that I'd failed.

And then I met Jack.

I will never know whether he turned up at my gallery that day by chance or because he was trying to extort money out of my husband. I'll never know if he loved me as much as he claimed or if he'd have abandoned me the moment Dominic handed him fifty grand. I've convinced myself that the truth lies somewhere in between: that Jack began the affair with me with nefarious motives but, somewhere along the line, he fell in love with me too. If Dominic had paid up there's a possibility Jack and I would have started a new life together but I'd have discovered the truth about Jack's past at some point and it would all have fallen apart. Or would it? If Dominic could keep me in the dark for so long there's every chance Jack could have too.

Was I gullible or was I just trusting? While I'd lived my life playing by the rules, I'd inadvertently surrounded myself with liars, manipulators and criminals: a fraudulent husband whose real name I didn't know, a lover who'd been in and out of jail, a best friend who would have left me for dead and a personal trainer who stole five years of my life. Some people will claim that I wasn't an innocent in what happened, that I deserved to be punished for falling in love with a man I wasn't married to. But did the punishment fit the crime? I lost my freedom, my career, my reputation and the most precious thing in my life, my child.

I don't think it did.

When Dominic and Nancy were arrested I was confronted with the biggest decision I'd ever faced: should I reveal that I'd been framed, attempt to prove my innocence and step back into my old life – one I barely remembered, safe, predictable and quiet? Or should I try on a new life for size? Maybe it would be interesting to be the perpetrator instead of the victim? To be in control instead of controlled? To mix up the pencils and walk away without a second thought?

'Mum!' Grace strolls in from the balcony, her long limbs glistening with sunscreen and a light film of sweat, her blonde hair swept up in a bun. 'Can we go down to the pool? It's boiling in here.'

'You're the one who chose Bermuda!'

'Yeah.' She pads across the tiled floor to the villa's kitchen area and takes a Diet Coke from the fridge. 'I didn't say I regret it. I said I'm hot.'

We've been here for less than forty-eight hours and she's spent at least ten of them in the pool or the sea.

'Let's see what Smithy wants to do. She's just getting changed.'

'Oi oi! Do I hear my name being taken in vain?' On cue, Smithy appears in the doorway in a blue bikini with a white sarong slung around her hips. The raised ridge of her surgery scar that runs from just above her bikini bottoms to her waist looks red and angry against the pale hue of her skin. She sees me looking and grins.

'I'm gonna tell the girls a shark did it, next time I'm inside.'

I raise an eyebrow. 'What do you mean, "next time"?'

'I know, I know.' Her grin widens. 'I'm starting my course when we get back. Jeez, you're worse than a screw. Anyway,' she rubs her hands together excitedly. 'When are we going shopping? I've got a hundred grand to spend.'

Grace, sitting cross-legged on the kitchen counter, lowers the can from her mouth and gawps. 'That's a fifth, Mum.'

'Good to see you've been paying attention in maths lessons. Yes, I gave Smithy that much because she earned it and I gave some to Lee and Ayesha as well. And no,' I add before she can respond, 'I'm not going to tell you how much.'

THE GUILTY COUPLE

Difficult decisions can be made quite quickly, as it turns out.

After Dani arrested Dominic I spent a couple of hours at Ayesha's house then, after a brief visit to Lee's apartment and a charity shop, I took Grace to Smithy's place to lie low. The police came knocking soon after. They were investigating a case of mortgage fraud, they told me, and they'd been informed that I was in possession of a suitcase that contained a significant amount of money. I handed it over, telling them my daughter had mistakenly grabbed it as we'd left the airport after my ex-husband was arrested. They took away Nancy's case, filled with charity shop clothes. Several days later, I returned to Lee's flat – ensuring I wasn't followed – to retrieve the cash I'd stashed.

Ayesha steadfastly refused to take the money. She took one look inside the parcel I handed her and gave it straight back, telling me it was the proceeds of crime and there was no way she could take it. I told her to think of it as my compensation money for being wrongly convicted. She could donate it to a charity if she didn't want to keep it. She still said no. At some point she'll discover the package under one of her sofa cushions. I slipped it there before I hugged her goodbye. What she does when she finds it is up to her, but I'm guessing she won't hand it in to the police. Lee cried when I gave him his parcel. No more dead-end jobs, I told him. You can start up your own gallery or your community art project. When a dream dies sometimes you get the opportunity to resuscitate it.

'All right then,' I say decisively. 'We're going shopping. Put something on over your bikini, Grace. You can't go round the shops like that.'

She rolls her eyes at me but she slides off the counter, slips past Smithy in the doorway, and her feet slap against the tiles

315

as she makes her way to her room. My phone vibrates on the glass coffee table where it's lying next to *The Right Way to Do Wrong* by Harry Houdini. I slide the phone nearer to look at the screen.

'Mate!' Smithy steps closer. 'What are you doing with that shitty old burner phone? You can afford a gold-plated iPhone now if you want!'

I laugh and pick up the phone. 'A gold-plated iPhone? This is worth much more than that.'

Chapter 56

NANCY

Nancy is lying flat on her back on a mattress so thin and uncomfortable she wouldn't give it to a dog. She's trying to remember the words to 'You'll See' by Madonna in an effort to block out the sounds of the health wing of HMP Bronzefield: the groaning, the moaning, the sniffing, the coughing and the swish-splosh-swish of the cleaner's mop. When that doesn't help she returns to her favourite subject: planning her escape.

She'd come to on the cold tiles of Dominic's kitchen to the sound of hammering from elsewhere in the house. Moments later a team of uniformed officers and plainclothes detectives burst into the kitchen and stared at her in surprise. She told them she'd discovered that Dominic Sutherland and Olivia, his ex-wife, had murdered Olivia's lover Jack Law and that Dominic had attacked her after she'd threatened to tell the police. Then she burst into tears and said she couldn't move her legs.

The part about her legs was true. The tears were all part of the act. The doctors in A&E asked her lots of questions

317

about her medical history and what had happened, examined her and then sent her for a CT scan. The doctor who spoke to her afterwards was grim-faced. The pain Nancy had been feeling in her leg before the incident was due to bulged discs and, when Dominic had thrown her against the wall, the discs had ruptured and were lodged in her spinal cord. There was only a sixty percent chance she'd regain the use of her legs after spinal fusion surgery and she'd require months of rehabilitation. The police returned, several hours later, and she was interviewed under caution. Seventy-two hours after that she was arrested and given a police guard. She tried to joke with him that she wasn't exactly going to run off, but her attempt at humour fell flat.

She wiggles her toes under the thin prison blanket, then, keeping an eye on the cleaner in the corner of the room, rolls her feet inwards and then back out. When everyone's asleep at night she'll get out of bed and do a few laps of the ward.

It's been a couple of months since her operation and, despite some pretty intensive rehabilitation, she's still paralysed from the waist down. At least that's what her therapist and the guards think. She's also in pain, terrible, terrible pain, so bad she screams the ward down and requires a morphine injection.

It's irritating, drifting into an opioid haze, when she'd rather keep her brain sharp and alert, but it's all part of her plan. Since she arrived at HMP Bronzefield she's been a model prisoner – polite, helpful and patient – but all the while she's been watching and listening, mentally noting the details of the guards' comings and goings and when the health-wing nurses clock on and clock off. She knows that agency staff are used to cover sickness and that the staff on the front desk have different shift patterns. That means the same person who checks an agency nurse in, won't necessarily be the same person who signs them out.

Nancy smiles a self-satisfied smile as the cleaner's swish-splosh-swish grows closer. All she requires to action her escape plan is a morphine injection, snatched from a nurse's tray. She's already hidden some bandages to use as restraints and, once she's jabbed the next agency nurse that attends to her, she'll strip her of her uniform and pass, then dress herself up and make her way to the exit and sign herself out.

She takes a deep happy breath and closes her eyes. She's made so many wonderful plans for when she gets out. The first thing she'll do is write to Dominic. She won't see his expression as he reads her carefully coded message but she's got a pretty good idea how he'll react. She chuckles to herself as she pictures his face – the dropped jaw, the wide eyes and the surge of anger that will flush his whole face red.

She'd realised she was on borrowed time with Dominic long before Jack came on the scene. The first flush of their affair was over: the longing, the anticipation, the frenzied shagging was gone. They no longer ripped each other's clothes off the moment they were alone, and Dominic had stopped ogling her as though he couldn't believe his luck. Their plan had been to divorce their respective partners and set up home together but Dom had itchy feet, she could feel it. He'd already started making excuses why he couldn't see her: working late, doing something with Grace, a trip to the gym. Sex no longer bound him to her the way it once had. She needed something weightier, more permanent to keep him in her life.

The solution came to her as Dominic ran up the stairs to get his phone and Jack, bleeding and silent, stared up at her from the fireplace with fear in his eyes.

The only thing more powerful than sex was death.

Jack tried to fight her off as she pinched his nose shut and clamped a hand over his mouth but his injuries had made him weak and his arms became tired, glancing off her body

before they dropped to his sides. When Dominic returned
with his phone Nancy was forcing out tears.

'You killed him,' she sobbed. 'Now what do we do?'

Now, a sharp pain in her shin makes her eyes fly open.
The cleaner – a mousey-haired woman with breasts that sit
on her waistline – is standing at the foot of the bed holding
a pin in one hand and a full bed pan in the other. The smell
– of blocked toilets and decay – drifts towards Nancy and
makes her stomach turn.

'Awake, are you?' the woman says.

Nancy narrows her eyes. 'Piss off.'

The woman laughs and puts the bed pan down on the tray
at the end of the bed and tucks the pin into the seam of her
prison sweatshirt. 'I know who you are. You were all over
the papers.'

'I'm surprised you can read.'

The smile freezes on the woman's face and anger sparks
in her eyes. She picks up the bed pan and hurls the contents
at Nancy, covering her face, hair and chest with a day's worth
of urine and faeces, then throws the pan at her too.

'I'll see you soon, Nancy.' She turns to go, leaving Nancy
gasping and retching, trying to shake the shit from her hair.
'I'm keeping an eye on you.'

Chapter 57

Dani turns off the shower, wraps a towel around her body and steps out of the cubicle and into the ladies' changing rooms. She dries herself quickly then opens her locker and takes out her clothes and her bag. The bag bleeps as she places it on the wooden bench and she closes her eyes briefly, steadying herself before she takes out her phone. The name on the notification says 'Dom'. It's not him but changing the name would mean acknowledging that she's trapped. It would mean accepting that she missed the most vital piece of evidence that connected her to Dominic Sutherland. This is her life now, and the lack of control makes her feel sick.

She clicks to open the message. It's a single word:

Well?

Done, she types back.

It hadn't been difficult to discover what time Dominic's flight was. In the hospital corridor Olivia had mentioned that he was leaving in the afternoon, and there was only one flight to Dubai between lunchtime and evening the next day. When she arrested him and destroyed the SIM cards and the repayment plan, she thought it was over – the shitstorm she'd found herself in. DI Fielding accepted her bullshit reason for being near Heathrow when the APB had come through, and there was no way Dominic could throw accusations her way without digging himself a bloody great hole. But when Olivia Sutherland turned up at New Scotland Yard to be interviewed, Dani's relief morphed into fear. Evidence or no evidence, if Olivia told the investigating officer that Dani had helped frame her to disguise the fact Dominic had murdered Jack there would be a full investigation supervised by the IOPC.

Only nothing happened.

No whispering in the corridors, no suspicious glances from the DI, no snide remarks from Reece Argent. Maybe Olivia was waiting until the trial to drop Dani in it? She listened to every word Olivia said in the witness box with her nails digging into her palms, but the accusation never came and when Olivia walked out of the court she cast the briefest of glances in Dani's direction. There was a look in her eyes that Dani couldn't read. Maybe Olivia had let her off the hook because she'd let her leave the airport with Grace. Or maybe Olivia just wanted to move on and put what had happened behind her. Dani could relate. She wanted to get on with her life too – her life with its Casey-shaped hole.

Good, comes the reply now.

Dani grinds her teeth in irritation. Good? That's it? She had to shell out five hundred quid of her own money to pay off Beth for moving a prisoner to cleaning duty on the health ward of HMP Bronzefield. So much for her being a mate.

Her phone pings again. Did Theresa do as she was asked?

Yes. Beth had described in great detail what Theresa had done to Nancy Ritchie. Apparently, the smell was so vile that the whole ward had to be deep-cleaned.

THE GUILTY COUPLE

As she should. I protected her in prison and she owes me for the punches I took.

We're square now then? Dani replies.

Square? Olivia's reply is typically speedy. We're not done yet, Dani. Not by a long shot. You work for me now. And you're not getting paid.

Acknowledgements

Huge thanks as always to my editor Helen Huthwaite for her positivity, hard work and uber efficiency. Also for her 'pernickety' edits (her words not mine!) that helped polish the *The Guilty Couple* and pull it together. Thanks also to Thorne Ryan who stepped in when Helen went on maternity leave. Thank you Thorne for steering *The Guilty Couple* (and me) through publication. Helen couldn't have left us in safer hands.

A huge thank you as always to everyone in Team Avon for all your hard work: Sammy Luton, Ellie Pilcher, Hannah O'Brien, Becci Mansell, Elisha Lundin and Charlotte Brown. And to freelancers Rhian McKay, Anne Rieley and art designer Henry Steadman. Thank you to all at HC360 for introducing my books to readers in the US and Canada: Jean Marie Kelly, Hannah Avery and Peter Borcsok.

Thank you to my incredible agent Madeleine Milburn and everyone at the agency, especially Liane-Louise Smith, Rachel Yeoh, Liv Maidment, Hannah Ladds, George Simmonds, Valentina Paulmichl, Giles Milburn and Emma Dawson for your support and hard work finding new homes for my books. I couldn't have written this book without the help and advice from the following people: solicitors Martin Bourne and Jackie Phillips (partners at Knights plc) for clarifying how prison licences work and the legal issues Liv would face when she tried to reconnect with her daughter. Criminal lawyer Helen Da Silva and barrister (and author) Tony Kent for answering my sentencing and court questions, ex-detective (and author) Neil Lancaster for being incredibly patient and helpful when I bombarded him with questions about bent cops and how much they could realistically get away with, and the kind of duties they'd do day to day. Thank you to ex-probation officer (and author) Noelle Holton for answering my questions about the role of a probation officer.

Thank you Sabrina Oitoju for talking to me about cleaning rotas and security in a building like The Radcliffe Building and to Jo Simmonds (and her mum), Lynsey James (and her brother) and @Joanie170 for answering the cleaning question I asked on Twitter. Finally, thank you to ex-journalist (and author) Fiona Cummins for answering my questions about press coverage of crimes.

A huge thank you to Kate Harrison for being my sounding board when I got stuck in plot holes and to Claire Douglas for being my writing buddy for this book. Checking in and comparing word counts kept me motivated and accountable. I won though, didn't I?!

A huge thank you to the crime community for keeping me entertained, to my quiz team who kept me laughing and humbled (I almost always come last). Thanks to the Rothbury Geriatrics for reminding me that we haven't grown up much since uni, and to the Ellerslie Girls who have known me forever and are always a listening ear.

Thank you Helen Kara, Leigh Forbes and Jenny Beattie for hot tubs, hot meals and the perfect combination of chat and rest. You are my kind of people.

THE GUILTY COUPLE

As ever, the biggest thanks go to my family: my parents Reg and Jenny Taylor, Bec Taylor, Dave Taylor, Lou Foley, Sami Eaton, Frazer, Sophie, Rose, Oliver, Mia, Ana Hall, James Loach, Angela Hall Meza and Steve and Guin. All my love to Chris and Seth who are far too noisy but I couldn't live without you, Lily, stop whining.

Finally, a huge thank you to all the booksellers and librarians who stock and recommend my books, the magazine and newspaper reviewers, the bloggers who shout about my books on social media and most of all the readers whose loyalty and lovely comments make all the hard work worth it. And thank you to YOU for buying this book.

If you'd like sneak peeks at my new books, exclusive competitions and a free eBook please join the C.L. Taylor Readers' Club: www.cltaylorauthor.com/newsletter

To keep in touch with me on social media follow me on:

twitter.com/callytaylor

facebook.com/CallyTaylorAuthor

instagram.com/CLTaylorAuthor

YouTube.com/CLTaylorAuthor

The Guilty Couple Book Club
Questions

These questions may contain spoilers

1. Was Olivia Sutherland a relatable character? Did you agree with all the decisions she made?

2. How much sympathy did you have for Dani? Do you think she received a just punishment at the end of the book?

3. Would you have trusted Smithy with such precious evidence after she'd colluded with Dani? Was Olivia foolish to trust her?

4. Dominic only acted the way he did because he was black-mailed and manipulated by other people and forced into a corner. Do you agree or disagree with that statement?

5. At the end of the book Olivia states that Jack may have set out to seduce her in order to blackmail Dominic but he ended up falling in love with her. What do you think would have happened if he'd survived?

C.L. TAYLOR

6. Nancy, Dominic, Jack and Dani were all villainous in their own way but how would you rank them, from most villainous to least?

7. At the end of the book Olivia decides to 'mix up the pencils' and embrace the criminal label she was so desperate to shake off at the start of the book. Why do you think that is?

8. If you'd been sent to prison for five years how would you cope? What kind of strategies would you employ to survive the experience?

9. When people leave prison it's impossible for them to get back on their feet because of the way society treats them. Discuss.

10. What other books would you recommend to readers who enjoyed *The Guilty Couple*?

The addictive and suspenseful
psychological thriller.

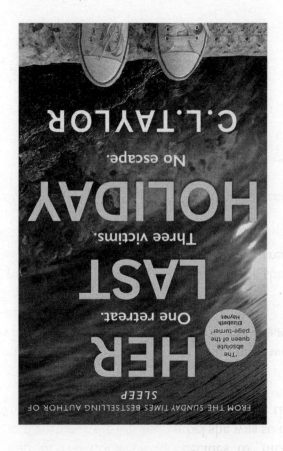

FROM THE *SUNDAY TIMES* BESTSELLING AUTHOR OF
SLEEP

HER One retreat.

LAST

HOLIDAY Three victims.

No escape.

C.L.TAYLOR

'The absolute queen of the page-turner'
Elizabeth Haynes

You come to Soul Shrink to be healed.
You don't expect to die.

A gripping novel that will keep you guessing until the end
from the million-copy bestseller.

Three strangers. Two secrets.
One terrifying evening.

Seven guests. Seven secrets.
One killer.

The addictive Richard & Judy psychological thriller
from the *Sunday Times* bestseller.

Sometimes your first love won't let you go . . .

The sensational thriller from the *Sunday Times* bestseller.

What do you do when no one believes you . . .?

A nail-biting, twisty thriller from
the bestselling author C.L. Taylor.

The unputdownable psychological thriller to leave
you on the edge of your seat.

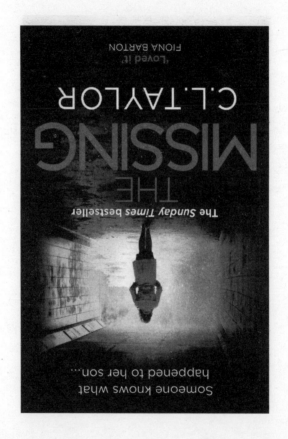

'Loved it'
FIONA BARTON

C.L.TAYLOR

THE MISSING

The *Sunday Times* bestseller

Someone knows what
happened to her son...

You love your family. They make you feel
safe. You trust them. Or do you . . .?

She trusted her friends with her life . . .

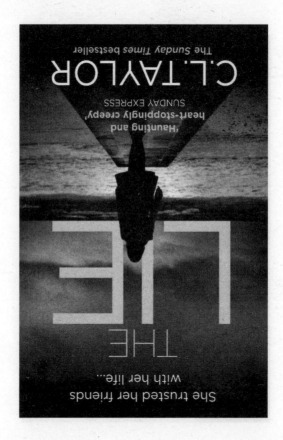

A haunting, compelling psychological thriller
to have you hooked.

Keeping this secret was killing her . . .

A riveting psychological thriller from
the *Sunday Times* bestseller.